FLIGHT OF THE SKYHAWK

A THRILLER

NATHAN GOODMAN

THOUGHT REACH PRESS

This book is a work of fiction. Names, places, incidents, characters, and all contents are products of the author's imagination or are used in a fictitious manner. Any relation or resemblance to any actual persons, living or dead, events, businesses, agencies, government entities, or locales is purely coincidental.

THOUGHT REACH PRESS, a publishing division of Thought Reach, LLC. United States of America.

First Thought Reach Press printing February, 2019

For information regarding special discounts for bulk purchases, or permission to reproduce any content other than mentioned above, contact the publisher at support@thoughtreach.com.

Printed in the USA, Canada, the United Kingdom, and Australia except where otherwise noted.

ALSO BY NATHAN GOODMAN

The Special Agent Jana Baker Spy-Thriller Series

Protocol One

The Fourteenth Protocol

Protocol 15

Breach of Protocol

Rendition Protocol

Peyton Phoenix Thrillers

Phoenix Fatale

John Stone Thrillers

Flight of the Skyhawk

DEDICATION

To my wife who supports me in everything I write. And to all those military pilots who risk their lives every day to keep us safe. Godspeed to you all.

The following was inspired by true events

1

Aboard the USS Ticonderoga. *The Philippine Sea. Eighty nautical miles from Kikai Island, the Kagoshima Prefecture. 5 December, 1965.*

LIEUTENANT JUNIOR GRADE Golan Stiel lay in his bunk and braced against the rail as the aircraft carrier pitched in the rough waters. He had just returned from the flight deck where the temperature was below freezing, and ocean swells were beginning to top forty feet. An alarm blared over his head and pierced the tightly confined quarters. "God loves the Navy," he said as he hopped off the bunk.

"What was that, Pickle?" Lieutenant Carlton Waters said through the open doorway. To Naval aviators, the term *pickle* referred to the releasing of bombs. But during an early training flight, Stiel had come back one fuel tank short. He had inadvertently released the tank instead of the weapon. The nickname stuck.

"I said, 'God loves the Navy.' That means *me*. You? Not so much." Stiel smiled at his wingman. He hurriedly grabbed his flight suit, a one-piece made from fireproof Nomex fabric, and stepped into it, then zipped it up. He picked up his anti-G suit and jammed in one leg followed by the other. The suits were designed to apply pressure to a pilot's lower extremities to prevent loss of consciousness when under heavy acceleration.

"Hurry up. Flight line in two. The Cold War isn't going to wait for you," Waters said as he darted from the stateroom.

Stiel threw on a torso harness and chased it with a survival vest. Once both were properly affixed, he stuffed a .38-caliber pistol into a chest pocket and zipped it tight.

The alarm continued to pulse. A booming voice came over the speakers, reverberating through every compartment on the ship. "General Quarters, General Quarters. All hands, man your battle stations."

"I hope this is a drill," Stiel said to himself. But part of him hoped it wasn't.

The carrier's primary Cold War mission was to defend against the ultimate doomsday scenario, one in which the Russians would launch a nuclear attack. But with the Vietnam war now in full swing, the carrier had double duties. Stiel had already made fifteen combat runs, expertly placing explosive ordnance onto military targets in North Vietnam. The adrenaline spikes had become almost addictive.

The first several attack missions had been targeted at supply depots, but the last was a munitions dump. Stiel's Zuni missiles had been right on target that day. He could still picture the secondary explosions in his mind.

But right now, time was not on his side. He stuffed a water-filled baby bottle into a pouch on the leg of the anti-G suit, grabbed his helmet bag and broke into a run. His destination was the hangar deck. Situated one level below the flight deck, the hangar deck served as the primary location where aircraft were stored, repaired, and armed for combat.

With so much gear and supplies strapped to his body, extra ammo, pencil flares, cigarettes, a knit cap, heavy gloves, signaling cloth, hat, and a long jungle knife strapped to his leg, his dash to the hangar deck felt more like a weighed-down slog.

The ship pitched from one side to another in the heavy seas. Under General Quarters conditions, sailors ran in various directions in what looked like disorganized chaos. Yet the response was textbook.

Stiel blew past the ready room and descended a narrow staircase, known onboard Naval vessels as a ladder well. With so many sailors running for their duty stations he called ahead, "Make a hole! Down ladder!" He shuffled past a dozen sailors coming up. He was on the hangar deck and running for his plane seconds later.

When he got to the craft, however, he hesitated. A B43 nuclear bomb was strapped to the underbelly. *Oh shit*, Stiel thought.

"Get your ass in gear, JG," Waters yelled from the cockpit of his A-4 Skyhawk attack aircraft.

Stiel slung his helmet bag into the hands of an airman already standing on the wing, waiting for him. He climbed the exterior ladder and jumped into the cockpit of his Skyhawk. The airman, known as the plane captain, handed him his helmet. Stiel snugged it over his head and began adjusting the oxygen mask. The airman leaned in and affixed Stiel's shoulder and leg straps, then pulled a pair of safety pins from the ejector seat.

Adrenaline pulsed into Stiel's veins the way it always did in the harried moments before being flung from the deck of the carrier.

The airman said, "Good to go, sir?"

Stiel nodded then his fingers instinctively found several switches. The process of preparing the plane for flight was on.

The airman gave him a thumbs up and shimmied down the ladder.

With so much noise emanating from the flight deck above them, Stiel held his oxygen mask over his mouth and keyed his radio. "Hey, LT, this isn't a drill, is it?"

"What makes you think this isn't a drill?" Waters replied. "The carrier's cruising for Yokosuka, Japan for a little R and R."

Stiel looked to the side of the hangar and saw them, three sailors known as ordnance men, red-shirts charged with moving, mounting, and arming weapons. But these were no ordinary officers. Known as "the W," the elite Special Weapons Division was comprised of those trusted to handle nuclear weapons. They were flanked by a detachment of Marine guards who stood in close watch.

Stiel smiled. "What makes me think this isn't a drill? Well, let's see. There's a Mark 43 on my wing for starters."

"Oh, you noticed that, did you? You got a problem with a tactical nuclear weapon strapped to your balls?"

"And we're not doing an exterior pre-flight?"

"That's a negative, Pickle. The island says this is priority. You just better hope that bucket of bolts you're flying is in good shape. Kick the tires then light the fire. Run your interior pre-check, and do it fast. Ejection seat safety pins out?"

"Affirmative."

"Fuel level?"

Stiel checked his gauge. Since a fully fueled tank would make the plane too heavy to launch, Skyhawks launched with half-capacity and were refueled in mid-air. His gauge read 2,734 pounds, almost perfect.

He flashed a thumbs-up to Waters.

"The tanker just launched from CAT A," Waters said. An enormous roaring sound came from overhead as another aircraft launched from the catapult. "That would be a Crusader. There's another F-8 to launch, but you're number two on CAT B, right behind it."

A vehicle called a tug detached itself from the front landing gear. Tugs had the singular responsibility of moving aircraft into various positions on the ship, but once a plane was ready to be backed onto the elevator, planes were moved the old fashioned way, by hand.

A dozen sailors ran into position and began to push. Stiel's plane rolled backward toward the carrier's single deck-edge elevator where it would be raised to the level of the flight deck.

Stiel hurried through his interior pre-flight checklist, flipping switches and checking gauges. As the plane was backed onto the open-air elevator platform, the wheels bumped across the leading edge of the elevator.

Stiel glanced over his shoulder at the raging seas behind him. A wave slammed into the side of the massive ship, and freezing, salt-laden mist blasted across the elevator and into the hangar deck. The ship lurched in protest, and Stiel felt the roll tilt him forward. He pulled the canopy actuation handle and lowered the jet's canopy to the closed position, forming an airtight seal.

Stiel's wingman came over the radio again. "Island says we've got two bogeys inbound. Probably Russian MiG-17 fighter aircraft. They're moving at subsonic speeds, just below Mach 1. Position is one hundred nautical miles and closing. That's what they're launching the Crusaders for. But those MiGs launched from somewhere. If there's a Russkie carrier group out there, it could get ugly. It's time to earn your pay."

"Bogeys?" Stiel said. "Christ, I expected it when we were in the Gulf of Tonkin, but out here? If you ask me, the Cold War ain't so cold."

"Did you just say *Christ*?" Waters said as he laughed into the comm. "Aren't you Jewish?"

Stiel extended the middle finger on his right hand and used it to salute Waters. He glanced at a small black and white photo affixed to the top of the instrument panel. His sweetheart, Evelyn, a trim brunette dressed only in a two-piece bathing suit, smiled back at him. "See you in the air, LT."

Several sailors, plane handlers in blue shirts and a safety director in yellow, shielded their faces against the freezing mist. As the plane was pushed back, the safety director eyed the position of the front wheel relative to the painted yellow line on the floor of the elevator. But as the massive wave passed underneath, the ship began to lean in the other direction.

Stiel felt his plane roll backward, toward the edge. With nothing between him and the rolling seas but a thin metal safety bar, he jammed his foot onto the brake pedal. Instead of feeling pressure, however, his foot went straight to the floor.

"Shit! No brakes!" he yelled into the comm.

The plane's front wheel rolled past the yellow line and the safety director blew his whistle. Men on the hangar deck erupted into motion. Two sailors, known as chock men, one positioned under each wing, threw large wooden chocks behind the landing gear, an attempt to thwart the roll.

Two other safety men blew whistles just as the plane's wheels bumped over the chocks. Frantic blue-shirts ran onto the elevator and grabbed at the plane. But the elevator platform tilted further and they could not arrest the rearward motion.

Jamming his foot on the brake pedal in repeated succession had no effect. The platform tilted past the critical threshold.

Waters watched from his plane and his eyes flared wide. His best friend was about to fall over the edge. He sat bolt-upright against his shoulder harnesses and his voice boomed into the radio. "Pickle, no!"

Stiel felt a violent jarring accompanied by the sounds of metal on metal as the huge fuel tanks under his wings tore through the safety bar. Blue and yellow-shirts let go and leapt to the side to keep from being pulled overboard.

Stiel's heart rate exploded as he felt his rear landing gear slide over the edge. It was too late to bail out. The bulk of the plane slid off the platform, hung momentarily by the nose gear, then toppled thirty-nine feet. It landed on its back, slamming canopy-first onto the thrashing water below. Stiel and the plane were upside down.

Inside the cockpit, the impact was jarring. The plane began to sink beneath the surface of the thrashing water. Stiel scrambled to get his bearings. The lights illuminating the instrument panel went black. Out of instinct, Stiel reached for the ejection handle, but being below the surface, realized instantly the canopy would not be able to jettison clear. With the canopy still in place, deploying the ejection seat's rocket motor would cause flames to erupt inside the cockpit. He would either burn to death or be crushed against the closed canopy.

With lightning speed, he unbuckled his safety harness, pressed the canopy actuation handle forward, and jammed his hands into the canopy. The plane slipped into the dark, watery oblivion. He pushed as hard as he could, but the water pressure holding the canopy closed was too much. What little light he had vaporized into inky blackness.

The plane descended deeper, and Stiel pushed against the canopy. After a few moments, it began to pop and groan under the pressure. The canopy would not budge. Stiel's mind frantically searched through every emergency training scenario he had gone through, but this was not a contingency anyone had planned for.

Stiel propped a boot against the canopy and pressed with everything he had. A small amount of water began to leak in around the seal. He could feel the plane descend deeper and deeper.

The canopy, however, remained like a rock. The plane rolled end over end into the depths below. Stiel no longer could tell which direction was up. Exhausted and out of options, there was nothing left to do, and Stiel knew it. He unbuckled his oxygen mask then fumbled in the pitch darkness for the photo of Evelyn.

The metallic groaning of water pressure against the canopy intensified, and he held the photo to his lips.

"Goodbye, my sweet Evelyn."

2

Mossad Headquarters, Tel Aviv, Israel, Nuclear Detection Lab. Present Day.

THE PHONE RANG for the fifth time in the past five minutes. Talia Stiel looked at it and shook her head. She knew the calls were for her but had been trying to ignore them. Her work to develop a technology to detect nuclear material was so close to being finished that she could no longer stand the repeated interruptions. But on the fourth ring, she stood and tightened the band holding her long black hair into a ponytail. She snatched the phone off the receiver.

"Talia Stiel," she said.

"Dr. Stiel?" a female voice on the other end said. "We've been trying to reach you. This is Ayala, in Human Resources? We've got an emergency call for you. It's a family emergency, I'm afraid. You'll need to call Sourasky Medical Center right away."

Talia's posture straightened. "Family emergency? Is it Moshe?"

"No, ma'am. We notified Director Himmelreich as well."

"But I don't have any other family."

"Please," the woman said, "it sounded urgent."

Talia shook her head. "I said I don't *have* any other family. You've made a mistake."

"No, ma'am. They said—"

"Your parents can only die once." Her slightly warped sense of levity went nowhere, and all she heard was silence. "Fine, whatever," she said. "You have a number?"

The woman relayed the phone number and reiterated the urgency of the call. Talia stood from behind a wide research table and caught the reflection of herself in the glass wall lining the laboratory. Ever since her last birthday, the "big three-oh," as she had called it, Talia found herself more conscious of her looks.

Like many Israeli women, she was trim and often found men looking at her. But today, in the final stages of her research project, she decided the long hours were beginning to take a toll. She stared into her reflection and smoothed a wrinkle in her form-fitting skirt. She dialed the number. "I still don't see how I can have a family emergency," she said to herself.

The phone rang twice, and on the other end, a female voice answered in a hurried, yet polite, tone. "Tel Aviv Sourasky Medical Center, Intensive Care Unit."

"Yes, my name is Talia Stiel. I think there's been a mistake, I've been asked to call this number. Some kind of family emergency?"

"Yes, Miss Stiel. We've been trying to reach you. It's about your grandfather. He's here in the intensive care unit. I'm afraid it's quite serious. You'll want to get here as soon as possible."

"My grandfather?" Talia said as she pressed the phone harder to her ear. "I don't have a grandfather. Both my grandfathers died years ago."

"Miss Stiel, please. He's calling for you. It's all we can do to keep him calm. The doctors say his condition is grave. You must come immediately."

"I appreciate your concern, but you've got the wrong person. Like I said, I don't have a grandfather. I don't have a mother or father anymore, for that matter. I'm the only Stiel left." Across the phone line, Talia heard what sounded like the woman standing up from a swivel chair.

"He said you wouldn't believe it." The nurse's voice sounded course, like one trying to choke down the day's frustrations. "Here, I wrote it down so I wouldn't forget." She sounded like she was reading from a piece of paper. "You are Talia Stiel, are you not?"

"Yes, but—"

"And your mother's maiden name was Mizrah?"

Talia's voice flattened. "Yes."

"Your father was Avraham Stiel?"

Talia swallowed. "Yes."

"The patient here is named *Yosef* Stiel. He says he's your grandfather. He's insistent about it. He's the one who told us where to call you."

Her legs wobbled. "But . . . " Talia said as she sat. "Yosef Stiel died when I was five years old. I distinctly remember it."

"No, ma'am. He's lying right here, and he's asking for you." A moment of awkward silence played out. "He said if you still didn't believe it was him to tell you he used to call you *Peanut*?"

Talia dropped the phone, then clutched her hands to her mouth.

The nurse on the other end of the line said, "Hello? Miss Stiel? Miss Stiel?"

3

Thirty-five minutes later, Talia Stiel half-jogged down the sterile, white hospital corridor. She skidded to a halt in front of the nurse's station, wobbling on her high heels before grabbing the counter top to stabilize herself. "I'm looking for a patient, Yosef Stiel?"

"Yes, ma'am," a nurse in surgical scrubs said as she looked up from a computer monitor. "Mr. Stiel is in pod seven, just that way."

Talia ran past pod five, then six. When she came to number seven, she stopped. She could see through a bay of large glass windows into the room where an old man lay. Tubes and wires were connected to his arms and chest. His face was obscured by an oxygen mask, and Talia squinted to get a better look.

She clutched her purse, then pushed the door open and stood staring at the man's face. Its warm familiarity flooded over her. It was her grandfather, a man who, until now, only existed in faint, time-washed memories. It was Yosef Stiel.

Talia placed her hand on a handrail against the wall as a wave of dizziness swept over her. She steadied herself when a different nurse, a woman with wrinkled skin and gray hair pulled back into a tight bun said, "Are you all right, Miss?" The woman spoke softly, as one might in a public library.

"Oh, yes, thank you. Vertigo. Comes and goes."

"Would you like to sit down?"

"No. This will pass. The dizziness comes sometimes when I'm under stress. I'll be fine."

The nurse smiled. "The ICU can be overwhelming." For just a moment, the woman's warmth reminded Talia of her own mother.

Talia looked back at the old man on the bed. His eyes were closed. Several digital monitors hung on the wall, each making its own, distinct bleeping sound. She walked closer and looked down at him.

A moment later, his eyes flickered open as he registered her presence. "Talia, Talia!" the old man said, his voice crackly and hoarse. "My little Peanut. Look at you." He pulled the oxygen mask from his mouth.

Talia startled, but the voice, it rang true in her mind; it was really him. "Grandpa?" she said as she leaned closer.

His face softened, and he reached for her hand. "My glasses," he said, his voice raspy and dry. "I need my glasses. I want to see your face."

She reached to the side table and picked up the glasses, and that's when she noticed her own hands were trembling. When he had donned the glasses, a warm smile spread across his wrinkled face. "Come closer. It's really you, isn't it, Peanut?"

"I don't, I don't understand. You're . . . dead."

"I'm so sorry, sweet pea. It was your parents, you see? I had to lie to you. I had to lie to you all. I know what they told you." He began to cough violently. When the hacking abated, he drew in a deep breath. "They told you I had died. But there was a lot at stake. I had to disappear. Otherwise, they would have found me."

"Who? Who would have found you?"

"That's not important right now. I'm just glad to see you. My little Peanut."

The face, the familiar voice, it was all starting to feel so real. And the reference to her childhood nickname brought a lump to her throat. "Grandpa, I'm so lost. Ima and Aba told me you had died. You're saying my own parents lied?"

"Do not place blame on them. They were simply trying to protect you."

"Protect me? Protect me from what?"

Her grandfather cocked his head to the side. To Talia, it appeared he had lost his train of thought.

"None of this is important now."

Talia decided to try a different tack. "What did you mean when you said they would have found you?" Talia shook her head. "Why don't you start from the beginning."

"No, no," he said as he began coughing. It was worse this time. "There are other things I must tell you—"

His coughing fit exploded, and a nurse walked in. She replaced the face mask over his mouth and nose and connected one of the tubes to a nebulizer pump.

She opened a small white box of medication labeled *Salbutamol Teva 5mg Solution for Inhalation*, then pulled out one of the vials of clear liquid. She poured a bolus of the liquid into the nebulizer and turned the machine on. A medicated mist began to blow into the face mask.

The nurse said, "There, there, Mr. Stiel. Just breath in slowly. That's it. You've got to stay calm now." She waited as the coughing subsided, then walked back out.

He pulled the mask down again. "There's not much time," he said as he gripped his rib cage and held it. The underlying pain's intensity magnified across his face. "But you have to know. You have to know everything. Otherwise, it will be too late." He stopped, apparently lost in thought.

"Grandpa?"

He took a few breaths through the face mask, then pulled it down again. "There is something I must tell you, something that has pained me all these years. I can't hold it inside any longer. It's been eating me alive since I was a young man. And," he coughed, "as it turns out, you, you are the only one left, the only one who can help me."

"Wait. Are you-"

"Dying? Yes, my dear. That's why I must tell you now before it is too late."

She pulled a chair closer to the bedside and sat, then placed her purse on the floor. "Um, okay." Talia studied his face a moment and found herself entranced with its familiarity. "Is this something I want to hear?"

"That is for you to decide." He drew the face mask closer and allowed the nebulized medication to waft into the air near his face. He covered his mouth and coughed again. "It was 1965. I was young, and so was Israel. You've got to understand, things were much worse back then. We had enemies on all sides. None of our enemies had wanted the state of Israel to come into existence in the first place. There was very little time."

"Time for what?"

"The Land was in great danger. We knew if Israel were to be invaded, we wouldn't stand a chance. We had to have a means of defending ourselves."

"But, Grandpa, we had an army. It was formed with the country's inception in 1948."

"When your tiny country is surrounded on all sides by enemies, just *having* an army is not enough. Even in 1965, our army was small, ill-equipped. We were facing the distinct possibility of being annihilated. It had become a matter of urgency."

"What did you do?"

"I did what had to be done, everything in my power. We had to obtain what we really needed, the one thing that would secure the security of The Land for generations to come."

Talia's head turned to the side as the statement played forward in her mind. "Which was?"

He coughed, but only mildly. "We needed a nuclear weapon."

Talia shifted in her seat.

He continued. "Your work at the Mossad as a nuclear physicist means you are in a scientific role, but from what I know about you, you've been something of a historian your entire life. You've studied the country's history, even to the point of accessing Mossad case files in order to learn all you could."

"How do you know that?"

He placed the mask over his mouth and waved the question off. "It's not important."

"But you haven't seen me since I was five."

He ignored the question. "You know that in 1965, Israel did not yet possess such capabilities. Not only did Israel not have nuclear weapons, but at that time we were not *allowed* to possess them in any form."

"Yes, yes," Talia said, "that was part of how the deal to create the State of Israel came about in the first place." The old man opened his mouth to speak, but Talia spoke over him. "Wait. You worked in the bakery with Ima and Aba. What do nuclear weapons have to do with a pastry chef?"

He coughed again yet a smile widened across his face. "Ah, Peanut. I am so glad you grew up with that picture of me in your mind. You were so young and innocent." He looked out the window a moment. The smile abated, and his eyes became glassy, like one lost in a memory. "I wouldn't have wanted you to know who I really was. Who I *am*."

There was something laced in his words. It sent a cold shiver up Talia's spine.

"But this is not why I wanted to talk to you." His face furled a moment as if assembling the words he wanted to use next. "We appealed to the United States, Canada, Great Britain, France and Norway for help obtaining a weapon, but none would defy the treaty."

"Well, sure," Talia said, "The United Nations Special Committee on Palestine made the recommendation for the creation of Israel after a lot of compromises. No one would have wanted to go against the agreements set aside in the Partition Plan."

"I was right. You do have a love of history. You are correct, my dear. Nonetheless, by 1965 our intelligence sources feared an invasion was imminent, an invasion we could not survive. We *had* to obtain a weapon, without which we would face utter annihilation."

He coughed again and gripped at his ribs. Talia stood and squeezed his hand. His face grimaced as he braced against the pain buried somewhere deep within his side. "I've got to tell you something," he gritted out, then his voice quieted. "It's a story you'll have a hard time believing, but it is true, every word of it. In 1965, I was a Mossad agent."

Talia's head turned, and she peered down at him out of the corner of her eye. "*What*?"

He began to hack and pulled the mask over his face and inhaled the bronchodilator medication until the coughing settled. "I was assigned a very specific mission."

"No, no," Talia said as she shook her head. "You worked in the bakery. Am I supposed to believe that all those times I saw you kneading dough and making pastries were all just my imagination?"

She stared at him a moment and studied his expression. When it was clear his story was not about to change, she said, "I work at the Mossad as a research analyst, but you are telling me you were an *agent*?" The word came out as if it tasted of spoiled milk.

"Do not judge me, dear Peanut. I was determined The Land was to survive, and it was up to me to obtain a device."

Talia's brow flattened. "A *nuclear* device?"

"The weight of the entire nation was on my shoulders. The Land," he said, referring to how most Israelis refer to their country, "needed me, and I was not going to fail it." His voice became dry, like the winds of the Negev desert. "I was to obtain the device using any means necessary."

Talia knew the types of covert operations the Mossad was involved in. "Any means?" She crossed her arms over her chest. "What did you do?"

"I killed a man," he said. "But not just any man. I killed . . ." his eyes crunched shut, "my own brother."

"You killed . . . but you don't have a brother."

"Your father probably never talked about Golan because of what he did with his life. To the family, he was a disgrace, and they carried the shame around with them as if it were a curse. But it wasn't. Golan Stiel was a great man."

Talia shook her head. "You're telling me I had a great uncle named Golan?"

Yosef spoke as though recounting a horror. "My brother didn't fail at his life. There was no disgrace. He was murdered at my hands, though no one knew it. In fact, the Israeli Prime Minister and the Director of the Mossad were the only ones who knew the truth, besides myself."

Yosef's eyes started to shift back and forth, and Talia wondered if the man was telling the whole truth.

"The truth you murdered my uncle, or that Israel was trying to obtain a nuclear device?"

"Both, my dear. In those days, I was recruited for the mission, a mission of such importance the future of the State of Israel hung in the balance."

"All right," she said as she turned around. "Grandpa, this is all a little too much for me to take in."

"You must hear this. You are the only one that can know. You must hear the story of how my brother died. It is my dying wish."

The old man studied the ceiling tiles a moment, then began.

4

Tel Aviv Sourasky Medical Center, Pod Seven.

Yosef started, "When my brother was of age, he chose to emigrate to America. The family was very upset with him leaving, but he insisted. It was the late 1950's. He became a US citizen and then went to university at the United States Naval Academy as a cadet. After graduation, he served in the Navy as a fighter pilot." He grinned. "He was so proud. His aircraft was an A-4E Skyhawk, and from what I was told by the others in his squadron, he was the best."

Talia turned and walked to the wall, lost in a swirl of thoughts. Her historical knowledge of the Israeli Mossad afforded her not only an extensive understanding of Israel's military capabilities and past actions but that of her allies and enemies as well. She turned to him and said, "Skyhawks were fighter-bombers."

"That's right. And during the Cold War, when tensions were high enough with the Russians, the United States would arm Skyhawks with tactical nuclear weapons, secured to the underside of the plane, and launch them from the decks of carriers. The weapons were *thermo*nuclear, and depending on the fusing options chosen, were capable of detonating in a variety of ways."

Talia crossed her arms. "Yes, I'm well aware. But how do you know —" She stopped herself. "Tactical devices are meant to be used in any number of situations. They can detonate in air burst, ground burst, can be dropped free fall, could detonate on contact, or even be used under laydown delivery."

"Your Ph.D. has not gone to waste," he said with a cough. "And depending on the fusing option chosen, the explosive yield of a single device could be adjusted from seventy kilotons up to—"

"One megaton," Talia said as she nodded. "And I'm not a Ph.D. yet."

"And that was exactly the type of weapon Israel was desperate to possess. Since a foreign aggressor could approach us from any side, by the time their attack was detected, it would have been too late for our Army to thwart. We needed a tactical nuclear weapon just like that to neutralize the threat. And the fact that the weapon carried by the Skyhawk could be varied in yield when detonated made it ideal. We would have a weapon which could be tuned *on demand* as the situation warranted."

Talia nodded, but her shoulders slumped. "And I suppose Israel would have made sure all of our enemies knew we were in possession. That way, they would think twice before invading."

"Exactly."

She exhaled. "What did you do?"

"I enlisted."

"In what?"

"In the United States Navy."

"Hold on," Talia said as she held an open palm to Yosef. "Your brother, Golan, if he did exist, may have been a US citizen, but you weren't. You couldn't have enlisted."

Yosef grinned. "You are correct. My brother had become a US citizen after a year-long process. I, however, did not have that kind of time. The details of how I was able to enlist are not important. Let's just say I had help."

Talia nodded. *The Mossad,* she thought.

"In the Navy, I became a Chief Warrant Officer and requested assignment to a particular aircraft carrier, the same carrier Golan was assigned. Since I also had obtained a brand new identity, no one knew we were siblings. And since my sole directive was to get my hands on a nuclear weapon, I figured, the best thing to do was to become a weapons specialist. It would give me direct access to the weapons themselves."

"You're telling me you were going to attempt to steal a nuclear weapon from the United States Navy? Were you insane?"

"I was trained to load, unload, and store armaments of all types, including those with nuclear tips. And as a Warrant Officer, I had authorization to be in restricted areas where others were not permitted."

Talia looked down as if lost in thought. "Which carrier was Golan assigned?"

"The *USS Ticonderoga*."

It took a moment, but then Talia's mouth opened. "The *Ticonderoga*? Wait a minute. We studied this in grad school. That's the ship that in 1965 lost a nuclear device. They were in the, ah, the—"

"The East China Sea. We were part of Attack Squadron 56. We had departed Subic Bay in the Philippines, performed a combat tour in Vietnam, and thirty-one days later were eighty miles from Kikai Island, the Kagoshima Prefecture."

She pointed at him. "You were on board the *Ticonderoga*?" But she stopped herself. "Wait. First, you lead me to believe you were a baker, that you died when I was five, and now this? This must be what Moshe was talking about."

"Ah, Moshe. What did your godfather tell you?"

"He always said you were crazy." She crossed her arms again. "I don't believe a word of what you're saying."

Yosef nodded. "Moshe has his own motivations. He and I never really saw eye to eye." Yosef continued with the story. "It was a bitter, cold December day. The seas were hell, I don't mind telling you. I remember it like it was yesterday."

Talia's tone sharpened. "Fine," she said as he sat in the chair then threw one leg over the other. "Go on then. Tell me how you did the impossible, stole a nuclear weapon from a naval warship. I'd *love* to hear this."

"I didn't."

"But you just said—"

"I failed."

Talia shook her head. "You failed? At your mission?"

He nodded.

"All right then," she said, "tell me how you *thought* you were going to steal a nuclear device from a US warship."

"At the time, my brother, Golan, had no idea I had entered the United States. He certainly did not know I was a Warrant Officer deployed aboard the same vessel as him. I tried, and I tried, but when I finally came to the conclusion there was no way to steal the weapon outright, I knew I would need help. So I approached him."

The old man stared off into nothingness. "Just seeing me shocked him to his core. You see, Golan and I never really saw eye to eye either." He wafted a hand. "Those feelings between us went back a long way. As a child in Tel Aviv, I always believed that since he was older, the family loved him more than me. And as you know, in Israeli households, to a certain extent, that is true."

He coughed but was able to settle himself before it could go further.

"On board the *Ticonderoga*, I had no other choice than to try to recruit him into the operation. After all, he was Israeli. If I could convince him to work covertly for Israel, his true homeland, we could accomplish the mission together.

My plan was that he would take off from the deck of the carrier with the weapon attached. He would fly off-course to a remote location we would coordinate with the Mossad where he would land. The weapon would be offloaded, and he would take off again and report a weapons malfunction. It wouldn't be the first time a bomb had come accidentally detached from its mounts and dropped into the sea."

"But he didn't go along with it, did he?" Talia said, as her foot bobbed back and forth.

"No," the old man replied as he again began coughing. This time, as he gripped at his ribcage and doubled over, the coughing intensified to a point at which a digital alarm began to pulse on one of the monitors.

Talia stood. "Grandpa? Are you all right?"

The hacking continued, and the nurse rushed in and helped him lean back. She repositioned the nebulizer mask across his mouth, then checked his vital signs. "You need to stay calm, Mr. Stiel. Perhaps you should rest now?"

"I will be fine," he said as he cleared his throat.

"All right then," the nurse said. "But please stay calm. And it's very important you get some rest." She glanced at Talia as if to say, "Visiting hours are over," then walked out.

He waited until the nurse was out the door before continuing. "At first, my brother was torn between service to his homeland, and service to his new home, America. He loved the United States, you see. Eventually, he refused."

"And you murdered him for that?"

He scowled at her. "Working in an air-conditioned laboratory may afford you the ability to stand back and pass judgment. You have the advantage of looking behind you, then evaluating decisions that were made in real time. Without the weight of a million tons of tanks, artillery, and boots standing on your head, it is easy for you to think in terms of black and white, right and wrong. But when faced with utter annihilation, nothing is that simple."

His eyes formed into slits.

"You have no idea what it's like to have the future of a nation in your hands." His voice stiffened further. "Israel was in imminent danger. Hundreds of thousands of lives were on the line, and I had sworn to protect them!"

Talia rubbed her temples. "All right, all right."

After a few moments of calming down, Yosef continued. "My brother may have initially been torn between loyalty to his homeland versus his new home, but once he made the decision to honor his commitment to the United States, he was clear. He struggled internally with what to do with the information, that an Israel operative was on board and was trying to actively steal a nuclear device."

"He was deciding whether to turn you in or not."

"I could see it in his eyes. There was inner conflict. Eventually, I couldn't risk it anymore. Even though he was my brother, I knew I had to honor The Land over my own family. I had to kill him."

Talia shook her head. "You were trying to save your own skin."

He pointed a crooked finger at her. "That, my dear, is where you are mistaken. I would have gladly traded my life for Golan's. I think about it every day. But if the United States were to discover the operation, Israel's chance of obtaining a weapon would be severely damaged."

"If this is true, you are a murderer." Talia snatched her purse from beneath the chair.

Yosef's voice descended into a gravelly whisper. "And Yahweh will judge me for my sins."

"As will I." She started to walk out.

His hoarse voice escalated. "I will be dead soon." Talia stopped just before she reached the door but did not turn around. "I am a man of sin. I admit that. But I am dying. Please hear me out."

She turned to face him. "What do you want from me? Why have you dumped all this on me?" A wave of emotion pushed tears against the backs of her eyes.

"I want you to do something that I cannot. I want you to honor your uncle. I want you to clear his good name." He stared at her a moment. A tear welled in his eye, then fell. "You must have Golan's remains returned to Israel."

She walked back to the bedside and dropped the purse onto the chair. "Returned? Where are his remains now?" But then she put her hands into the air. "No, wait a minute. I want to get this over with." Her teeth clenched. "You want to unburden yourself? You want to dump all this on me? Fine. I want to know how you murdered my great uncle."

"My dear, the details are not—"

"I'm tired of all this evasive double talk. Tell me!"

The up and down movement of Yosef's chest increased and his eyes filled with fear. "Don't make me retell it," he said shaking his head. "It is too painful."

Talia reached down for her purse, but Yosef grabbed her other wrist. "I will promise to tell you everything if you promise to stay."

Talia stared at him a moment, then nodded.

"As weapons specialist, I had direct access to the devices. In my mind, I had run through every scenario of how I could smuggle one off the ship. But nothing was feasible. Security was too high.

"Originally, I had reasoned that if I could have uninterrupted time, I would be able to physically separate the internal components of one of the bombs. I had training that would enable me to remove the warhead from inside the nose cone and reassemble it.

"I would have had my hands on the nuclear tip, and, looking at the bomb from the outside, there would be no way for others to tell the nuclear components had been removed. But there would also have been no way to get the warhead off the ship.

"The bomb itself is large, over twelve feet long, with a weight close to twenty-one hundred pounds. But the warhead is only about yay big," he said as he held his hands about two feet apart, "and weighs eighty pounds. But as I mentioned, security around those devices was high. We had a roving Marine guard on board at all times. Officers would inspect each weapon as it was loaded or unloaded from a plane."

"Let's fast forward. Once you knew you had no chance at stealing the warhead, and you had made the decision to kill your brother, what did you do?"

"I had to ensure his death looked like an accident."

She held her hand up to stop him. "An accident?" She turned and studied the floor until her memory recalled what she had learned about the *Ticonderoga*. "I remember this," she said as she began to pace the floor. "My Military Studies professor used it as an example in one of his lectures. The device the *Ticonderoga* lost was attached to the underbelly of a Skyhawk."

She snapped her fingers. "There was an accident on the elevator." Her voice trailed off as the thoughts played forward in her mind. "Something went wrong and the pilot and plane were dumped overboard, and the weapon with them."

He turned his head, a veiled attempt to hide his eyes.

She pointed at him. "You *caused* the accident, didn't you?"

Yosef's voice choked. "We had completed a combat tour in Vietnam and had rotated off. The ship headed for Yokosuka, Japan for a little R and R. But on the way, the captain received orders for what is called a nuclear strike plan. A Russian carrier group was nearby and tensions were high. The temperatures were below freezing that day, and we were in the middle of a huge weather front. The ocean swells were at thirty feet. Even with the massive size of the aircraft carrier, the ship pitched from side to side. I knew where my brother's plane was. I knew when and where it would be moved from below decks, topside to be launched."

He swallowed and covered his eyes with a crinkled hand.

To Talia, it looked as if he was picturing the scene in his mind.

"The plane was rolled from the hangar bay and onto the number two elevator. The elevator sits on the edge of the ship and lifts multi-ton aircraft to the flight deck to be launched."

He began to cry, and his words came out in fits and starts. "Once on the elevator my brother would have applied pressure to the brake pedal to stop the plane from moving backward. But I had sabotaged the braking system. In the storm, as the ship leaned to port, the plane rolled off the elevator platform and was dumped overboard."

"And your brother with it."

"Yes," he whispered as he covered his eyes. "One of the sailors standing right there describe it to me. He said everything happened so quickly. My brother knew immediately he had no brakes. The look in his eyes was frantic. The sailor said the blue-shirts threw wooden chocks behind the plane, and grabbed at it, but it was too late. The plane rolled right over the chocks and through the safety rail. The back landing gear dropped off the edge and the front gear caused the plane to hang for just a moment. Then the plane dropped. It fell on its back. I picture it in my nightmares. I picture myself strapped into the cockpit, a helmet over my head, then being dumped overboard into the wet darkness." He looked up at Talia. "The canopy would have held for quite a while as the plane plummeted like a rock toward the ocean floor. Oh, it's so horrible!"

She walked the floor in front of the bed. "You knew once your brother's plane had been dumped overboard, he would have had no chance to escape." She stared at him, her mouth hanging open. "And in the high seas, no one would question the accident."

Yosef nodded. "His plane had a nuclear bomb attached to it at the time. The reason they never attempted a recovery was because of the ocean depth in the area."

Talia's voice descended into resignation. "That is correct. The depth was something like 4,900 meters, three miles down. Far too deep for a recovery." She put both hands on the top of her head "I studied that incident in graduate school. No public mention was made of it at the time. It wasn't until 1989 that the US admitted a one-megaton bomb had been lost. The Japanese were pretty pissed off about it as I recall. And now you're telling me it was deliberate?"

"After the accident," he said, "I went to—"

"*Accident*?" she said, interrupting. "History may record it as an accident, but you *murdered* him. That was no accident."

"I am sorry, my dear. You are correct." Yosef cleared his throat. "Having failed my mission, I needed to get off that ship and pursue Israel's goal another way. I went to the First Officer and told him that Lieutenant Junior Grade Golan Stiel, the pilot that had just perished, was my brother."

"They sent you home on bereavement leave, didn't they?"

"As a matter of standard operating procedure, yes. I was horrified at what I had done. I knew I had to honor my brother. My plan was to go home and bury him."

"Bury what?"

Yosef did not address the question. "And that is where my plans went awry. You see, my brother had dual citizenship, Israeli, and American. But our family were all in Israel."

"Wait, wait, wait," Talia said. "Bury *him*? His body was at the bottom of the ocean. What were you going to bury?"

Yosef shut his eyes. "His footlocker."

Talia's eyes wandered. "*His personals*. The Navy would have sent his personals home."

"That is correct. It was my wishes to place his personals into a casket to be returned home. I at least wanted to pay him that honor."

The old man looked away. His labored breathing punctuated the silence. Without looking up, he said, "But that is where the story takes a turn."

5

"What turn?" Talia said.

"The Navy honored my request to have Golan's personal items placed into a casket. But that casket was not sent to our home in Tel Aviv."

"It was sent to the United States, wasn't it?" She looked at him. "You thought the Navy would ship the casket to Israel."

"That is correct," the old man replied. "Since Israel wasn't yet officially recognized by the United States as a sovereign nation, it was the policy of the Navy to ship remains back to the States."

"But," she pointed at him again, "you were sent on bereavement leave. And since your family was in Israel, that's where they sent you, didn't they?"

"Yes. My brother's casket in one direction, myself in another. While we were at sea, the casket was offloaded to a sister ship and taken to the harbor. But our shore leave was canceled and it was months before the *Ticonderoga* itself came to port and I was allowed to disembark. All I could think about when I arrived in Tel Aviv was going to the US to recover my brother's casket so I could return him to Israel, to his final resting place. But two days after I got back, on June 3rd, 1967, that's when—"

Talia interrupted. "The Six-Day War erupted."

"Yes. It was the invasion Israel had feared. The Land was thrown into chaos. Invasion forces came at us from all sides. You can't imagine how terrified we were. With no nuclear device, we believed we would be overrun. But in the end, our military was able to defend our borders. To this day, it's considered a miracle of God that Israel wasn't destroyed. There is no other explanation. At any rate, the Director of the Mossad, one of the only people with operational knowledge of my mission, was killed."

"So no one besides you knew about the mission, and no one was interested in seeking the return of your brother's remains."

"That is correct."

"If Golan's casket was sent to the US, where was it interred?"

The old man looked away. His eyes pooled again, but no tears fell.

"The United States, if nothing else, is brilliant at honoring its dead. Even without a body, the American military wishes to honor those that have served and paid the ultimate sacrifice for their country. Golan's casket was laid to rest in the cemetery of his beloved United States Naval Academy in Annapolis, Maryland."

He paused a moment, and he folded his hands together. "There," he said, "my secret has been revealed to you. Now, it is up to you. You must go to the United States and retrieve Golan's casket and have it brought home, to its proper place, here in The Land."

"Tell me this, if it's so important to you that your brother's remains be moved to Israel, why don't you make the request yourself?"

The old man's eyes darted around the room as if he were searching for a lost item. "It is not possible," he finally said. "The United States, they knew . . ." He struggled to finish the sentence. "They found out about my involvement."

"But you said the US had no idea of the plot."

His words quickened. "You must retrieve your uncle's remains!"

Talia put her hands into the air and shook her head. "I'm in the middle of finishing my dissertation. I do not have the time, nor the inclination, to traipse off to a foreign country and retrieve the empty casket of an uncle I'm not even sure I have. In fact, I don't think I believe a word that's come out of your mouth."

She picked up her purse and started to leave in earnest.

"If you don't believe me," Yosef said as he reached a hand out, "please, go back to Mossad Headquarters. Pull the case file. But tell no one what you are up to."

Talia's shoulders dropped. "The case file about the fictitious mission you were talking about? You must be out of your mind."

"Peanut?" he said, an attempt to stop her in her tracks. "At least go discover for yourself that your uncle, Golan Stiel, was a real person. You have the access. You have the clearance. Once you discover that he was real, perhaps then you will believe me."

His coughing erupted, and a heart rate monitor let out a shrill cry.

The nurse rushed in, and this time injected a bolus of medication into his IV drip. She turned to Talia. "I'm afraid visiting hours are over. Mr. Stiel needs to rest." Moments later, the pulsing of the heart monitor subsided, and Yosef's eyelids began to droop. The medication was taking effect.

"What did you give him?" Talia said.

"It's just a mild sedative," the nurse replied.

Talia stopped in the doorway and looked back at Yosef, her emotions in a swirl. His eye flickered open, and for just a moment, she saw a twinkle, and it catapulted her back to her childhood.

6

Talia walked out of pod seven in a state of half-shock. Just the knowledge that her grandfather was alive was enough to disrupt her equilibrium. But the wild story was so detailed, she couldn't help but wonder if any part of it was true. She stopped at the nurse's station and leaned against the desk.

"He must have lost his mind," Talia said to herself.

"Are you all right, Miss?" the nurse in her later years asked.

Talia startled. "Oh. Fine."

"You don't look fine," the nurse added. "The intensive care unit isn't an easy place."

"I'm agitated, I guess. He just doesn't seem like he . . . You'll look after him? Mr. Stiel, I mean."

"Of course. Your grandfather is in good hands. We'll keep him as comfortable as we can."

"Thank you," Talia said, her voice leaking telltale signs of mental exhaustion. She started to walk but turned back. "Has there been any psychological evaluation?"

The nurse cocked her head. "Psychological? Let me look at his chart. Hmmm, no, there's nothing here. There hasn't been a need to from what I've seen. But I want you to know he's under the care of our top oncologists."

"So, when you've interacted with him, there hasn't been anything that made you feel like he's not all there, mentally, I mean?"

"Most patients in the ICU who are lucid are under a great deal of stress. We get everything from critically ill patients like your grandfather to traumatic injuries. I wouldn't let it bother you."

Talia nodded. "Is the oncologist here? I'd like to speak to him."

"The doctor should be making rounds in a few hours. That would be the time."

"Thank you. I'll be back." Talia rubbed her temples. "I've got to go somewhere and process all this." She hadn't realized how quietly her words had come out.

"I'm sorry?" the nurse said.

Talia looked up. "Oh, nothing. Can I leave you my cell phone number?" She turned and wrote the number on a pad. "Please, call me if his condition changes."

"Of course."

Talia walked down the hallway and boarded the elevator. It was time to get some fresh air.

* * *

Pod Seven. Thirty minutes later.

The elderly Yosef Stiel's eyes cracked opened as an orderly approached his bed. To Yosef, the dark-complected man appeared to be around thirty years of age, of obvious Israeli decent, yet the look in his eyes decried something between toil and deadness.

Stiel felt groggy, but drew back as the man reached underneath his pillow and pulled out a small black device about the size of a cellphone.

"What are you doing?" Yosef said.

The orderly pressed a button on the device. From a tiny speaker on the device, Yosef heard his own voice, and that of Talia's, replaying their earlier conversation.

"You recorded me?" Yosef blurted.

The man removed a tiny earpiece and held it up. "And I've been listening in. You have served your country well, old man. Your government owes you a debt of gratitude."

But as Yosef's mind began to clear, he realized he recognized the man's face. The right side was pockmarked, as though it had been drug across gravel, and a long scar ran the length, starting at the base of the jaw, crossing over the eye, then continuing onto the forehead. "I have always been loyal to The Land. My country owes me nothing. You and I have communicated with one another a half-dozen times. You never said anything about being here when my granddaughter arrived. How long have you been listening?"

The man's face hardened. "I heard every word. You revealed too much to her. The mission is now in jeopardy."

"No, no. The mission will be fine."

The man looked over his shoulder. "You should have just told her that her uncle's remains needed to be moved to Israel, and that was all."

Yosef's voice quivered. "She was not believing me. She didn't even think she had an uncle. She needed to be convinced. I thought—"

"You told her of the original plan to steal the nuclear tip from the device. And then you made the mistake of telling her the United States found out about your involvement. You have said too much, her curiosity will be our undoing."

"No," Yosef said as he thought back to the conversation. "You don't think she would—"

The man's tone sharpened. "You told her to look into the records to verify that her uncle did, in fact, exist. When she does that, what do you think she's going to find? Play it forward in your head, old man. Once she discovers he's real, she'll try to find out if there was a covert operation in the first place." His eyes narrowed to slits. "She will try to access the case files."

Yosef's eyes flickered from one side of the room to the next as his mind scrambled to come up with something to say. "No, she will find out her uncle does exist, and that his casket is in the US and should be moved. That is all. I have done exactly what our mission requires. She will have the casket exhumed and sent to Tel Aviv. Then, the operation can go forward, as planned."

The man laughed, and the sound of it curdled Yosef's stomach. "A fighter, till the last," the man said. "Tell me, how many others know our secret?"

"No one. No one knows," came the raspy reply. "I've held this secret for over fifty years and have never divulged it to anyone. And now that the casket will be brought here, the final objective can be completed."

"You are weak, old man. No one knows besides your granddaughter, you mean?"

"She had to be told. She didn't believe me." But as the thoughts played forward in Yosef's mind, he grabbed at the man's jacket. "You stay away from her!"

A sickening grin painted his face. "I have no intention of staying away from her. Once she is out of the way, we will move forward with the final objective in a different way."

"She is my granddaughter!"

"Tell me, do you know who I am? Who I truly am?"

"Of course I know who you are. I have known from the beginning. Your name has circulated within the shadows of the intelligence community for years. You are the one they call *the Raven*."

"And what am I known for?"

"You follow orders. That's what we all do."

"That is not what I am asking."

"You are an assassin."

"Go on."

"They say, they say you are insane, that you have no soul."

The Raven began to laugh. At first, the laughter was reserved, but then it escalated to an almost maniacal level.

The old man drew back, but the laughter suddenly stopped as if a switch had been turned off. The Raven towered over Yosef, and his eyes narrowed. "Insane? Is that what they say? Tell me what I want to hear!"

"They say you murdered your own parents!" Yosef blurted. He leaned further away, fearing a blow may come at any moment. When none came, he said, "You are known for killing your victims with a—"

"Coming out of the shadows was a mistake, old man."

Yosef's eyes flared, and he reached for the nurse call button, but the Raven slapped it out of his hand. Yosef drew back.

"You have failed your country for the last time." The Raven snapped his left arm down, the action causing a six-inch stainless dagger to slap into his hand. The steel dagger, which had been concealed under his sleeve, was honed into the cylindrical shape of an ice pick, but with a flat handle on the end.

Without hesitation, he yanked off Yosef's oxygen mask and covered his mouth to contain the screams. Yosef struggled, but the Raven plunged the blade into the base of the neck, forcing it in. The upward direction of the blade caused it to pierce Yosef's brain stem and cerebellum.

Yosef's eyes crunched shut against the pain, then the rigidity in his body abated. The Raven glanced at the heart monitor above Yosef's bed.

The jagged line representing Yosef's heartbeat slowly flattened. Then a piercing sound began to blare, a warning sign that the patient's heart had stopped. The Raven reached up and turned the knob to quiet the noise, then slid behind the room's open door.

An instant later, the elderly nurse, having seen the alarm on a monitor at the nurse's station, rushed in. The Raven grabbed her from behind, cupped his hand over her mouth, then plunged the blade into the base of her skull. The woman thrashed, but then her body went limp.

The Raven held her upright and closed the door. He then dragged her to the opposite side of the bed. He let her body flop to the ground where it landed out of sight. He took a hand towel from the bathroom and cleaned the blade, then wiped the blood from Yosef's neck. He stood back and studied the scene a moment as if to ensure that someone glancing into the room would see nothing out of the ordinary.

He walked out with the lackadaisical air of a person strolling in the park, then stepped behind the nurse's station. He switched off the monitoring equipment and glanced over his shoulder. He nodded to an orderly pushing a cart of supplies, then walked toward a stairwell door. He was gone.

7

Talia pulled into the underground parking deck at Mossad Headquarters. She parked in her spot but sat with the engine running, her hands still vice-gripped onto the steering wheel. "My grandfather?" she said to herself. Her senses were overwhelmed.

A rap on the window tore her out of her own fog. She startled at a uniformed soldier with an automatic rifle standing just outside her driver's window.

"Dr. Stiel?" he said as he glanced at the marker in front of her parking space. "Is everything all right?" He looked up, and his eyes scanned the other cars the way a Secret Service agent scans a crowd.

Talia nodded and glanced at his shoulder insignia. He was a member of the famed Sayeret, an elite unit within the Israeli Defense Force. In practice, Sayeret units typically specialized in commando and other special forces activities, but they also served as security for the Mossad. As far as Talia was concerned, they were everywhere.

She was so close to finishing her dissertation that her coworkers had begun calling her *Dr.* Stiel. It had become a bit of an office joke. They had even gone so far as to repaint her nameplate over her parking space. "I'm not a doctor yet," she said.

"Please kill your engine," the guard said. His tone was curt but polite. "Carbon monoxide."

She nodded then turned the key and opened her car door. The soldier nodded back. "Ma'am," he said, then continued his foot patrol.

She remained seated, and her mind drifted back to childhood. Memories of her grandfather came to her in fits and starts, like the flickering of an old newsreel. She remembered certain things. Him pushing her on a swing set behind the house, coming to the dinner table and finding he had placed a small gift there for her, a magnifying glass, and the smell of his aftershave, a cross between fresh earth and mint.

Something in the rear-view mirror caught her eye and Talia looked up. The military guard had returned but was simply on foot patrol. He nodded as he passed and she got out.

"Have a nice day, ma'am," the guard said.

"You, too."

Talia grabbed her bag and walked past the elevator bank to a heavy steel door, then scanned her badge across a digital card reader. When she heard the door's bolt thrown clear, she pulled it open and went through.

She walked down a long, starkly-lit hallway before entering the lobby. The lobby of the building served as the main security checkpoint, and was massive. Despite the volume of foot traffic traversing the floors daily, the dark marble was polished to a fine shine.

Talia found herself glancing down at the crest of the Mossad embedded into the floor. It consisted of a menorah, the seven-lamped ancient lamp stand, and was surrounded by Hebrew writing.

As Talia recalled the conversation with her grandfather, which had taken them back to the year 1965, she thought about the meaning of the menorah and the words surrounding the crest.

The menorah is described in the Torah as being made of pure gold. It was said to be used in the portable sanctuary set up by Moses in the wilderness, then later in the Temple in Jerusalem. Believers would pour fresh olive oil into its lamps and light them.

The Hebrew words on the Mossad crest, however, foretold something far more ominous. The words roughly translated to "*By way of clandestine strategy thou shalt do war.*"

She thought about that in light of the wild tale her grandfather had just woven.

Talia walked behind several other Mossad employees that had queued at the security checkpoint. About a dozen heavily-clad soldiers holding automatic rifles looked at each in turn, studying the faces, identification cards, and body language. Although this was just an average day at the Mossad, the tension was palpable in their faces.

She placed her bag onto a conveyor belt so it could be scanned, swiped her badge on a card reader, then placed her hand, palm down, onto a biometric scanner. The scanner lit up in yellow light as it searched the database for a matching hand print.

After a moment, the light turned green, an indication her identity had been verified. A Kevlar-laden guard standing next to the scanner studied her ID a moment, then compared the photo to her face. "Thank you, Dr. Stiel," he said. The guard smiled politely. Talia couldn't help but notice the man's eyes flick down to her chest.

Considering where the man was looking, she said to herself, *Hey, I'm up here*, but said, "I'm not a doctor yet."

"That's not what the computer says," he replied.

Talia shook her head then picked up her bag and walked through the metal detectors.

A man wearing a light gray, three-piece suit and bow tie speed-walked over to her. His steps were short, almost effeminate. "Talia, my dear," the man said with a slight lisp. "I just heard about your grandfather. Are you all right?"

His name was Moshe Himmelreich, and to Talia, he always reminded her of what Albert Einstein would have looked like had he trimmed his hair and grown a beard. He had been a close friend of the family, and when Talia's parents had died, he had raised her as if she were his own child.

Himmelreich's title was Director, Political Action, and his years of service were evidenced by the gray of his hair and beard. He was the de facto head of the Mossad Intelligence Services.

"I'm fine," she said. She put her arm around him and gave him a quick hug. Even in the halls of one of the world's most revered intelligence services, a hug between father and daughter wasn't frowned upon. "Just a little shaken up, I guess."

"I came as soon as I heard," Moshe said as he placed a hand on his flushed cheek. Moshe had never married, and although he would never admit it, Talia believed he preferred the same sex, not that it bothered her in the least. "It's shocking, just shocking. The fact that he's alive I mean."

As they walked down the corridor, he removed a finely pressed linen handkerchief from the breast pocket of his suit jacket and dabbed his forehead. "An ugly business this is," he said. "I was so worried when I heard. I thought it would upset you."

She looked at him and smiled. "I'm fine, Moshe."

"You know how much I like it when you call me Aba," he said referring to the way Israelis often address their fathers. "It must have been awful for you. Just awful."

"I don't have words for it." As they walked, she looked over her shoulder to ensure no one was behind them and waited until they had walked past another military guard. "Aba," she whispered, "there's something else."

"What is it, my dear?" he said as he took her by the arm. "You know you can tell Aba anything."

"He told me things, a wild story."

Moshe stopped her. "Oh dear. I was afraid you would find out one day."

"Find out?"

They began to walk again. "Your grandfather, he's, well, he's not all there." He looked at her with the eyes of a father. "It pains me to tell you this, dear, but there's mental illness in your family."

It took a moment for the thought to settle in Talia's mind. "You've made comments here and there, why didn't you tell me."

"Well, I suppose I didn't want to hurt you. I'm afraid whatever story he told you is likely a fabrication."

"I know. It's just, he was so detailed. And it sounded like a story you couldn't make up."

Moshe seemed lost in his own train of thought. "The man was always a little off-kilter, a real Meshugana if you ask me. I'm shocked he's still alive. Are you *sure* it was him?"

"Positive," she said with a tone of resignation. "I remember him from my childhood. I can see it in his eyes, the resemblance, I mean. It's uncanny."

"Well, you would know. We were all together when you were a child, your parents, your grandparents, and me."

"He's in the ICU at Sourasky. Cancer."

They continued down a corridor then turned toward Talia's office.

"Tell me what he said."

"It's . . . almost too much to believe. But, interestingly, it folds into my research."

"How so?"

Talia retold what Yosef had revealed. That he had been a Mossad agent, that he had tried to steal a nuclear weapon, the murder of his brother, all of it.

"That's astonishing," Moshe said, yet his tone was more mocking than supportive. "You know you cannot trust such a tale."

"I just—"

"My dear," Moshe interrupted, "Whatever he told you was a manipulation of his own warped mind. This is not the first time the man has gone off the rails. I mean, think about it. He was always a bit of an eccentric, never staying in one place, disappearing for months at a time. And apparently, he faked his own death." Moshe shook his head. "I was at his funeral. In fact, my dear, so were you."

Moshe dabbed his brow with the handkerchief again.

"Do you think any of it could be true? What about his brother?"

"Yosef Stiel *had* no brother." He stopped just outside her office. "I'm so sorry he caused you this much upset. Put it out of your mind."

"Aba, do you realize what it would mean if the story were true? I mean, I've researched every nuclear device that's gone missing since the Cold War. Are you sure he didn't have a brother?"

Moshe's tone sharpened this time. "It's a fabrication from an old man that doesn't deserve your attention. He was never there for you as a child, particularly after your parents died, God rest their souls. You're upset over the sudden appearance of this madman, and it has affected your judgment."

"But Moshe, I—" She studied his face a moment, and when a cold shiver ran her spine, she stopped herself. It was a look she had never seen before. Her shoulders slumped. "I'm sure you're right. It's been a very upsetting morning."

Talia opened the door to her office.

Moshe let out a long exhale, put his hands on her shoulders and smiled. "I raised you as if you were my very own daughter. I hate to see you this way. Perhaps you should go home and rest?"

"No. No, I'm fine," she said, a curt smile easing onto her face.

"All right. But if you need to, don't hesitate. I want my top Ph.D. at her best when she presents her dissertation to the Directorate next week."

"I'm not a Ph.D. yet. My report is almost done. I've rehearsed and rehearsed."

"Very well, my dear. And no more talk of wild stories."

Talia watched as he walked away. But there was something in her gut that wouldn't settle.

8

Talia sat at her desk. She still felt a little uneasy and began to second guess herself. The story her grandfather had retold had been wild. But at the same time, she couldn't help but notice a number of things she knew to be true.

As a graduate student, she had spent an entire semester studying the various incidents involving nuclear materials from around the world. She also knew that globally, over one hundred devices had gone missing over the years. Most had been lost during the Cold War between Russia and the United States and were still unaccounted for.

During that time period, tensions had been so high between the nations that it had become common to load nuclear weapons onto military aircraft. It was a practice still in use in Israel today.

Although a few of the devices had disappeared under suspicious circumstances, the majority had simply been lost due to accidents at sea or in the air, just like the accident Yosef had described. Several had been separated from the underside of Naval aircraft which had either undergone mechanical trouble or had been involved in mid-air collisions, usually with members of their own squadron. At the end of her research, Talia had been shocked at the sheer volume of them.

But in the case of the USS *Ticonderoga*, Yosef Stiel had been accurate about so many things. The dates he spoke of were precise. December 5, 1965. On that date, the USS *Ticonderoga* did, in fact, lose an A-4E Skyhawk fighter-bomber with a nuclear bomb strapped to its belly.

The location of the accident had been accurate as well. And even Talia's knowledge of naval operating procedures added up.

She took a few deep breaths, a futile attempt to blow out the jittery feeling in her stomach. "You *know* Moshe is right," she said to herself. Yet it wasn't two hours later that her curiosity got the best of her.

She stopped in the middle of re-reading her dissertation paper for the hundredth time. "The man is obviously a nut-job, but is it going to kill me to confirm he didn't work for the Mossad?" She tapped at her laptop and accessed a classified section of the Mossad's vast computer network. She clicked into a directory labeled, "Personnel," then typed in the name *Yosef Harel Stiel*. When her query returned a hit, her spine stiffened.

There she sat, face to face with a headshot of a man who was a much younger-looking version of her grandfather. "You've *got* to be kidding me," she said. She let her finger trace the monitor as she read.

NAME: YOSEF HAREL STIEL
DATES OF SERVICE: 2 FEB 1965 - 9 MAR 1993
MILITARY OCCUPATIONAL SPECIALTY: REDACTED

"REDACTED?" she said. "What's that supposed to mean?" Never in Talia's experience had she come across a personnel file where the job description was *Redacted*. "I don't get it. Where's the rest of this file?" She clicked on the hyperlinked tabs at the top: Background, Role, Human Resources, but they were grayed out as if there was nothing to click. And she knew, someone had purposely removed the records. Talia's eyes drifted to the bottom of the page.

The final entry said:

CURRENT ASSIGNMENT OR OUTCOME: DECEASED

"DECEASED, MY ASS," Talia said as she leaned back in her chair. "That was him. No one else called me Peanut. No one could have even known about that." The thoughts played forward. "So he *was* in the Mossad. I can't believe it." But believe it she did. "This record has been heavily altered."

Her next thought was to tap into the operational records system, a separate area of the network. It took a moment, but after clearing three security challenges, she was in. The familiar warning message painted the screen.

UNAUTHORIZED ACCESS PROHIBITED
UTILIZATION OF THIS SYSTEM IS GOVERNED BY THE PROTECTION OF PRIVACY LAW
CODE SECTION 5741-2981
DATABASE CLASSIFICATION: HIGH SECURITY
BREACH NOTIFICATION: UNAUTHORIZED ACCESS WILL BE PROSECUTED
LEVEL: HIGH TREASON
AUTHORITY: ISRAELI LAW, INFORMATION AND TECHNOLOGY AUTHORITY (ILITA)

She clicked through the warning screen and placed her cursor into the search box. She started by limiting the query to one date, December 5, 1965, the date of the *Ticonderoga* accident. After typing the date into the search box, her finger hesitated over the Enter key on her keyboard. She clicked it. A single record popped onto the screen.

CODE NAME OR DESIGNATION: RED SCORPION
INSTANTIATION: 5 DEC 1965
VISIBILITY: EYES ONLY

"There *was* an operation on that date."

She heard a small commotion in the hallway and glanced up.

When she looked back at her monitor, the screen had inexplicably gone blank. Talia's brow darkened at the sight. The laptop was still powered on, and the browser was still active, but the webpage had simply gone blank.

"What the hell?" She tapped at the keyboard to refresh the browser page. The browser again painted a blank screen. Her eyes flickered up at the hallway. But when she hit the refresh button on the browser a second time, this time it read:

FILE DELETED OR REDACTED

"WHAT?" Talia whispered.

A man appeared in the doorway. The bottom of his rumpled suit jacket splayed wide as he tried to close it over what must have been one hundred pounds of unneeded body weight. His eyebrows were heavy like thick, fuzzy gray caterpillars. But what caused her to cock her head to the side was the fact that he was flanked by several military guards.

"Dr. Stiel?" the man said, his voice thick.

"I'm *Miss* Stiel, yes?" Talia replied as she closed the lid on her laptop.

"Pardon me. May I come in?" he said, but walked in without waiting for a reply. His tone was harsh, yet disarming at the same time. He squeezed his enormous frame into a chair in front of her desk and said, "Let me introduce myself. My name is Pakad Avraham Zaret. I'm with the *Mišteret Yisra'el*."

"I'm sorry, what's a Chief Inspector of the Israel Police doing in my office?" Talia became suddenly aware of a wave of heat rising from her blouse.

Inspector Zaret looked over his shoulder at the armed guards flanking the door. He flicked at a fluorescent orange visitor badge that was clipped to his top pocket. "My apologies about the armed escort. The Mossad doesn't take kindly to visitors inside their headquarters. At any rate, I'm sorry to be the one to tell you, but I am the bearer of bad news. It's your grandfather, I'm afraid."

Talia stared at him a moment then her vision washed free of all color. "He's . . ." she searched for the words, "gone? I just saw him. So soon?"

"Yes, ma'am."

He pulled out a notepad and pen from inside his coat. "The incident occurred approximately one hour and fifty minutes ago."

"Incident?"

"Your grandfather was murdered."

9

Talia stared at the inspector. "He couldn't have been murdered. No, he has cancer. His illness is terminal." When the inspector did not reply, she said, "I was just in his room. He wasn't murdered. Why would you say such a thing?"

The inspector glanced at the notepad. "Another individual, a Mrs. Shira Doron, a nurse, was a victim as well. The coroner estimated their times of death to be identical. Surveillance video shows that you exited the room twenty-nine minutes before another individual, a male. Who else was there with you, Miss Stiel?" His tone had drifted to the accusatory.

But Talia's was still transfixed. "Why do you say he was murdered?"

"In twenty-nine years working homicides, I have covered plenty of stabbings."

Talia's face paled, and she sat with the information a moment. "Stabbings?"

"Now, the coroner will list the *official* cause of death at a later time, but right now, I need you to tell me who that man was."

"What *man*?"

He rattled off a description as if he were reading, "Dark-complected, one hundred and seventy pounds, twenty-five to thirty-five years of age, dark coat, dark trousers, a scar running the right side of his face."

"What are you *talking* about?"

"He was in there nearly at the same time as you."

"You're accusing *me*?" Her volume had escalated higher than she had intended and one of the armed guards at the doorway looked in. Talia stood and turned to the window. She put a hand over her mouth. "I'm sorry, I didn't mean to yell. This has all been just too much. He's really gone?" she said. "I only found out he was alive this morning."

"I don't follow you."

"I don't have any family, Inspector. Well, no real family anyway. My parents died when I was a child. And from what I knew, all my grandparents were gone as well. I got a call this morning from the hospital telling me my grandfather was alive. And now, you're telling me he's been murdered?"

Thoughts swirled in her mind: her grandfather laying on the hospital bed, the twinkle in his eye, a memory of the two of them in Moshe's little dingy on Dalton Lake, and then, the sudden redaction of the classified document she had just accessed.

The inspector looked over his shoulder at the guards. "Miss Stiel, this is a murder investigation. I am not comfortable here under the prying eyes of the Mossad. I'll need you to come to headquarters. I have some further questions for you."

"Frankly, I don't care for your tone."

"Miss Stiel, in Israel murder is *my* jurisdiction. It's a matter of national law. If I need to question a person of interest, that decision is mine and mine alone." Zaret pushed himself up from the chair. Given his considerable body weight, the act took him a moment. "Gather your belongings, please."

The hallway came alive as a small commotion erupted just outside the door. Talia looked out.

"Oh, let me through," a man said. The voice was effeminate, and Talia recognized it as Moshe's.

"Identification, please," one of the guards said.

"Identification?" Moshe replied. His normally timid voice had quickened. "You know damn well I'm the Director of Political Action. Now step aside. What's all this about anyway?"

"Orders, sir," the guard replied after examining Moshe's ID card, then handing it back to him.

Moshe walked into Talia's office but stopped at the sight of Inspector Zaret. "Oh, my goodness, am I interrupting?"

"Moshe, no," Talia said as he motioned toward the detective.

"Inspector Zaret, this is Moshe Himmelreich. He's the number two in command."

The two men shook. Moshe removed his cloth handkerchief and dabbed his forehead with it. Talia couldn't help but notice he seemed to be having trouble figuring out what to do with his hands.

"Is everything okay?" she said.

"Fine, I, I just wanted . . ." He couldn't peel his eyes from Zaret. "There's been some . . . I need you to . . ." Finally, he clasped his hands behind his back and smiled. "Dr. Stiel, when you are finished, would you please join me in my office?"

"Actually Moshe, I was just telling the inspector here that I'm not leaving Mossad HQ. I'm sorry," Talia said as she looked at Zaret. She looked back at Moshe. "Apparently, my grandfather has been murdered."

"I know dear," Moshe said. "I just heard. That's what I was coming to tell you."

"The inspector seems to think I knew something about it."

"What's this then?" Moshe blurted. "Inspector, I can assure you Dr. Stiel is not a murderer." He pushed his wire-rimmed glasses higher onto his nose. "How dare you accuse her of such. She is an esteemed member of the Mossad, a true servant of The Land."

Zaret held up a stiff palm to Moshe. "Miss Stiel is a material witness in a murder investigation, and I'm taking her in."

"You'll do nothing of the kind," Moshe said. "This is a federal facility." He turned his head to the door. "Guards?" Two Kevlar-laden soldiers entered. "Escort Inspector Zaret to the front gates."

"Yes, sir," came their stilted reply.

Four of the guards inserted themselves in front of Zaret, and one took him by the arm.

Zaret smiled politely to the men in uniform. He patted one on the shoulder. "Ah, our fine soldiers. That is all right, my dear boy. You are just doing your job." He looked back at Moshe. "I play golf with the Interior Minister on Saturdays. Perhaps you'd like to join us this weekend? I'm sure he would be *fascinated* to ask why you interfered with the investigation of a capital crime." Zaret held out a hand, "It was nice to meet you, Director Himmelreich."

The guards took Zaret out.

10

The next morning as Talia pulled her car into her assigned parking space at Mossad Headquarters, she rubbed sleep from her eyes. She had tossed and turned the prior night as the stress of day's events took its toll. She glanced at her makeup in the rearview mirror, grabbed her bag, hopped out of the car and affixed her security badge to a pocket on her dress.

But as she scanned her badge across the steel door, she stop. She took one glance at the elevator door to her right and the sign that read "Fire Evac Only." The elevator led to one place, the sub-basement level. It had been installed years prior as a means of secondary escape in the event of a fire.

The reasoning at the time suggested that if a person should find themselves in the underground recesses of the records room when a fire alarm was sounded, the high-security doors would lock to protect the contents from being destroyed. The elevator provided a person's solitary means of escape.

The elevator was only accessible from that level, but just looking at the doors made her think about the records stored there. Something haunted her from yesterday:

CODE NAME OR DESIGNATION: RED SCORPION

Red Scorpion. The code name of a project of top-secret status. Yesterday's events swirled in her mind. Yosef had been murdered just after telling her about an operation that took place on the exact date as Operation *Red Scorpion*. And her access to the digital records of that operation had been redacted just as she'd opened it.

A brief wave of nausea wafted over her but was quickly replaced by familiar dizziness. Her vertigo had kicked in, but she could tell it wouldn't last. She put a hand against the wall to brace herself and took a few deep breaths.

As her equilibrium stabilized, she walked through the corridor, and her thoughts railed forward. The project's instantiation date corresponded exactly to what Yosef had told her. Talia knew she'd have to dig this out for herself. And she also knew there was but one way to proceed: she would have to go to the records room and find the physical case file the old-fashioned way.

As she walked to the security checkpoint, she thought to herself, *You're going to be distracted all day until you go down there.*

Once past security, Talia tossed the strap of her tiny purse over her head and walked to the facility's main bank of elevators. Several Mossad employees waited there, all headed to upper floors of the building. Talia was the only one headed down.

She boarded an otherwise empty elevator and swiped her identity badge through the scanner inside. The buttons controlling access to the below-ground floors lit up, and she pressed a button labeled SF-5, a level five stories below ground.

Talia's research had taken her to the sub-basement levels on numerous occasions, and as the elevator descended, she rubbed her eyes again. "What am I doing?" she murmured. To her, it felt as though she were on a wild goose chase.

Up to this point, she hadn't allowed herself to believe her grandfather's wild claims. In fact, if she allowed herself to believe them, that would mean he was not the man of her memories, the one who took her for ice cream, who visited on holidays, and had brought her the gift of a hand-carved rocking horse. The dichotomy was something she couldn't reconcile.

And, if any part of the story were true, it would cast a sickening pallor over her employer, the Mossad. She knew full well the Mossad was involved in clandestine activities, but she couldn't picture the authorization of unjustified murder.

She distracted herself by thinking how many times she'd pulled records out of storage. In research for her dissertation, fact-finding was her favorite part. Each box filled with records had a history all its own. Discovering once forgotten secrets was fascinating.

Although she had to admit, the vast majority of files housed in the highly secured sub-floor were more boring than most people would imagine. Instead of cases involving international espionage and intrigue, many were operations that simply recorded movements of various people of interest.

The Israeli government, in its desire to protect itself, had long made it a practice to spy on individuals whom it believed may be plotting against it. A not uncommon reaction to the dangers of a country surrounded by enemies.

The elevator doors opened, and Talia walked to the security desk. Behind the desk was a wall of tinted fire-proof glass separating the small lobby area from the massive collection of records.

The storage space itself was gargantuan, particularly for an underground facility. The entire span of the building, approximately the square footage of a European football field, was occupied by row after row of warehouse shelving. Shelves, packed from top to bottom with boxes, files, and other items, rose to a uniformed height of eighteen feet and fit snugly beneath the twenty-two-foot ceilings.

The desk was manned twenty-four hours a day by security officers, all of whom were familiar with the layout of the stacks. Only one officer was on duty at any point in time, yet never in her experience had Talia found the security desk unoccupied. She wondered how these "librarians," as she thought of them, ever had a chance to go to the restroom.

Talia recognized the uniformed man posted there. He looked up from his work and glanced at her badge. "May I help you, *Dr.* Stiel?" the man said with a grin.

Talia smiled. Although the name on her badge did not include the title of Doctor, the inner-office joke lived on.

"I'm looking for an old case file. I don't have the case number this time, but its name is *Operation Red Scorpion*? I not sure it even exists but —" Talia stopped mid-sentence as the aroma of cinnamon, and sweet yeast wafted over her. She was catapulted in her mind back to childhood, back into the kitchen of her parents' bakery.

Sights and smells from those carefree days flickered into her mind's eye. Her as a little girl covered in white flour, giggling with her mom. Sneaking a chocolate chip when her Ima wasn't watching. The smell of yeast as the bread was rising.

And then she saw it. Sitting on the security desk was a Krantz pastry. With countless layers of thin yeast dough interspersed with a not-too-sweet chocolate filling, the delicacy had been one of her mother's favorites. The babka-like pastry lay on a disposable plate, half eaten.

"*Red Scorpion*?" the guard replied, shaking Talia from her memories. "Hold on, let me look." He tapped at a computer keyboard and ran his finger across the screen. "Case number 8076. Wow, a four-digit case file. Considering the cases are sequentially numbered, that *is* old."

"Wait, it's a real case file?"

"Well certainly." His head tilted to the side as he studied the screen. "Hold on a minute. This file is in the active group. That changes things. I'm afraid I'll have to call for authorization before you can access the active section."

"There must be some mistake. Even if it does exist, this is a historical file. It dates back to 1965. It can't be active."

"We don't make mistakes, ma'am. I'll need to hold your credentials, please."

Talia shook her head and handed the young guard her badge. Yet her eyes wandered back to the Krantz, and she thought about the bakery. Her mother's smile had been so wide, her eyes so large. Nothing in real life could account for the beauty she remembered in her mother's face.

She cleared her throat to avoid it tightening and distracted herself with thoughts of her grandfather. The idea that *Operation Red Scorpion* existed lent his story credibility. But then again, according to Moshe, that would be just like her grandpa. He had apparently always been an expert at weaving bits of truth into his lies.

The guard picked up a phone and dialed. As Talia waited, she strolled to the glass wall and stared at the shelves. They were stacked so full that a person couldn't see from one row through to the next.

After a few moments, the man hung up. "Sorry about that, Dr. Stiel. I'm required to get authorization for anyone accessing the active stack. Regulations." He glanced at his computer monitor. "I see that looking at your past access, you've never requested an active file?" His eyes flashed at her chest, but just for a moment.

Talia crossed her arms. "Well, no. Is there a problem?"

"No, ma'am. You have all the access you need. But you are aware that all the files in the active section are eyes-only? You must be cleared to view each file individually. If you need to view other files, besides this one, please just return to the desk, and we'll make the appropriate call."

Talia glanced at a second computer monitor in front of the man. It displayed the view from multiple independent security cameras. He continued. "You'll find the active stacks at the far end, all the way in the south-east corner, closest to the wall." He took the scrap of paper and jotted on it. "Your file is on row forty-nine, stack fourteen, shelf nine, space eleven. That's almost at the top of the shelving. The active sector is separated by a glass wall similar to this one. To enter you'll need to walk down row thirty-five. That's where the entrance is. Just scan your badge to gain entry."

"Thank you," Talia said as he handed her ID back. He pressed a button, and the glass door slid open. Talia walked in and could feel his eyes on her backside. The way men looked at her body often made her uncomfortable, but in the male-dominated world of the Israeli government, it was such a common occurrence, she had hardened to it.

The temperature of the records room was kept at sixty-five degrees year round, a sometimes pointless effort to thwart mold and mildew from forming. Talia crossed her arms against the cold and walked down the center aisle all the way to row thirty-five, then turned left.

She walked about three-quarters of the way and stopped at the glass wall separating the secure area. The walk had been so far that, in her heels, her feet already hurt.

The wall of bulletproof glass lined the entire periphery and a sign posted on the door read, "Authorized Personnel Only." Talia looked up at a security camera then scanned her badge. The heavy glass door wafted open with a *swish,* and she walked in. As the door closed behind her, she couldn't help but notice the quiet. It was so quiet, in fact, that she couldn't even hear noise coming from the air conditioning vents.

She walked into the rows, her heels clacking on cold cement, and glanced at the paper in her hand. Again she thought back to childhood. More flickers of the bakery popped into her mind. The feel of her mother standing behind her, guiding her little hands as they pushed a rolling pin back and forth. Her mother slipping a hand onto Talia's rib cage, tickling her while she rolled. Talia would let go of the rolling pin and giggle.

"Come on, my sweet Talia," her mother would say as she too laughed. "We must roll the dough."

"But you're tickling me!" Talia would reply as she began to roll again.

Her mother would tickle her other side, and Talia would giggle and withdraw her arms again.

"Ima!"

The smell of fresh yeast, the glow of her mother's smile, a smile that, to Talia, symbolized warmth, love, and a feeling that *everything's going to be all right*. Those had been good days, days when Talia knew she was loved. And it all had ended so abruptly.

11

When Talia finally reached row forty-nine, she walked down it and read labels on the shelving until she got to stack eleven. She looked up and squinted. Shelf nine was indeed almost at the ceiling. Talia walked over to a heavy rolling metal staircase and pushed the monstrosity into position.

"Even if there is an *Operation Red Scorpion*, I'm sure it's going to turn out to be something else." But her curiosity had piqued. "What wild story has grandpa concocted this time?"

She ascended the stairs until at the top of a small level platform. From there, she located shelf space eleven. Two cardboard boxes with lids sat nestled against one another. One was of a different style of box and was covered in a thick layer of dust, yet Talia noticed what appeared to be relatively recent finger smudges across the top. The label on the older one read:

CODE NAME OR DESIGNATION: RED SCORPION
CASE NO: 380987
DATE CLOSED OR TERMINATED: 2 NOV 1965
VISIBILITY: EYES ONLY

"SEE?" Talia said to herself as she removed the dusty lid. "It says right there. The operation terminated even before the Six-Day War. Why is this in the active section?"

A smell of must wafted out. It reminded her of when she would spend a week each summer at Moshe's tiny cabin on the edge of Dalton Lake in Israel's north country. She had gone there on numerous occasions with both Moshe and her grandfather.

She closed her eyes a moment and inhaled. She could picture Moshe's smile, his face much younger in those days, her grandfather sitting on the porch cleaning fish, and the little dingy tapping gently against the dock.

She glanced inside the box. Not unlike others she had opened, it was stocked full of old button-and-string style manila envelopes, each tied shut.

"This might take a while," she said as she let out a long exhale. There were seven large envelopes in total. All were yellowed and worn. But then something occurred to her. "Actually, this shouldn't take any time. *Operation Red Scorpion* might have been an actual codename, but it has nothing to do with grandpa." She shook her head. "I can't believe I walked all the way down here for this."

She picked up the first envelope and squeezed it to feel its contents. Aside from one bulge at the bottom, it seemed to contain nothing but paperwork. She untied the string and dumped the contents into an open hand.

A yellowed file folder, the type with a bonded, flat metal bar to hold its contents, dropped into her hand. She was about to look to see what else was in the envelope when her eyes traced the words on the outside. Stamped at the top, it read:

ACCESS RESTRICTION(S): TOP SECRET
USE RESTRICTION(S): EYES ONLY

"YEAH, YEAH," she said. "I've got your clearance right here."

THEN, further down, toward the center:

CLANDESTINE SERVICES HISTORY

SUBJECT OR OPERATION CODENAME: RED SCORPION
COMPILED: 1965 DECEMBER
GOVERNMENTAL ENTITY: MOSSAD
DEPARTMENT: CAESAREA
PROJECT UNIT: KIDON
PROJECT LEAD: YITZHAK HOFI
PRIORITY DESIGNATION: AT ALL COSTS

DO NOT DESTROY

"'At all costs.' My, my. I'll say this, grandpa certainly doesn't disappoint. Let's find out what *Red Scorpion* is." She read the rest of the manila folder allowing her finger to trace the words as she read. "Yup, the *Kidon*, literally meaning 'the tip of the spear.' That unit belongs to the Caesarea department of the Mossad. They run assassinations and infiltrations. This is the first time I've ever seen a Kidon file. And I'll be damned. Look at that, *Yitzhak Hofi* oversaw this operation." Talia thought for a moment. "He later became the Director of the Mossad. Back in the early '70s."

She flipped open the file and read the first page. There, she perused the table of contents:

PRINCIPAL PROJECT AND ACTIVITY

EXCULPATORY OVERVIEW: TAB A
INFILTRATION: TAB B
EXECUTING UNIT: TAB C
INTENDED OUTCOME: TAB E

Talia knew from experience that operational files tended to have a summary page at the front, containing the most pertinent details. This file was no different. She flipped to the second page and read.

**EXCULPATORY OVERVIEW:
STABILIZE BORDER SECURITY VIA HEIGHTENED MILITARY RESPONSE CAPACITY**

But then her eyes locked onto a type-written line written in a different font. Even the color of the ink appeared darker.

**OPERATIONAL CROSS REFERENCE:
OPERATION RED DRAGON EXECUTED IN CONCERT WITH OPERATION ABSOLUTION**

Talia liked to think out loud. She found it helped her clarify her thoughts. She read and reread the sentence. "That's weird. It looks like someone added this after the fact." She shook her head but knew the Mossad never revealed the details of related ops within the same case file. She glanced at the newer box beside her and knew this was going to take some digging.

"Wait a second," she said, again scanning the name of the operation. "Absolution? What's Operation Absolution?"

She glanced at the space number printed onto the metal shelving, then at the scrap of paper in her hand. "I'm definitely on the right spot." But when her eyes read the label on the outside of the newer box, the one sitting right next to the old one, she stopped. It was marked:

**CODE NAME OR DESIGNATION: ABSOLUTION
CASE NO: 380987**

"Both operations have the same case number? I don't get it." She glanced between the two.

The newer box read:

DATE CLOSED OR TERMINATED: N/A

"So *that* one is active. Okay, one old case file, *Red Scorpion*, one still active, *Absolution*. She shook her head and continued reading from the *Red Scorpion* case file.

MODE OF OPERATION - INFILTRATION.
HIDE IN PLAIN SIGHT. INSERT COVERT ASSET AS WEAPONS SPECIALIST / WEAPONS ASSEMBLY OFFICER.

"Well, that's interesting," she said as she thought back to her grandfather's words. *I was a warrant officer . . . a weapons specialist.*

INTENTION - INFILTRATE USS TICONDEROGA.

She stopped right there. Upon reading the words *USS Ticonderoga*, her mouth dropped open. "Oh my God." It was almost too much to take in. She placed a hand onto the railing to steady herself on the platform. "He wasn't lying?"

Then she heard a noise. It came from the other side of the wall, through the thick glass enclosure. To Talia, it sounded like a muffled *whump*, but it was barely audible. She looked up but then shook her head. "You're getting paranoid."

She read further and her eyes locked onto the page.

INTENDED OUTCOME: OBTAIN A NUCLEAR DEVICE VIA CLANDESTINE ACTION.

"OH, SHIT," Talia said as she covered her mouth with her hand. "So it's true. Israel did have an operation to steal a weapon, *Operation Red Scorpion*." She glanced at the newer box and knew she needed to know what *Operation Absolution* was as well. She dropped the manila file folder from *Operation Red Scorpion* into its envelope, but when it did not go all the way in, she pulled it out again.

That's when she noticed something at the bottom of the envelope. She turned it upside down and a small metal canister dumped into her hand. The canister had no labeling on it, was drab green in color, appeared old and scratched, and was capped. She held it a moment before shoving the old *Red Scorpion* box aside and opened the newer box.

The *Operation Absolution* box also contained manila file folders, but the printed materials appeared much newer, perhaps having been generated by a modern laser printer.

Talia opened the first file and scanned it. Several things jumped off the page at her.

RECOVER THE NUCLEAR DEVICE . . .

SECURITY OF THE NATION OF ISRAEL . . .

AT ALL COSTS . . .

ANY MEANS NECESSARY . . .

"ALL RIGHT," she said. "So, if what Yosef said was true, and Israel was trying to obtain a nuclear device in 1965, but *Operation Red Scorpion* failed, then why is *this* operation still active? I mean, 1965 was more than fifty years ago. We've got all the nukes we could ever want. And what do they mean *recover the nuclear device*?"

She scanned to the next section.

OPERATIONAL OBJECTIVE, REVISED

FURTHER DOWN IT READ,

COVERT PLACEMENT OF THE WEAPON . . .

BUT THEN A *SWISH* sound interrupted her concentration, and she looked up. It was the bulletproof door sliding open. *Someone else must be accessing the active stacks*, she thought. She glanced back to the file.

HEZBOLLAH . . . HAMAS . . .

A MAN APPEARED at the end of the row, and Talia turned. He was holding a box similar to so many others on the shelves and began walking in her direction. He nodded to her in a polite yet businesslike manner. But when she noticed a long scar running the length of his face, her mouth dropped open.

Upon seeing Talia's reaction, his stride increased in length and pace. It was as if he knew he'd been recognized. In one swift motion, he tossed the box aside, pulled out a handgun, and aimed it at her.

12

At first sight of the gun, Talia froze, virtually paralyzed. He fired a silenced round. Flame burst from the end of the barrel, and the bullet zipped through the file folder Talia was holding. It slammed into the older box. Shards of yellowed paper peppered the air.

Talia dropped onto the staircase's metal landing as a second bullet missed her head by a millimeter, blowing her hair back. The man continued his deliberate stride as he fired again and again. Silenced bullets smashed into the metal railing beside her.

Out of instinct, Talia flung the open case file boxes aside and leapt into the shelving. The man had closed the distance, and Talia heard the heavy *clank* of his heels on the metal staircase. She crawled deeper into the shelving and kicked two boxes, sending them flying in his direction. Both rained their contents on top of the gunman just as he reached the landing.

She scrambled to the other side of the shelving and yanked two more boxes out of her way.

He leveled the gun at her, and a lopsided, sickening grin painted his face.

Talia kicked the boxes in his direction. One of them knocked into the gun just as he pulled the trigger. The bullet, intended for her head, clipped the flesh of her left shoulder, but in the adrenaline-fueled terror, she didn't feel it.

She kicked another box at him and flung her body over the edge of the other side of shelving and grabbed the edge at the last moment. She hung from the shelves only long enough to get a foothold on the shelf below, then crawled down the outside of two more shelves.

Upon hearing the man shove boxes aside as he climbed through the shelving to come after her, Talia reversed course. Instead of leaping to the floor below, she scrambled back in the opposite direction, toward the metal staircase. As the man popped out on one side of the shelving, Talia popped out on the other. She shoved boxes aside and jumped down, a height of about eight feet. Her heels landed with a loud *clack* against the cement. She tumbled sideways then jumped up, flicking off her heels in the process. She ran barefoot down the row in the direction of the sliding door.

The man leapt down and landed like a cat. He then ran toward the end of the row.

Talia turned and sprinted for the door, about two rows away. Just as she reached it a bullet ricocheted off the bulletproof glass. She ducked just in front of the door, and the door whooshed open. She dove through then got up and ran through the stacks on the other side. She turned down one row, ran to the end, turned again, and continued her escape in a zig-zag pattern.

When she popped out onto the main walkway, she was two rows from the exit. She nearly tripped over the body of a guard. Her eyes locked onto the pool of blood on the floor below him and she froze for a second. It was the same man that had checked her in.

She started to turn to run toward the sliding glass door where the security desk sat, but a bullet slammed into the bulletproof glass in front of her. She ducked and ran in the opposite direction. She'd been cut off. Her mind scrambled, but then she remembered, *the fire-evacuation elevator.*

She ran for it and pressed the button. The door wafted open, and she jumped in just before the gunman rounded the corner. She repeatedly pressed the only button inside, one simply labeled "Up," in repeated succession.

As he ran in her direction, the sound of his footsteps slamming into the cement grew louder.

13

The pounding of footsteps escalated as Talia continued pressing the Up button. The elevator door slid closed a moment before the gunman arrived. As the elevator ascended toward its only destination, the parking deck level, Talia panted to catch her breath. A wave of heat flushed up her neck, and a brief bout of nausea ensued, chased with a dose of dizzying imbalance. She slumped to the floor and tried her deep breathing exercises.

So much adrenaline coursed her veins that her hands, arms, and even torso began to shake. The vertigo leveled off but did not relinquish its grip. She stood and leaned on the wall and looked for an emergency phone or call button, anything with which she could alert the Sayeret soldiers.

The imbalance in her equilibrium made it hard for her to hold her head up straight. She closed her eyes and breathed deeply. The elevator chimed once, indicating it had reached the parking level. The door slid open, and she braced its sides to step out, yet had trouble maintaining her balance.

She looked down the long expanse of cars until her eyes landed on the entrance where a guard shack was positioned. In her dizziness, it looked as though the ceiling of the parking deck was bending and waving in a rolling motion. She stumbled to the first car and used it for balance, then began to call out.

"Help!" she half-yelled, but being over one hundred meters away, the guards could not hear her. She struggled forward, moving in their direction. Her feet were unsteady, yet she pressed on, all the while trying to force the vertigo to abate.

She made it halfway down when from behind her, near the elevator, a stairwell door flung open and slammed into the wall. The scar-faced gunman burst from it. Talia dropped to her knees and shimmied toward the wall to hide.

She raised her head just enough to see the man through the glass of several cars that were between them. The man squinted toward the guard shack as if to check if he had been heard, then his head craned in all directions. He walked in her direction, and the distance between them closed.

Talia turned toward the guard shack and opened her mouth, but before she could scream, she stopped herself knowing they'd never hear her.

The sound of the man's footsteps grew louder.

Talia watched as he inspected the space between each car, then got down on his hands and knees to look underneath.

The closer he got, the more Talia's heart rate accelerated. He was just three cars away now. She ducked lower to avoid being seen but knew, once he bent down to look under the car, he would see her. He was now two cars away.

She stopped breathing. In the hollow-sounding deck, she could hear the quiet crunching of grit under his heels. He had reached the trunk side of the car she was hiding behind. He glanced down both sides of it.

Talia's only thought was to peer under the car and follow his feet, but the gunman dropped to the ground, and his face appeared. When he saw the terror in Talia's eyes, a crooked smile went across it.

Talia's mouth opened as if to scream, but no sounds came out. Her heart pounded, her breathing became erratic, and the vertigo intensified. Talia slumped, almost paralyzed with the spinning of the room.

The man walked between the cars with taunting slowness until he could see her. He stood and studied her a moment, almost as if to evaluate why she wasn't screaming.

"Where is it?" he said. He waited a moment. Talia was so frozen in fear, she could not speak. "I said, where is it?" The words were harsher this time. "I saw it in your hand." When Talia didn't respond again, he reached his right hand inside his opposing sleeve and began to pull something out. Talia's eyes caught the glint of a polished steel blade.

"Sir?" a male voice yelled from the guard shack. "Sir? Is there a problem?"

The man pushed the dagger back under his sleeve as the guard approached.

When he turned to speak to the guard, Talia saw the scar and pock-marked skin on his face.

The soldier approached the car and said, "Sir, I was asking if everything was all right. You'll need your identification badge displayed at all times." The guard held out his hand. "Break out your ID, please."

Talia's mouth moved, but no words came out.

"Oh, my fault," the man said. The corners of his voice sounded like cold frost. He patted at his pockets as if searching for his ID. And like a flash of lightning, yanked out the dagger and plunged it into the soldier's gut.

The soldier doubled over but quick-fired his rifle before falling. Inside the confines of the underground parking deck, the sound was deafening. The man turned to Talia and her eyes locked onto the blade, now covered in dark blood.

Two other guards at the guard shack yelled then broke into a sprint. The man looked at them, then turned back to Talia and slipped the ice pick into his sleeve. He ran in the opposite direction.

The guards screamed for him to stop. As they ran past the wounded soldier, one raised a rifle and fired. Out of instinct, Talia ducked, and the chase was on. But the moment her eyes landed on the wounded soldier, the vertigo abated. She went to him and found him curled into a ball.

"Let me see," Talia said as she knelt. The soldier pulled his blood-covered hand off his stomach. Talia pressed a palm onto the wound, an effort to stem the bleeding. "It will be all right," she said. "Help will be here soon." She looked back in the direction of the now empty guard shack. "Medic! We need a medic!" she screamed.

The soldier looked at her. Somehow, his face looked younger than she had thought. He was perhaps just nineteen years of age. "You are a doctor?" he said.

"Yes," Talia lied. "I'm going to take care of you."

"I want my mother," he whispered. But then his eyes went wild. "Don't tell the others I said that."

She heard more gunfire from the direction where the attacker had fled. When she looked back down, the young soldier's eyes had stopped moving. He was gone.

Talia stared at the boy. Laying like this, he didn't look like a soldier, he looked like a son. She placed a gentle hand onto his eyelids and pulled them closed then took his hand and held it in hers. She sat, allowing tears to run quietly down her face. She whispered, "You saved my life."

A few moments later several other Sayeret soldiers ran up as the sound of their boots echoed across the cement walls. As they stopped, one of them, a commander, barked orders to the others. "You four, set up a perimeter. Seal the facility. Every exit. I want it shut down!" He knelt to Talia. "Ma'am? Do you require medical attention?" he said as he placed fingers onto the soldier's throat to check for the presence of a pulse.

"No," she said.

"Ma'am? There's nothing we can do for him now." His voice was surprisingly soft this time.

Talia nodded, then placed the dead boy's hand onto his chest.

The bewilderment of the events had overwhelmed her senses. She stood, leaned against the car, and tried to process her thoughts. As the adrenaline eased, her thinking became more clear.

He tried to kill me, she thought. *But how did that man get in here?*

Talia startled to find the commander standing in front of her. She hadn't realized it, but he had apparently been trying to get her attention the whole time. "Ma'am?" He turned to another soldier. "She must be in shock."

"I'm sorry," Talia said.

"You'll need to come with us. We need to debrief about the incident."

"How did he get in here?" Talia said.

"Ma'am?"

"The gunman. How did he get into Mossad Headquarters?"

"I don't know, ma'am. We're still in the process of apprehending him."

"Has anyone ever penetrated HQ?"

"Not that I'm aware. But there was obviously a breach. There will be a thorough inquiry, however. We'll get to the bottom of this." He turned to the other soldier and issued several more orders.

A breach? she thought. She glanced at the blood on her hands. *Yeah, I'd say there was a breach.* Something in Talia's core shifted, and she felt an overwhelming need to get away from this place. She began walking toward her own car.

"Wait, ma'am, we still need to talk to you."

But Talia didn't slow. She walked to her car and to the driver's side door.

"Ma'am?" the commander yelled.

The sensor in the car detected the key fob in Talia's tiny purse, and the door lock popped open. She hopped in and locked the doors, then pushed the button labeled "Start."

"Ma'am?" the officer yelled as he and the other guard ran toward the vehicle.

Talia threw the car in reverse and jammed her foot on the gas pedal.

The tires squealed, and the soldiers stopped running to avoid being hit.

The car's tires barked again, and Talia accelerated toward the exit. She waited until the automatic security gate swung open, then sped into the street.

It was only then, as she gripped the steering wheel, that Talia noticed it. Still clutched in her hand was the small metal canister from the records room. She had been holding it the whole time.

14

As Talia sped from Mossad Headquarters, adrenaline spiked into her system again. She glanced at the small metal canister in her hand, then tucked it into her purse. She took the on-ramp to the Glilot Ma'arav Interchange, one of Tel Aviv's major highway arteries. From there she headed east toward Petah Tikva, a city in the Central District, toward her apartment.

Something doesn't add up, she thought, then began talking aloud to herself. "I mean, seriously, how did that guy get in there, all the way down to the sub-basement level?" As she changed lanes, she noticed a woman in the lane next to her staring. "Yes, I'm talking to myself. That okay with you?" she blurted and sped up. "That scar on his face. That had to have been the same man who killed grandpa." Talia began piecing the events together. "If that was the same man, that means he then came after me. But why? Why would anyone want to kill him, want to kill me, for that matter? This makes no sense."

Being past rush hour, traffic was light. She exited Route 5 onto Derekh Zvulun Hamer Road and wound around the long curve in the road surrounding Yarkon Cemetery, a sprawling circular property nearly one kilometer across, the final resting place for more than 100,000 people. As Talia took the curve, she glanced at the multitude of new construction projects at its center where multi-story cemetery tower structures were being erected to house up to 250,000 more.

She turned onto Rishon LeTsiyon and thought back to the records room. *He came all the way after me.* It was a thought that terrified her to the core. She took the last turn onto Zikhron Ya'akov Street. The residential road was well-populated but quiet. Talia particularly liked the trees that had been planted all down it. There were many Bengali ficus, but her favorite was a sycamore fig, a massive tree of at least four hundred years of age. Its canopy of green sprawled in all directions.

She parked on the street in front of her apartment at 32 Zikhron Ya'akov and got out. She glanced at her bare feet and thought back to when her heels had come off during the attack. *It wasn't random,* she thought as she slammed the car door. It was broad daylight, yet for the first time, Talia felt unsafe.

She walked barefoot to the apartment building, a four-story structure, strikingly well designed for a city known for its drab construction. But her inner turmoil railed on. *He had to have penetrated Mossad security to get there. How is that even possible?*

After ascending the open-air stairwell to the third floor, she reached in her purse for her keys. *Think of the risks he took to get in there. Why would anyone want to risk all that to come after me?* As she withdrew the keys, the tiny metal canister tumbled out with them, and she bent down to pick it up. She stared at it. "This?" she said. "He said something about *where is it* and that he *saw it in my hand.*"

She went inside and bolt-locked the door behind her. "What could possibly be in this that's worth killing for?" But the more the thoughts played forward in her mind, the more jittery she became. And finally, it hit her. "No one could break into Mossad HQ. Someone would have had to help him from the inside." Talia then began to fear that she had stumbled upon something she wasn't supposed to find, and someone wanted to kill her for it.

"Wait," she said as she walked to the tiny flat's one and only bedroom, "If someone helped him from the inside, then that means . . . that means he might know where I live. He could come after me here."

Her heart rate again accelerated, and she darted to the closet and pulled out the backpack book bag she used for school. She tossed it onto the bed and turned it upside down. Two thick textbooks and a large three-ring binder dumped out.

She yanked open a dresser drawer, grabbed several pieces of clothing, and jammed the stack into the bag. She threw on a pair of snug jeans and a casual top and running shoes. "I've got to get out of here."

She crammed toiletries into an outside pocket then stuffed the metal canister into a small zippered pocket.

She spun around the room, looking for what else she should grab. “Passport,” she said as she pulled open the top dresser drawer and grabbed her Israeli passport.

“Cash, I need cash.” With the backpack over her shoulder, she was out the door and down the stairs. When she got to the ground floor, however, a nondescript, four-door sedan pulled up on the street and stopped, double-parked right next to her car. Both doors popped open, and two men with tightly trimmed hair emerged. They wore crisp suits and black Ray-Ban Aviator sunglasses.

Talia clutched the straps of her backpack, then backed up until she was underneath the staircase, out of view. She peered through the bushes at them.

One of the men raised a handheld radio and spoke into it. Talia couldn’t hear what he said, but the other glanced at the back of Talia’s car. She heard him call out the numbers on the yellow license plate. “Niner-four, three-ten, two-three. That’s her all right.”

Talia clutched the strap of the backpack and watched as the men walked right at her.

15

As they got closer, Talia squinted at a pin affixed to one of their lapels. It depicted the Star of David encircled in a ring of woven leaves with thin wings angling downward. Her mouth dropped open. *Yamam*, she thought. *The Special Police Unit. What are counter-terrorism agents doing at my door?* She slid deeper beneath the cement staircase.

One said to the other, "Go around back."

"What for? Her flat is on the third floor. What do you think she's going to do, jump or something?"

They both began to ascend the staircase.

Talia looked at them from underneath, then followed the sounds of their hard-soled shoes across each step. When they were on the next level, she peeked out at the street. With her car blocked she scanned in all directions to find an alternate escape.

"*Ha-matzav khara*," she muttered under her breath, meaning *the situation is shit.*

Talia hugged the edge of the wall and moved toward the back of the complex, then made a break for it. No sooner had she ran across the thin green-space of the apartment's backyard, did she hear a booming male voice call out. "That's her!"

Talia stopped and looked up just as the other agent appeared at the third-floor banister. The man drew a Glock and pointed it at her. "Don't move!" the man screamed.

Talia took off in a blind run through the sparse assortment of trees toward a roadway on the other side.

The deafening report of the Glock shattered the otherwise quiet of the neighborhood. The round splintered a sapling ficus next to her when another shot rang out. Something impacted Talia in the back and spun her sideways. The force knocked into a tree, and she toppled over. Shocked, she got up and ran.

The men leapt down the staircase as Talia ran across the street. She dodged one car just as another slammed its brakes. She crossed behind a city bus and sprinted for the bus stop.

The Dan bus slowed as it reached the corner and two passengers disembarked. At about the time the agents reached the ground, Talia boarded the bus and slid her Rav-Kav mass-transit card across the scanner and sat behind the driver. She panted to catch her breath as she looked out the window in the direction of the agents. The bus pulled away and turned just as the agents reached the street.

She leaned back, and her eyes froze in their sockets. Her chest continued to heave in an effort to vacuum up enough air. As her breathing settled, she looked at the shaking of her hands.

A woman with a crinkled smile and a purse clutched on her lap said, "Are you all right, my dear?"

Talia looked at her, then clasped her hands together to hide the shaking. "Oh, thank you, yes." She paused a moment. "I was afraid I would miss the bus."

The woman nodded.

Talia turned and looked behind the bus, fearing the agents could have somehow gotten to their car in time to give chase. As the adrenaline eased, she began to feel pain in her left wrist. She rubbed it and looked at her digital watch. The watch face had a series of scrapes across it and didn't appear to be working. *Must have banged my wrist*, she thought. She tapped a finger on the top of the watch several times but to no avail—it had apparently broken under the impact.

She pulled off her backpack and found what she feared, a small hole was torn into the side. Apparently, the bullet had struck the pack at an angle. The force was what had spun Talia off balance and caused her to fall. She began shaking in earnest as her mind tried to process the terror of what had just happened.

It was only a minute before the stark truth gelled in her mind.

Someone wants me dead. She pulled out her cell phone and dialed Moshe's mobile number.

After a couple of rings, he picked up. "Talia, my dear. I'm so glad you called. Have they moved you to a secure location? Apparently, there's been some kind of incident and—"

"Aba, listen!" she blurted. "That was me!" She lowered her voice so other passengers on the bus would not hear. "Someone tried to kill me in the records room, and I think it's the same person that killed grandpa."

"What? My dear, that's impossible. It's true, we had a security breach on the parking level, and I'm afraid a Kidon guard was killed, but—"

"No! I was in the sub-basement, in the restricted section, and a man came in and started shooting at me. Aba, something is happening. Someone is after me, and I've got to get away."

Talia heard the sound of Moshe's chair sliding back as he stood. "*Ya Allah*," he murmured as though he had his hand over his mouth. "Are you sure?"

"Of course, I'm sure! I had to run from my apartment when two agents showed up. Aba, they shot at me."

"I, I, I . . ." He stuttered. "Are you hurt?"

"No, but I've got to get off this bus before they track it."

"Bus? Track it? What on earth are you talking about? Where are you?"

Talia looked at the street sign as the bus crossed a crossroad and started to answer, but stopped herself. "No," she said, "someone might be listening. Look, Aba, I'm going to go offline for a while. I've got to figure this thing out. But I need you to do something. I need you to pull the security video from the records room. You have access, right?"

"Well, certainly, but—"

"Pull the tape and run it through facial recognition. Find the identity of the man that tried to kill me. I don't know who else to trust."

"You trust your Aba, don't you?" His voice sounded like it might crack.

"I'll call you," she said. "I love you, Aba."

"I love you, too."

Talia hung up, then powered her phone off. She needed to avoid the use of anything that could be used to track her. Thoughts swirled. *Why would they try to kill me? If it's that metal canister, what could possibly be in it that's so important?*

But then she began to think back. *He murdered grandpa first. Why would anyone want to kill that sweet, albeit crazy, old man?* But then an opposing thought. *What if he wasn't a sweet, crazy old man?* "God, I'm going nuts," she said quietly.

As the bus slowed to a stop, Talia jumped up and exited. She waited on the sidewalk as it drove off then glanced across the street. One of her bank's branches, the Bank Mizrahi-Tefahot, sat on the corner. *I can't believe I'm doing this,* she thought.

She crossed the street then went inside. She was greeted by a cold waft of air that felt frigid compared to the outside. While two customers were being helped by bank tellers, a third teller, a young woman seated behind the counter nodded. Talia walked up and pulled open her purse. "I'll need to make a withdrawal, please," she said, trying to calm her voice.

"Yes, ma'am. Checking or savings?"

"There's not much in my checking. Savings. Here's my ID. Can you give me a current balance first."

The teller looked at it. "Certainly, Miss Stiel." She tapped at her keyboard. "The balance in that account is 18296.66 shekels."

Better get out of the country until I figure this thing out. With Israel bordered by enemies, Lebanon, Syria, and Jordan, that left Talia only one choice, Egypt. There, border crossing was not only possible for an Israeli citizen, but easy. "Okay, and what's today's exchange rate for Egyptian pounds?"

"Let's see, it's hovering right at four point nine."

"I'd like to withdraw eighteen thousand shekels. Let's convert four thousand to Egyptian pounds, twelve thousand to US dollars, and the last two thousand in shekels. Can you do that?"

"Yes, ma'am." The woman calculated the day's exchange rates and popped her cash drawer open. "That almost drains your account. I don't understand. Are you closing your account with us?"

"Oh, no. Nothing like that," Talia said with a nervous smile.

"Are you sure you want to carry all that currency?"

"Thank you, yes." Talia waited as the woman counted the three types of bills onto the counter. When she was done, Talia signed the withdrawal slip then tucked the various types of currency into separate pockets. She was out the door in under three minutes.

"I need a cab," she said to herself as she spotted one approaching from the east. But instead of raising her hand, the way she had learned on a trip to New York last summer, she did it the way Israelis did, by holding her arm at a forty-five-degree angle and pointing to the curb in front of her.

The yellow cab pulled up, and she got into the back seat.

"Where to, ma'am?"

"What's the largest bus station in Tel Aviv?"

"Tel Aviv Central," the driver replied.

Talia checked behind them as they drove down Em Hamoshavot Road through light traffic. After the third time she turned around, the driver glanced in the rearview mirror. "Everything okay, ma'am?"

"Yes," she replied. "How long till the station?"

"Well, traffic isn't bad. Maybe take about twenty-five minutes?"

"Cash okay?"

"My favorite kind," he replied.

The inner-city thoroughfare was two lanes wide on each side, separated by metal dividers. The road was lined with sidewalks and multistory buildings. Construction cranes towered in the blocks behind them. Finally, the driver turned onto Hagana Road.

The area adjacent to the train-bus depot was notably more urban: bars on windows, graffiti-adorned buildings, and trash littered the streets. The station itself was long and sprawling. A myriad of vans, cabs and other vehicles were each vying for a spot to pull to the curb. Talia's cab pulled underneath the building's overhang right next to a newsstand. Talia handed the driver a wad of shekels, grabbed her backpack, and hopped out.

As the cab drove away, she walked down the wide, tiled sidewalk and went inside. Talia knew one thing about travel to Egypt: the only options were plane or bus.

If there is something going on inside the Mossad, and someone is trying to track you, you've got to stay off the grid. That meant *a* flight was out of the question. There would be no way to purchase a ticket without producing valid identification. *A sure way to pop up on the grid,* she thought.

It only took a moment to spot a sign that read *Israel Egypt Bus Line.* She speed-walked toward the ticket counter up to a squat-heavy man with salt and pepper hair standing behind it. He had at least three days of stubble on his face and was holding a Shakshuka pita, an overstuffed pita-bread pocket filled with feta cheese, eggs, herbs, cream cheese, and lettuce. He flopped the mess onto a paper plate and wiped a small dollop of red sauce onto his already stained shirt.

"Help you?" he said in a deep husky voice.

"I'm looking to explore Cairo. Can you tell me the options?"

The man put a piece of paper on the counter and pointed. "Tel Aviv to Cairo. Tours run Thursdays and Sundays. Two departures, one at eight, the other at," he glanced at his watch, "four. You are wanting to leave today? I don't think you have time to catch that one."

Talia set her backpack on the ground. "How much is a ticket?"

"My, my, you are in a hurry to see the pyramids, aren't you? Four hundred shekels, round trip."

"How about one way?"

"You are not returning?"

Talia said nothing.

He continued. "Ninety shekels. But there's a two-hundred shekel border tax. You'll pay that separately as you enter Egypt."

Talia counted as she peeled bills onto the counter. The man took the cash and tapped at a keyboard. Her ticket began to print. "You'll have to run. Up those stairs, go left and down to the end."

Talia shouldered her backpack and took off. She had to make that bus.

16

Laurel Ridge Apartments, Annapolis, Maryland.

JOHN STONE GRABBED a beer from the fridge, slumped onto the couch, and cracked it open. But when he picked up the television remote, he stopped himself. He didn't want to watch TV, but the sight of the remote had produced an automatic response, like Pavlov's dog reacting to a bell.

He tossed the remote back onto the empty coffee table and glanced around his Spartan apartment. Nothing hung on the walls; nothing lined the shelves. Stone sat and listened to the abject silence. When he caught his own reflection on the polished glass of the television, he stared a moment. His sandy blond hair had grown unkempt and heavy, and the beard as well.

As was typical of the quiet times, his thoughts drifted back to the many deadly operations he'd been on. Stone was in his early thirties but felt much older. As an Army Delta Force operator, he'd traveled the globe: Turkey, Iran, Syria, Crimea, Ukraine; the list went on. In his way of thinking, if there was a hell-hole, he'd been there. His various brushes with death had left their mark on both his body and mind.

Eventually, he'd left the service and become a government contractor. His last assignment had taken him undercover for the Drug Enforcement Administration. At first, he'd thought of it as perhaps the best assignment of his career. Based on the Isle of Antigua he had been hired to infiltrate a ruthless drug cartel. The beautiful island and the constant presence of danger had swirled together to give him a sense of purpose, and he'd loved it.

He knew, however, the only reason he'd survived that, and several other assignments, was his uncanny ability to sense when something was wrong. On multiple occasions, he had felt something shift in his gut. His "sixth sense" would kick in and he would end up narrowly averting disaster.

Stone had fallen for a girl on the island as well, and sitting alone in his apartment, he couldn't help but smile at the thought of her. She had been an American, too, and as he'd later learned, she'd left the FBI in search of a quieter existence. Special Agent Jana Baker had tracked down terrorists with the Bureau but had paid the price, a set of her own inner demons that haunted her at night.

At one point, he'd asked her how she would describe him in an FBI report. He smiled as he recalled what she had said that day. "Six feet, 185 pounds. Long, curly blond hair. Lean, very lean."

Although the op on Antigua had been a success, it had gone terribly sideways—the firefight, the killing, and all of them narrowly escaping with their lives. In the aftermath, Stone and Jana had gone their separate ways, and now he wondered what might have become had they both led different lives.

His mind wouldn't settle and he knew going for a run would help clear it. He leaned down and slid on his running shoes, then laced them tight.

If one thing had proven true of his life, he knew he'd have to get back onto an active assignment before long—having too much quiet time was killing him.

17

Talia ran up the staircase taking three steps at a time. When she reached the top, she broke into a run toward the far end of the boarding area. She passed several buses then accidentally bumped into a woman. Talia yelled back, "Sorry!"

The last bus, the one she needed to board, had begun to pull out. Talia just caught up to the back of it, and she ran alongside, banging it with her hand. A teenager seated in the last row glanced down through the window then reached up and pulled the cord. A chime rang inside the bus, and the driver stopped.

The door swung open, and Talia boarded, holding her ticket out. "It's just a tour bus, ma'am." The driver said, apparently surprised at Talia's persistence.

She found an open row midway down the aisle, dropped her pack and sat by the window. She took a moment to catch her breath and was relieved to feel the air conditioning blowing from a vent.

The bus pulled out and began its twelve-hour slog to Cairo. It was scheduled for two stops, the first of which was the all-important border crossing into Egypt. Although Talia hadn't crossed into Egypt in several years, she knew the rules. Relations between the two countries were not great, but neither wanted to restrict travel and forgo tourist revenue. And thus, border agents were only interested in collecting a crossing toll and little else.

Talia slumped down in the seat. She hadn't realized, but with all the sudden adrenaline spikes, her body was feeling the effects. She knew the bus would not stop for several hours, and propped her head onto the window then closed her eyes. Her body needed sleep.

She thought back to the visit with her grandfather in the hospital. *The last thing he said to me was that I had to honor my uncle. I had to go to America and have his grave exhumed.*

The bus rattled through moderate Tel Aviv traffic. Talia opened her eyes and considered the route. Instead of there being a more direct way, travelers were forced to avoid the Gaza Strip which meant taking Route 40 all the way to Be'er Sheva. From there, they'd pick up Route 90 straight south until it hit the northernmost tip of the Gulf of Aqaba. And then it was a straight shot down the coast to the Israeli-Egypt border.

Talia though was lost in her own thoughts. *Even if my uncle's casket was buried in the US, his body isn't even in it. That's what doesn't make sense.* Talia's neck stiffened as she leaned her head on the window. It wasn't long before she drifted into a fitful sleep.

What seemed like moments later, she awoke with a start and looked out the window. They were on the banks of the Gulf of Aqaba pulling to a stop at the border crossing. She sat bolt upright and fear gripped her stomach. *It will be all right*, she thought to herself. *No identity check, just a crossing fee.*

The driver's voice came across the bus's PA system. "Welcome to the Israel-Egypt border, ladies and gentlemen. All passengers are required to disembark. The border crossing fee is nine hundred eighty-three Egyptian pounds, approximately two hundred shekels. Either currency is accepted. You may leave your belongings on the bus."

She fished through her pockets and pulled out the thin wad of shekels and counted them off. The driver continued. "You will need your passports."

Talia's stomach hit a flutter. She sat back down but knew she had no choice. She pulled out her passport and looked at it. *If they run this through, I'll pop up on the grid.* She stood and shuffled down the aisle with the other tourists and got off.

Despite being on the water's edge, the breeze that blew Talia's hair was bone-dry. She squinted into the bay. The first fifty meters of water was turquoise, but the deeper the water became, the darker it got.

She had been on several beaches on the gulf, and this one appeared no different. A thin strip of white sand edged in stones to protect the shoreline from erosion. Out across the bay, about five miles distant, she could see the country of Jordan. Its geography was not much different than where she was standing. A moderate flat lowland edged with rolling hills.

Technically, they were already in Egypt, but before the bus would be allowed deeper into the country, the Egyptian government first wanted to extract a little money. Egypt was rife with tourist destinations, and the government took full advantage of every one.

The group walked inside a small building with glass walls. Several border guards were stationed behind a long counter where queues had formed. On the wall behind the border agents were posters of tourist hotspots: the Giza Pyramids, the Great Sphinx, the Abu Simbel temples, and the Valley of the Kings.

Talia's group split into three different lines, and she craned her neck to see if she could tell what scrutiny was being applied to passports. When it was finally her turn, she stepped up to the high counter, and the Egyptian man behind it said, "Passport please."

She handed it to him and held her breath.

"You are here with a tour group?" the man said.

"Yes." He glanced from her passport to her face. *Have they forwarded my picture to all border crossings?* The thought was terrifying.

"I see you are an Israeli citizen. Have you traveled to Egypt before?"

"Yes, once. Several years ago, when I was young." She hesitated. "I wanted to see it again, as an adult."

The man smiled. "Two hundred shekels, please."

A feeling of relief flooded Talia's senses. She counted out the cash, and the man stamped her passport. "Welcome back to Egypt." He handed her the passport and a temporary entrance card, then looked over her shoulder. "Next in line, please."

Talia walked back to the bus and wiped a bead of sweat from her temple. "I'm not cut out for this," she said to herself.

The bus resumed the next leg of the trip, a six-hour drive to Cairo. Talia tried to figure out what to do next. The more she thought about it, the more she knew she had to have answers. She needed to get to America to find out what was in that coffin. But given her need to stay off the grid, the only question was how to get there.

18

The bus route took them through the town of Nekhel into a tunnel under the Suez Canal, through Madinati, and hours later into Cairo itself. The arid city spread out before Talia's eyes. There were more trees inside the city than she remembered. Yet, for the most part, things hadn't changed. Decaying rail lines ran in various directions through the center of wide thoroughfares choked with cars.

The buildings, most of which were four or five stories tall, were painted in the same drab sand color, and cars were jammed into parking spaced all along them. In Talia's view, it wasn't an attractive place.

The bus turned on Hussein Kamel Road and pulled into the Almaza Bus Station. The driver's voice came across the PA. "As we disembark, please stay together. A member of our staff will guide the group to the next bus so your tour of Egypt's wonders can commence. I hope you have had a pleasant ride into Cairo . . . "

Talia's mind wandered. *I've got to separate from these people.* She wanted to be at the back of the line, so she shouldered her backpack and waited until all the passengers had moved past. She glanced out the bus windows at the station. Throngs of people crowded the sidewalks as each vied for a better path through the mass of humanity. She stepped off the bus and waited. It wasn't long before she was able to slip to the side and disappear from the tour group.

She was on her own now. She ascended a wide, crowded staircase to get into the main terminal then glanced at a map on the wall. It depicted the grid of bus routes throughout the city. Fortunately for Talia, one, the El-Orouba bus line, frequented the only place she wanted to go, the Cairo International Airport.

She had reasoned that her only true mode of transport to the States was via air. The only other viable route was to board a ship, and that would take far too long. Her belief was that her passport would not be scanned in Egypt but instead only when she landed in America. Her hope was that when the US Border Patrol scanned her passport, she would be able to disappear into the vast country before whoever was tracking her was able to react.

It was a risk she could not avoid.

* * *

THIRTY MINUTES LATER, Talia walked into the sprawling Cairo International Airport. Despite the lackluster appearance of much of Cairo, the ultra-modern air hub stood in stark contrast. Sweeping glass vistas curved up from the ground to form an overhang where cars, buses, and other vehicles dropped off passengers. The airport was the busiest in Egypt and served as the primary hub for EgyptAir, and that was where Talia knew she'd find a suitable flight.

She walked through the sliding doors into the glass and marble terminal, then straight to a massive digital board which displayed upcoming departures.

Most outbound flights were those of EgyptAir, but as the screen flipped from one page to the next, dozens of other airlines came into view: Emirates, Eritrean Airlines, Kuwait Airways, Lufthansa, Oman Air, Royal Jordanian; the list went on.

But what Talia was most concerned with wasn't the airline, it was the destination. She reasoned that she should take the first flight available to the States, but knew she wanted to land in the northeast, closest to the United States Naval Academy.

She pictured what her uncle's headstone might look like sitting atop a grave and surrounded by others. The difference being, this one did not contain a body. *What am I doing?* she thought as she looked over her shoulder. *I'm getting paranoid, that's what I'm doing.*

Several flights piqued her interest, yet one stood out:

EgyptAir
CIA - JFK
Nonstop
Departure: 10:45 p.m.
Arrival: 9:54 a.m.

She walked to an area teeming with computerized kiosk terminals, went up to one, and searched the flight. She tapped the touchscreen until it popped up.

EgyptAir : Economy : Boeing 777 : MS 985
EGP 15,136

She did a rough calculation. "Fifteen thousand Egyptian, that's about what, three thousand shekels?" She walked over to a row of leather bench seats and pulled her backpack off, then unzipped the main compartment. She discretely removed a wad of Egyptian pounds from her back pocket and lowered the cash into the open compartment. She didn't want prying eyes to see as she counted what she had left. "Not quite enough," she said, but then looked at the far end of the terminal and spotted a National Bank Of Egypt kiosk and walked to it.

After exchanging her remaining Israeli shekels, she got in line at the EgyptAir desk. When it was her turn, she said to the agent, a man in a yellow-gold blazer and tie. "Your flight MS 985 to JFK? Have an available seat?"

"You are not ticketed? Oh my, and that flight departs in less than an hour," he said as his eyes flickered to her chest. "No, I wouldn't think so, but let me check." He tapped his keyboard a moment. "I'm sorry. It appears the flight is sold out."

Talia's shoulders slumped.

When he saw her reaction, he added, "But there are a few passengers who have not checked in yet." He pointed down the terminal. "If you go to the gate, sometimes those seats free up. The gate agent will be able to assist you. Gate F19."

"Thank you," Talia said as she headed in that direction. She looked over her shoulder. It was as if she thought she was being watched. *Calm down. No one knows where you are.* Her pace quickened. *I've got to get on that flight. I've got to get as far away from here as possible.* She walked down the long hallway and boarded the moving sidewalk and began to take notice of airport employees. What stood out most was that only one was female. The male-dominated culture of Egypt, in contrast to that of Israel, was on full display.

Minutes later she arrived at the gate. A long queue had formed, and passengers were already boarding. She stepped up to the gate agent, another male, and said, "Do you have any available seats?"

He smirked at her and shook his head. "Completely sold out."

"The ticketing agent said you had a few that hadn't checked in yet?" Talia again caught herself looking over her shoulder.

"That may be but . . ." He stole a glance at the trimness of her form-fitting jeans, then tapped at his keyboard. "Yes, we have one. But that passenger may be here now but has not yet checked in. Let me make an announcement. If they are a no-show, the seat is available."

Talia stood back and couldn't help but notice that as the man spoke into the microphone, calling across the PA system, his eyes ran up and down her body. She turned and studied the people in line to board. Although a few looked European, and several others American, most were Egyptian. Several were staring at her and Talia suddenly became self-conscious.

It was of no surprise that her attire did not meld well with the locals. She thought it would have been the Egyptian men that did not approve, but it was the women. Most wore long flowing garments and hijabs over their hair. The Egyptian men, however, seemed to be more interested in studying her feminine form than casting disapproval.

"Passenger Nubia Saliba, Nubia Saliba," the agent said over the PA system, "Please report to the ticketing agent."

Talia couldn't bother with the glares of other passengers. Her more immediate concern was getting on that flight.

19

Several minutes passed, and the majority of passengers had already boarded. Talia again approached the ticketing agent. "Now?" she said with a smile.

"Yes, ma'am. I believe it's safe to say that the seat is yours." He tapped at his keyboard but glanced down at her backpack. "You only have the one carry-on?"

"I travel light."

"Name?"

Talia's stomach jumped. *Why didn't you think of a false name in advance?* Her mind scrambled for a name. "Gamila Rahal."

He glanced her up and down. "But you are Israeli, no?"

This is never going to work, she thought. "Uh, my mother is Israeli, but my father was Egyptian." Her heart rate accelerated.

His tone shifted, and Talia could tell he thought the whole thing odd. "That's most unusual," he said, but then continued typing. "The fare is 15,136 Egyptian, Miss Rahal."

Talia knelt down to pull out the cash. As she counted it onto the counter, she could feel his eyes looking down her shirt. He took the cash but then hesitated. "Passport, please?"

"Oh," Talia replied, "I didn't think we needed them for departure."

"It's only a formality." He waited.

Talia pushed some hair that had fallen forward behind one ear. "It's in here somewhere," she said as she fished around in the backpack, stalling for time. *Think, dammit, think. I can't pop up on the grid.*

A man carrying a suitcase in his hands came running up. He was out of breath.

"Did I miss it?" he blurted to the agent.

Oh shit, Talia thought. *Now I can't buy the ticket at all? I've got to get on that plane!*

"No, sir," the boarding agent said. "You're just in time."

The man handed the agent his ticket.

The agent studied it a moment then looked up. "I'm sorry, sir. This gate is flight 985 to New York. You're looking for the flight to Athens. Gate F20, just behind us."

The man recovered his ticket. "Oh, thank you." He shuffled off.

Talia's shoulders relaxed.

The agent tapped at the keyboard. "Looks like that seat is still yours."

He continued processing her ticket and seemed to have forgotten about the passport. She paid the fair, and he scanned her through. "Thank you," she said as she hurried down the jetway to board the plane.

Once aboard, she found most passengers already seated. She hurried down the tight aisle to a middle-row seat where she would spend the next eleven hours. Two passengers stood to let her through. She tucked the backpack under the seat in front of her and sat. Only then did she feel the perspiration on her scalp.

20

Hours later, as the plane cruised across the Atlantic, Talia's mind wandered. She was exhausted, but her thoughts wouldn't settle. *Grandpa had to have been killed for a reason. But why?*

She heard his voice in her head. *Go to America and recover your uncle's casket. What am I, insane?* The thoughts kept coming. *I still don't understand. Even if my uncle's casket is there, his body isn't.*

But as the thoughts played forward, she sat upright. *Does someone want what's in that casket?* She sat back. *What could possibly be in there that's so valuable it would be worth killing grandpa for, killing me for? And if someone wants it so badly, why would they come after me? Wouldn't I be the most likely person that could get their hands on the casket? I'm family, for God's sake.*

She couldn't reconcile the question. *Well, whatever is in there, it must be valuable.* That was the only explanation.

During the middle of the night, Talia tried everything to fall asleep, but nothing was working. She couldn't settle. By the time the plane was an hour from touchdown in New York, she finally drifted off.

Her dreams picked up where her conscious mind had left off. She saw a picture of her uncle, a man she not only had never met but a person she hadn't known existed in the first place. His face betrayed a hint of her father. But then thoughts and images began bouncing across the dream like a pinball.

She saw flickers of her uncle in his Naval flight suit climbing the ladder to board his fighter jet. She saw herself in the records room, the terrifying gunman with a scar running the length of his face, shooting at her. Then she saw images from her apartment: the agents pointing handguns at her, and beginning to fire. In the dream, she felt the impact of one of the bullets as it struck her backpack. Her body jarred in the seat and she sat bolt upright.

The plane had just touched down on the runway at New York's JFK and the jarring she felt was the landing. Bright light streamed into the cabin from windows on both sides of the plane and Talia could hardly believe she had slept. Moments later, a flight attendant's voice came across the PA system. "Welcome to New York. I've got updated flight connection information . . ."

But Talia's mind drifted. *What do I think I'm going to do? Walk up to the caretakers of the cemetery and say, I'd like to dig up my uncle, please*?

But the first thing she needed was to get clear of the airport. Once her passport was scanned by agents of ICE, the US Immigration and Customs Enforcement agency, her identity would show up on the grid. Once that happened, time would be short. If it was the Mossad that was after her, it would take them no time to see she had entered the United States.

A shiver rode her spine, and she knew she'd have to disappear into New York fast to avoid being tracked down by Mossad agents.

* * *

THE QUEUES for Customs were long. Talia took the time to think. Being on the run wasn't something she was accustomed to. To her, it felt as though she were on a covert mission of her own. And as a researcher, she had no idea how to proceed. The one thing she kept thinking about was finding out what was in that coffin. If she was right, there was something in there worth killing for.

She waited behind the white line taped to the floor and watched as other passengers spoke to customs agents. Then an agent waved her forward. She approached the desk with her passport and a paper copy of Customs Declaration Form 6059B in her hand. The agent, a female with tight curly hair pulled behind her head, looked Talia up and down.

To Talia, the woman's uniform was not dissimilar to that of a police officer — black, button-down shirt and badge, name tag, and a patch on each shoulder. The woman's waist was wrapped in a thick black gun belt. Talia glanced at the weapon, a Glock just like the one that had fired at her outside her apartment in Tel Aviv. The memory of bullets whizzing by caused goose bumps to rise on her arms.

The agent studied the passport. "You are traveling alone today, Miss Stiel?"

"Yes."

"And what is the purpose of your visit?"

"Oh, just sightseeing."

"I see. And is that your only luggage?" the agent said as she waved the passport under a scanner.

"Yes," Talia said as she watched. *That's it*, she thought. *My passport is on the grid now.* The clock had just begun ticking.

The agent's brow turned down as she flipped through the pages of Talia's passport. "May I see the boarding pass for the flight you just came in on, please?"

Talia fished in her pockets, and her heart pounded a little harder. She handed the agent the boarding pass.

"You are arriving through Cairo today?"

"Yes, ma'am," Talia said. She locked eyes with the woman. "Is there a problem?"

"Your passport is Israeli, yet the computer finds no record of your entry into Egypt."

"Well, yes. I took a bus. They looked at our passports at the border, but I don't think they scan them in or anything."

"I see," the agent said as she tapped the passport on the desk in repeated succession. To Talia, it seemed as though the agent was thinking. "And they didn't stamp your passport either. You traveled by bus, you say?"

"Yes, ma'am. But I don't see why—"

"Can I see your bus ticket please?"

The agent held out a hand.

Talia searched her backpack and pulled out the bus ticket and handed it to the agent.

"I see. This was a tour group?"

"Yes, mostly Israelis like myself who wanted to see the sights."

"A tour of the pyramids and such?"

"Yes, ma'am," Talia said as she swallowed.

The agent exhaled. "What bothers me is that this ticket is for a tour package, not just transportation into Egypt. And yet it appears that a few hours after the bus arrived in Cairo, you're suddenly on a flight to the United States. Why would you pay for a full tour package when your intent was to miss the tour?"

Talia's mind scrambled to come up with an answer. "I, uh—"

The woman waved another agent forward. "Place your bag on the desk, please."

She's already scanned my passport. I can't be held up by these stupid questions. Talia placed her backpack on the counter. The other uniformed Customs agent took the bag, zipped it open, and began removing contents. He and the female agent inspected the items. "And this is the only bag you brought with you?" the male said.

"Yes, but I don't see why that matters."

The female responded. "I find it very unusual. For someone who says they're here sightseeing, you didn't bring much with you. Not to mention the fact that you apparently paid cash for both the bus tour and the flight to JFK." The agents continued to pull items from the backpack.

"Is that against the law?" Talia said a little too quickly. She bit her lip.

"What's this?" the male said as he removed the small metal canister from a side pocket. He pried off the lid and dumped the contents into his hand. He studied the tiny roll of microfilm that fell, then unrolled it and held it to the light. The female agent waved over two other Customs agents. These two were Kevlar-laden and wore fatigues. Both had automatic weapons attached to their chests. They walked up behind Talia and stood.

As the male agent squinted into the microfilm, the female said, "What is that?"

"Some kind of microfilm," he replied. "But from the looks of it, whatever is written on it is encrypted. Letters, numbers, symbols, all jumbled together."

Talia began to panic but knew there was no way out. "Oh, that? That's just . . ." But her words trailed off.

Then the female agent pieced through some of Talia's clothing items. She said, "Why are some of these torn? Look at that," she said to the male. "And this streak of something dark around the tears."

The two agents looked at each other and immediately began searching the outside of the backpack. The female then said, "Here it is." She spun the pack around toward Talia. "What is this?" she said as she poked her finger through a small hole on the outside of the backpack.

Talia stuttered, but no words emerged.

The male continued inspecting the outside of the pack. "I don't see an exit hole," he said as he pulled out another wadded article of clothing from inside the pack. He squeezed it until his fingers landed on a small, hard object. He unrolled the clothing and pulled out a mangled, mushroom-shaped bullet. "Would you care to explain to the United States Immigration and Customs Enforcement agency why there's a bullet lodged in your bag?"

Talia began shaking, and one of the Kevlar-laden agents pulled her arms behind her back and handcuffed her.

"And look at this," the female said as she pulled out Talia's Mossad identification badge.

The male glanced at it. "You are being detained," he said with a smile. "These fine agents will escort you."

The steel of the handcuffs against Talia's wrists felt like the cold of death. She walked away under the stares of most every passenger in the area.

21

The Raven glanced down at his cellular phone to see who was calling. He immediately recognized the caller as the one he knew only as Codename *Vipera*. He tapped the screen to answer, held it to his ear, yet said nothing.

"How could you have fucked this up so badly?" Vipera said. "She's disappeared. She fled her apartment, right under the noses of those two you sent after her. Now the local Tel Aviv police are investigating the shooting, which occurred in broad daylight, I might add."

The Raven's jaw muscles clenched. He was unaccustomed to failure, much less being spoken to in such a manner. Referring to his narrow escape from Mossad headquarters, he said, "I got out of there, didn't I?"

"That isn't good enough!" Vipera's voice boomed. "You have no idea what is at stake here. There is no room for error. *Ya Allah!*" The man exhaled then said. "As it is, you will have a second chance."

"We know her location? Where?"

"You're on the next flight to New York." An uncomfortable silence punctuated Vipera's anger. "Don't screw this up. Put an end to her before word of our plan leaks out. Everything depends on it."

22

Customs Interrogation Room C, John F. Kennedy International Airport, Queens, New York.

After waiting three and a half hours on a cold metal bench, Talia was escorted into a sterile room and placed on a metal chair. The walls were painted stark white with the exception of one that was made up primarily of a large mirrored window. Talia looked at her own reflection and was almost certain she heard the creaking of a metal chair from behind it. It was a two-way mirror.

The heavy door opened and she turned. A man with a mustache, wearing dark slacks, polished shoes and crisp, button-down shirt and tie walked in followed by a woman. The woman was much smaller in stature but appeared to be about the same age as Talia. Her facial features and long blonde hair were striking, but everything in her demeanor was all business. The double-breasted suit, the hair pulled back into a tight bun, gave Talia a sense of ominousness.

The man leaned against the wall, and the woman walked to the opposite side of the table from Talia and dropped her leather attaché onto it. She pulled a chair forward and sat. "My name is Special Agent Jana Baker," the woman said as she removed some paperwork from her attaché. "I'm with the Federal Bureau of Investigation."

Talia tried to sit upright but ended up squirming in her seat. She couldn't quite decide where to place her handcuffed hands. She waited for Agent Baker to continue. But when the woman interlocked her fingers and leaned her elbows on the table, Talia said, "I'm sorry. This is all a little unsettling for me. I don't understand why I'm being detained."

"The FBI is often involved when US Customs authorities identify a person of interest."

"I am just traveling here as a tourist."

Agent Baker looked at the document in front of her. "You'll want to be aware, Ms. Stiel, that in the United States, lying to a federal agent is a crime, punishable by up to two years in prison." Agent Baker did not wait for a response. "You were flagged by ICE for multiple reasons, one being your travel history. It's quite interesting, to say the least." She flipped the page and read, "You are an Israeli citizen, yet you travel to Cairo without evidentiary of your border crossing, then hop a plane to New York. All paid with cash. Kind of makes it look like you're trying to hide something."

Talia's mind raced to come up with a plausible story but had nothing.

"Then there's this," Agent Baker said as she plopped a mangled bullet onto the table. "Then this." She dropped Talia's Mossad identification down. "And my personal favorite." She emptied the small metal canister, and the microfilm dumped out. "But before we get to all that, I'm confused, Ms. Stiel."

Talia looked down, and her throat tightened. She knew there was no plausible explanation, other than the truth. "About what?"

"You work for the Mossad, one of the most premier covert agencies in the world, and someone apparently took a shot at you. If I were in your shoes, I would have sought the help of my employer. Yet you jumped on a plane. Why?"

"How do you know I didn't seek the help of my employer?"

"The US State Department placed an inquiry to your government."

Talia's heart jumped a beat. *They know,* she thought, *the Mossad knows where I am. I've got to get out of here.*

Jana nodded to the other agent. He walked out. But a few moments later, Talia heard a squeak from the chair on the other side of the two-way mirror.

"Yes, I work for the Mossad. Is that a crime?"

When Talia received no response, she went on. "I'm not an agent. My official title is Technical Analyst."

Agent Baker slid a piece of paper in front of her. It was Talia's Mossad employee record.

She already knows everything, Talia thought.

"And what do you do as a technical analyst?"

Talia's voice came out fluttery. "I'm not at liberty to say." She knew she was in danger, but revealing state secrets was not what she had in mind. "I need you to release me right now."

But the questions kept coming.

"Why was there a bullet lodged in your backpack?"

"I, I don't know. Have I done something illegal?"

"What are you doing with this microfilm?"

Talia's mouth dropped open. It was as if she was unable to speak.

Jana pointed a sharp finger at her. "You had better start cooperating with this office, or things will go badly for you."

"I, uh . . . "

"Why is someone shooting at you? Might it be this that they're interested in?" Jana said as she held the microfilm to the light. "It appears to be encrypted. You know, Ms. Stiel, the United States government gets a little irritated when foreign agents enter our borders with bullet holes and encrypted documents."

"I'm not a foreign agent!"

Jana slid the chair back and stood. "I don't have time for this. Right now, I've got to go call the Central Intelligence Agency and inform them a foreign operative was just been apprehended in possession of encrypted data. And the US Attorney's office isn't going to be too thrilled about your complete lack of cooperation either." It was a not-so-veiled threat. "It might take a few hours, but they'll hand down an indictment."

"An indictment?" Talia said as her cheeks flushed red. "But I haven't done anything!"

Jana slammed her hand into the desk. The sound reverberated against the cold cement floor. "Oh no? In the United States, it's known as *U.S. Code, Title Eighteen, Gathering or delivering defense information.*"

Talia bristled at Jana's escalating volume.

"Would you like me to quote it for you?" Jana walked around the table until she was directly behind Talia. Her words came out laced in venom. "Whoever, with intent or reason to believe that it is to be used to the *injury of the United States* or to the advantage of a foreign nation, communicates, delivers, or transmits, any document, writing, code book, or information relating to the national defense, shall be punished by death or by imprisonment for any term of years."

Talia's breathing became erratic, and her eyes flared wide. She glanced up at Jana.

"You may as well get comfortable," Jana said. "You'll be here quite a while." She picked up her attaché and started to walk out.

"Wait!" Talia blurted.

Jana stopped.

"Something is happening. I don't know what exactly. My grandfather was murdered, and someone is trying to kill me, too."

Jana returned to the table. "So you've decided it's in your best interest to talk to me now?"

"Yes," Talia replied.

"Then start from the beginning, and don't leave anything out, or I'll know."

23

"My work at the Mossad involves nuclear physics," Talia said. "But let's just start with the last two days of my life." Talia began to recount the emotional roller coaster of terrifying events: the story her grandfather had revealed, his murder at the hands of a scar-faced man who had then come to kill her, followed by the two agents who had shot at her as she fled her apartment.

When she stopped, Jana placed her hands flat on the table. "That's quite a story."

"You don't believe me? Then why is there a bullet in my backpack?"

"I didn't say I didn't believe you."

"Then why are you threatening to arrest me?"

"It's what you didn't say that concerns me."

"What I didn't say?"

"Why?" Jana replied. "Why would there suddenly be a conspiracy to kill you, seemingly out of nowhere? And to hear you tell it, you seem to be directly implicating the Mossad itself."

"I already told you. The man that tried to kill me in the records room couldn't have penetrated Mossad Headquarters without help. It's impossible. And it's the same man that murdered my grandfather." She looked at Jana. "Has anyone snuck into FBI headquarters, past all the security, and started shooting?"

"No, but in 1992 an unauthorized male talked his way onto the grounds of the FBI Academy at Quantico. When he was stopped by security later for not having his identity on display, he was apprehended. They found automatic rifles and ammunition in his room."

"All right, but hopefully it makes more sense to you now."

"You're being evasive. Tell me why someone would want you dead."

"All I know is that my grandfather tells me this story about a 1965 mission he was on, one in which he was to steal a nuclear device. He tells me I have an uncle I never knew about, and the moment I go access the case file, people start shooting at me." Talia's eyes wandered. "It's got to have something to do with that casket."

"Casket?"

"My grandfather was desperate that I request the remains of my uncle be exhumed from a cemetery here in the US, and the casket shipped back to Israel. And that's the thing," she said but then raised her hand-cuffed hands to Jana. "Are these really necessary? You already know who I am and I hope you know I'm not here on some secret mission. You know I'm not field personnel. Besides, what am I going to do, overpower you and escape from this dungeon?"

Jana smirked as she stood with a set of keys and unlocked the cuffs. "It would be the biggest mistake of your life." The two sat again. "Explain to me what is on this microfilm."

"I have no idea what's on it. I told you. I was looking through the old case files, and that was in there. I didn't even realize it was still in my hand when the shooting started."

"You know I can't let you just leave here, and certainly not with this microfilm."

"Agent Baker, you've got to believe me! I'm as lost as you are. That's not some set of state secrets that I stole from the US after scaling the outside of a building with suction cups attached to my hands. That microfilm is ancient. It came out of the 1965 case file at Mossad Headquarters. If anything, those are details about the mission my grandfather talked about."

Jana said, "I think I've heard enough." She stood. "I haven't been honest with you. When I said earlier I had checked your identity, I did a little more than that."

"What do you mean?"

"Our countries are allies, Ms. Stiel."

As Talia stared at her, Jana pulled out another sheet of paper and read. "Talia Kailea Stiel, born 2 February 1993 in Tel Aviv at Ichilov Hospital, later renamed Tel Aviv Sourasky Medical Center. Mother,

Gavriella Mizrah Stiel, father, Yoel Doron Stiel. Undergraduate studies at the Technion-Israel Institute of Technology where you studied physics. Your graduate work was at Weizmann Institute of Science, where you studied Condensed Matter Physics, the same institution where you are now pursuing your doctoral degree in nuclear physics."

Jana looked up and said, "Your colleagues tell me you are close to completing your thesis. The office joke is that although you are not yet a Ph.D., everyone addresses you as Dr. Stiel? Is that correct?"

Talia's mouth hung open.

Jana looked down at the paper again. "Tell me, Miss Stiel, what exactly is condensed matter physics?"

But Talia's eyes remained wide, and she shook her head. "Who did you talk to?"

"What do you research for the Mossad?"

Talia's volume escalated. "Who did you talk to?"

"You can relax, Miss Stiel. I spoke with one," she glanced at the sheet, "Moshe Himmelreich, the Mossad's Director of Political Action. As I understand it, that's part of the intelligence services?"

Tension vacated Talia's shoulders. "Oh, thank God," she said as she pressed a hand to her heart.

"Yes, our State Department put me into contact with Director Himmelreich. He's quite an outgoing man, isn't he? He was quite worried about you."

"Well, he's my godfather. He raised me. He thinks of me as his own daughter. He must be worried sick."

Jana looked at the paper, and her eyes traced the words. "I see here it says your parents died when a bomb exploded? I lost my parents at an early age as well."

"That's *not* fair," Talia said as she pointed an angry finger at Jana. "You can't just pull a dossier and pry into someone's life." But as memories of her parents flickered into her mind, Talia softened. "Hezbollah," she whispered. "They took my parents from me. And for what? My parents were simple people. They ran a little bakery. Everyone loved them, the whole community, I mean. I don't like to say it out loud, but I've hated those terrorists my whole life. Wait a minute. Are you arresting me?"

"And I'm sorry about your grandfather. I was able to verify that part of your story, at least the fact that he was murdered at the hospital. Witnesses outside your apartment also corroborate your statements regarding the shooting event." Jana flicked a glance at Talia. "Director Himmelreich pulled the case file from your local police for me."

Talia's earlier emotion seemed to vaporize, and she crossed her arms. "You knew all this? And yet you put me through those questions?"

"Standard procedure, Miss Stiel. We like to make sure actual events correspond to statements provided."

Talia sat back down and buried her face into her hands. "If you believe me, then you've got to let me out of here. Whoever is trying to kill me has help from inside the Mossad. I don't know, there's a mole or something." She pointed toward the door. "When my passport was scanned, the killer would have been alerted to my presence. That's why I paid cash for the bus and plane tickets. That's why I chose to enter Egypt at a place that didn't scan passports. I had to stay off the grid for as long as possible. As it stands now, you've detained me for *hours*. They know where I am and they'll come. They certainly have agents here in the United States who are now looking for me."

"We're going to have to get this decrypted," Jana said as she held the microfilm to the light.

"Agent Baker, have you not heard a word I said?"

"It's Jana. Call me Jana. And we're way ahead of you. Like I mentioned earlier, our governments are allies. The US State Department has asked the FBI to lend its full cooperation in this matter."

"What?"

"Apparently, Director Himmelreich did his undergraduate studies with our Attorney General," Jana said with a smile. "Come on. I've got some friends that can tell us what's on this microfilm." Jana walked to the door, opened it, then held it for Talia. "You coming?"

Talia stood and shook her head. "This is not what I expected at all."

As they walked down the hall, Jana smiled. "Suction cups on your hands? Nice touch."

24

"Where are we going?" Talia said as she and Jana walked into an underground parking area at JFK.

They got into Jana's Bureau car, a nondescript, heavy four-door sedan. "To a place that can decrypt this microfilm. Might as well get comfortable. It'll take a few hours to get there."

Talia thought about it a moment. It was a well-known fact that the bulk of the decryption work done in the United States was handled by the National Security Agency.

Talia fastened her seatbelt. "Fort Meade?" But Jana didn't answer. "You're really going to help? Moshe must be asking for a big favor. But now that I think back on it," she said as the car pulled past an armed guard into the stark sunlight and mid-afternoon New York traffic, "it makes a little more sense."

"How so?"

"I remember Moshe mentioning your attorney general a long time ago."

"They must have been good friends," Jana said.

Talia smirked. "Oh, I think they were more than good friends, but don't tell him I said that."

"What do you mean?"

"Your attorney general is male, correct?"

"Yes."

"I think they were . . . close, if you know what I mean."

"Oh," Jana replied as she nodded. "Wait, so they dated? You know, I never thought about it. Our attorney general isn't married, but the thought that he might be gay never crossed my mind. Not that it makes any difference."

They slogged through Brooklyn and across Staten Island until finally reaching I-95, the New Jersey Turnpike, then headed south.

"Well, Moshe was always very secretive with me about his dating life. For a long time growing up, I just figured he was too busy raising me. But later I figured out he just wanted to keep a low profile, because of work, I suppose."

Jana kept her eyes on the road but said, "What's the attitude toward the LGBT community in Israel?"

"Not great," Talia replied, "but it's night and day compared to elsewhere in the Middle East. Even though it's moderately well accepted, in the military and places like the Mossad, it's never mentioned."

A few hours later they drove through Newark on their way to Baltimore, then ultimately arrived in Fort Meade, Maryland. They cleared the extensive security gate, and Jana parked the car. "What should be a three-hour drive done in four."

"And I thought traffic was bad in Tel Aviv," Talia replied.

They got out and entered the lobby of the expansive building complex where Jana flashed her credentials at one of the many armed security officers.

"Nice to see you again, Agent Baker," the officer said.

Jana handed him Talia's Mossad credentials, and he scanned them. After a moment, he handed Jana her badge and Talia a visitor badge.

"You've been here before?" Talia asked as they headed to a set of elevators.

"A million times," Jana said. "We're going to the command center. It's the heart of decryption and surveillance, and where we'll find Uncle Bill."

"Uncle Bill?" Talia said as they boarded the elevator.

Inside, Jana swiped her badge, and the doors wafted shut, then began to descend toward the lowest sub-level. "Bill Tarleton. He's section chief. He and his crew have been the tip of the proverbial spear on countless investigations. Well, at least as far as surveillance and decryption go."

The elevator doors opened, and they walked into a vast, almost cavernous room. The space was easily one hundred feet across and had ceilings of over thirty feet. Hanging from above was a myriad of computer monitors. People were scattered throughout, some at desks, others computer terminals where they pecked away at keyboards. Talia's mouth opened at the enormity of the operation.

Jana said, "You'll like him. He's been like a father to me. Well, a grandfather, anyway," she said with a smile.

A man with heavily graying hair and an enormous beard walked up. His mouth was buried somewhere beneath the mass of facial hair, but his smile was so large, it spread to his eyes. In a voice that betrayed his age, the man said, "Hello, young lady."

Jana hugged him. "Hello, Bill."

Bill put her at arm's length. "Are you eating?"

"Oh, Bill," Jana laughed.

Bill looked at Talia. "She doesn't take care of herself."

Talia smiled.

Jana leaned closer to Uncle Bill. "Oh, I don't take care of *myself*?" she said as she plucked a tiny orange crumb from his beard. She swept another off Bill's short-sleeved plaid button-down covering his protruding spare tire. "Just as I suspected." She held a crumb up for further inspection. "What is Mrs. Uncle Bill going to say when I tell her you're eating orange crackers again?"

Bill grinned. "It will be our little secret?" He looked again at Talia. "You must be Miss Stiel. It's a pleasure. Welcome to NSA. William Tarleton." Bill shook Talia's hand and began walking into the space. "Everyone around here calls me Uncle Bill. You can call me Bill, or Uncle Bill, or just 'hey, old man.'"

Talia laughed.

They stopped at a desk where a young man typed away at a keyboard. His head, however, craned up to see the results of his work on the monitor high above. The boyish face, unkempt hair, wrinkled t-shirt and Converse high top All-Stars made it appear to Talia, that he wasn't older than seventeen.

"This is Knuckles," Uncle Bill said. "Knuckles, you know Agent Baker, but this is Miss Stiel. Son, introduce yourself."

Talia wanted to comment on the boy's name but stopped herself.

The boy stood, and Talia couldn't help but notice the peach fuzz on his chin.

Knuckles seemed to become instantly lost in the depth of her dark eyes. "Uh," he mumbled, "it's nice to meet you," he said, then shook Talia's hand.

Jana smiled. "It's okay, Knuckles. She doesn't bite."

His face turned a shade of crimson. "Hi, Agent Baker, I mean, Jana."

And referring to the way Knuckles had handled the introduction, Jana added, "You're actually getting better at this."

"Come on," Uncle Bill said as he started to walk, "let's take a look at that mysterious microfilm I've heard so much about."

25

NSA Headquarters, Laboratory.

"Knuckles," Uncle Bill said, "you do the honors."

Knuckles took the canister of microfilm from Jana and dumped the contents into a flat, stainless steel dish on the countertop. He then donned a pair of cloth laboratory gloves and picked up the yellowed strip of film. He stretched it flat underneath a huge magnifying lens and peered through the eyepiece. He looked up. "Well, this is going to take some digging. This has really seen some age. How old is this supposed to be?"

Talia replied, "The original operation began in 1965, so I suppose it dates back that far."

Knuckles squinted through the magnifying lens. "If I'm not mistaken, this appears to be broken into two sections."

"What do you mean?" Talia asked.

"From the looks of it, this bottom section has really deteriorated. I'm not sure we're going to be able to read this. But I'll scan it in, and we can let the computer crunch on it. The top half is different. It appears to be encrypted in a classical cipher."

Uncle Bill smiled as he watched the kid work.

Knuckles continued, "But it doesn't look like substitution or transposition. Hmmm, this could be more of a polyalphabetic substitution." He turned to Uncle Bill. "Sir, want to take a look at this?"

"It's time for me to pass the gavel, son."

"But," Knuckles said as timidity crept out around the edges of his words, "what if this is some super cool important crypto stuff? What if I mess it up?" Bill nodded to the boy and Knuckles turned back to the eyepiece. "I'd say this is likely a Vigenère."

"A what?" Talia said.

Knuckles was in his element now. Once he warmed up, he loved to be the one who knew everything about everything. "A Vigenère cipher, first invented by and later improved by Blaise de Vigenère. It's a method of encrypting alphabetic text by using a series of interwoven ciphers, based on the letters of a keyword. It dates back to the mid-1500's."

"They encrypted details of a covert operation with five-hundred-year-old technology?" Talia said.

"It's harder to crack than you'd think," Knuckles answered. "And if this does date back to 1965, that might make sense. The data is fairly well encrypted, not something that could be read or even broken by just anyone. But fortunately for us, this is the NSA, and I'm the best code breaker here."

"Ahem," Uncle Bill said as if clearing his throat.

"Oh, well, yeah," Knuckles said to Talia as he looked at Bill. "Maybe except for him. I'll have this cracked in no time. But I need to . . . where is Cade when you need him?"

Upon hearing the name, Talia noticed Jana shift her posture.

"I'll get him," Bill said, but no sooner had he reached for a phone did the door on the far side of the room open.

A trim dark-haired man of about thirty years of age wearing a pair of jeans and wrinkled, untucked button-down walked in. Talia watched as he stopped in front of Jana. She didn't make eye contact. "Hello, Jana," he said.

She looked up. "Hello, Cade."

Silence hung for a moment.

"Well, that was awkward," Uncle Bill said. "Cade Williams, this is Talia Stiel. Miss Stiel comes to us from the Mossad with an interesting piece of history."

Cade shook Talia's hand, and Talia looked between Cade and Jana. She could almost feel the tension.

"It's nice to meet you," Cade said.

Knuckles, still holding the microfilm in both gloved hands, looked over his shoulder. "Cade, my faithful assistant. Can you get me a slide?"

Cade's eyes were still locked on Jana, but said, "Your faithful assistant?" He smirked then pulled open a cabinet drawer and removed a pair of laboratory gloves similar to what Knuckles was wearing. He fished inside the drawer a moment. "This about the right size?" he said as he held up what appeared to be a glass microscope slide, used to hold objects for examination under a microscope, only much wider and longer.

"Perfect," Knuckles said as Cade pried the coverslip off. Once the film was in place Knuckles took it and walked to a large piece of lab equipment about the size of a small refrigerator. The front was labeled:

MICROSCOPES INTERNATIONAL
USCOPE MXIII

He inserted the glass slide into the slit-like opening on the front. A digital monitor on the machine blinked to life, and the slide slowly began to be pulled in. "Just take a minute," Knuckles said. "Then, we can get the computer crunching."

"How long will that take?" Talia asked.

"Just a couple of minutes," the kid replied.

Uncle Bill piped up. "Ah, well, it may take a bit more time than that. Our decryption systems are the best in the world, but this kind of thing doesn't happen instantly." He looked at Talia. "You've traveled a long way. Perhaps you'd like some time to freshen up? Jana? Would you?"

"Of course," Jana replied. "Come on. There's a ladies room and a lounge where you can relax."

"Thank you," Talia said, though she couldn't help but feel Bill was trying to get rid of her. "I've been in these clothes forever. I need a shower."

The two walked off, and Jana said. "The Fort has plenty of those."

"The Fort?" Talia replied.

"Just something we call this place. I guess the US government couldn't think of anything else, so they built it in the shape of a big box.

We've got showers and sleeping quarters here, in the event personnel need to stay overnight."

"Do they ever get used?"

"Not much. Used them a time or two myself, though, when we were in the middle of a big case, and the threat level had escalated."

As they walked down a long, stark hallway, Jana stopped in front of a guard desk. She turned to a uniformed man stationed there. "We'll need an escort for Miss Stiel."

"Yes, ma'am," the guard replied, then picked up a phone.

"Sorry," Jana said to Talia. "Although you are a guest of the United States, visitors must be escorted at all times. They'll send a female guard down." She pointed. "Are you hungry?"

"Just exhausted."

"Down on the right are the restrooms and showers. Just across are the dorm rooms. The cafeteria is a little ways further, but the escort can take you down there. If you want to lie down in one of the rooms, feel free. They're not used that often, and it's first come, first served."

"I feel like I should be there while they decrypt the microfilm."

"Unfortunately, it's not like on TV where things happen instantly. I know Knuckles said it would be fast, but this could take a while. I'll have your backpack brought down so you can change."

Talia took Jana by the arm. "I feel like if I don't find out what's on that microfilm, I might explode."

"I'll go back and find out if they're making any progress. If they find something, I'll come get you. Otherwise, you should get some sleep."

Jana walked away, and Talia stared after her. She couldn't help but wonder if she was being left out on purpose.

26

Jana made her way back to the situation room and over to the desk where Knuckles was seated. Cade sat just across and turned as he saw her enter. They had been involved in a prior relationship, but that was a long time ago. The tension between them, however, was as palpable as ever.

Jana leaned over Knuckles and looked at his computer monitor. "How's it coming."

"Still working on it. I've got the digitized scan here. The computer is chewing on the crypto variable now."

Jana could tell the kid was dying to spill some more of his knowledge. It was his way of trying to impress her, so she humored him. "What's a crypto variable?"

"It's the key needed to decrypt the data. See, you start with a key, and that's used for the encrypting procedure. The encrypting procedure is varied depending on the key, which changes the detailed operation of the algorithm. A key must be selected before using a cipher to encrypt the message in the first place. And for us, without knowledge of the key, it would be extremely difficult, if not impossible, to decrypt the resulting ciphertext into readable plaintext."

"Knuckles," Cade said from behind them, "can't you just speak plain English when communicating to the humans?"

"Oh, sorry, Agent Baker."

"What have I told you to call me?" Jana said.

"Jana. Sorry, Jana. The key is required in order to decrypt a data set like this. We don't have the key, but fortunately, the computer will crack it shortly."

"So why are we involved in this in the first place?" Cade asked.

"Because we were *told* to be involved," came Jana's terse reply. She glanced at Cade. "She's Mossad and obviously in imminent danger. The United States has an obligation to its allies."

Cade crossed his arms and waited.

Jana continued. "And the US Attorney General apparently dated the now Director of Operations at the Mossad."

"And there it is. Wait," Cade said, "the attorney general is—"

"Gay?" Jana popped back. "Apparently so. You have a problem with that?"

"Whoa," Knuckles said, still engrossed in his work, "you two need to eighty-six the hostility."

Jana exhaled and looked back at Knuckle's monitor.

"Hey!" Knuckles said. "There it is. See, I told you."

"Got the crypto variable?" Cade said as he slid his rolling chair over.

"Yup," Knuckles replied. "Now that we have the key, we're golden. Watch this."

He keyed a few commands into his laptop, and the monitor refreshed the previously jumbled mass of letters, numbers, and symbols on the microfilm into a series of readable paragraphs.

They all stared at the screen and began to read.

After a moment, Cade leaned back. "Better call Uncle Bill and Miss Stiel over here."

"No, let her sleep," Jana said. "People have been trying to kill her for the last thirty-six hours. She needs some rest."

At a cubicle across the room, Uncle Bill was speaking with an analyst. He looked up and saw Cade waving him over. When he walked up, they began.

"Looks like an after-action report," Knuckles said.

"Meaning?" Jana said.

Cade spoke before Knuckles had the chance. "Even back in the day when microfilm like this was used, it would be common for operatives to write up a summary of what happened on an operation, or to pass data back to their handlers. The good news is, these are usually written in a conversational tone."

"Hold on there, Mister," Uncle Bill said to Knuckles. "Did we get a full transcription?"

"Just a partial," Knuckles replied. "There's a section of the microfilm that is fairly deteriorated. From that section, we got almost nothing."

Bill said, "We'll have to send it back to the lab to see what they can do with it. If we're lucky, they can reconstitute the deteriorated microfilm into something readable." Bill squinted at the monitor and repositioned his glasses. "God, I'm getting too old for this. Put it up on monitor seven, son."

Knuckles keyed in a few commands and the decrypted text from the microfilm displayed on a large computer monitor hanging from the ceiling in front of them. Knuckles read aloud.

Operation Red Scorpion.
Our original goal has not come to fruition. Removal of the warhead without being detected is possible, though highly dangerous. However, we were unable to determine any means of transporting the package without detection, thus rendering any direct attempt impossible. The original goal has failed.

UNCLE BILL SAID, "Hold on, what was that Ms. Stiel told us about the case file at Mossad HQ, before an assassin came in and started shooting, that is?"

Talia walked up from behind them. Her long black hair still wet from the shower. "That *Operation Red Scorpion*'s mission was apparently to steal a nuclear warhead from the *USS Ticonderoga*."

They all turned.

She smiled at them then looked at Jana. "Did you really think I could sleep?" She continued. "Just needed that shower. Been in those clothes since yesterday." She looked up at the screen. "Yeah, I couldn't read much of the 1965 case file before that psycho tried to kill me, but that's what it said exactly. And, that's what my grandfather told me in the hospital." Talia squinted at the words on the monitor. "I assume he's the one writing this."

Uncle Bill shook his head. "So the Mossad was really going to try and steal a nuke off a US warship? That's insane."

"Hey, don't look at me," Talia said. "I agree with you. I was told my whole life that my grandfather, Yosef Stiel, wasn't all there, in the head, I mean."

They looked back at the monitor and Knuckles continued reading.

At this point, we are in agreement. We see no path forward other than to proceed with CONTINGENCY PLAN BRAVO. ECLIPSE has initiated contact with instructions for an anticipated rendezvous on 16 DECEMBER at 25°57′N 131°18′E.

Uncle Bill glanced at Talia. She said, "I never saw anything in the file that talked about a Contingency Plan Bravo, or whatever Eclipse is."

Bill said, "Eclipse is likely the codename for another asset involved in the operation. Your grandfather would have needed help on board the *Ticonderoga* if there was any chance for success, which I'd have said from the beginning was zero."

"Apparently, given the danger Israel was in at the time, they thought it worth the risk," Talia replied.

"That's all there is," Knuckles said. "All we've been able to decrypt anyway. And I'd doubt the lab can pull anything off the lower half of this microfilm. It's just too deteriorated."

"Look up the coordinates, son," Bill said to Knuckles.

"Way ahead of you," Cade added as he spun around from his laptop. "Those coordinates center on a place called Kitadaitō Island, about two hundred nautical miles east of Okinawa."

Bill crossed his arms. "Bring it up on the map."

Knuckles pecked away at the keyboard, and a map depicting the island appeared. "Well," Knuckles said, "tiny little place. I don't get it. They were on board an aircraft carrier. What's this island got to do with anything?"

Cade read from his monitor. "Kitadaitō, also known as Kitadaitōjima, is the northernmost island in the Daitō Islands group, located in the Philippine Sea southeast of Okinawa, Japan. Ah," he continued, "it goes on with more general info about the island, cultivated for agriculture, no beaches or harbors, but it does have an airport.

It's roughly eight miles across by four miles wide, humid subtropical climate, yadda, yadda, yadda."

Uncle Bill asked, "Under Japanese control?"

"Let's see," Cade said as he continued. "Before World War II, the island was occupied by the Japanese, but after, the United States. Then, yes, it was returned to Japan in 1972."

"My grandfather said he was trying to convince his brother, the pilot of a plane that carried the weapon, to fly to a discrete location where the weapon would be offloaded. I guess that island is it."

Uncle Bill walked over to Talia. "Miss Stiel, as a courtesy to the Israeli government, we're glad to continue the analysis of the rest of the microfilm, but at this point, I'd say this is just a look into history. I'm afraid I don't see any reason to commit additional NSA resources."

"Bill," Jana said, "her life is in danger."

"Yes, I am aware," he replied. "But since we have no credible evidence of an imminent threat to the United States, nor Israel for that matter, that's as far as we can take it."

"But I thought—" Talia said.

Bill interrupted. "I'd suggest Miss Stiel be given protection, and if needed, she should apply for asylum here." He turned to Talia whose mouth hung open. "I'm sorry. I really am. There's just nothing we have to go on. This is a matter for the Israeli government. Here at NSA, we're up to our eyeballs in terrorists and the like. We have to stay focused on our charter. Of course, we'll contact you if we are able to read anything else on the microfilm. For the meantime, Agent Baker will be your liaison." He walked away.

27

"Wait, that's it?" Talia said as Bill walked off. "I thought, how am I supposed to . . ?" She struggled to continue her line of thought.

Jana said, "Let me go talk to him," and followed Bill.

"I'm sorry, Miss Stiel," Cade said.

Then Knuckles nodded. "Yeah, me too. I was hoping we would work together. I mean, I've never worked with a real Mossad agent."

Talia forced a smile. "You still haven't. I work in R and D, remember?"

"I never was told," Cade said, "What is your specialty?"

"I'm really not supposed to talk about it," Talia replied as she watched Jana speed-walk after Uncle Bill.

Knuckles spun his chair back to his laptop and began typing away. "Hold on, Jana sent us the data package." He read the screen a moment. "She's a technical analyst. She's finishing her Ph.D. in condensed matter physics."

"Hey!" Talia said.

"Yeah, Knuckles," Cade added. "Don't be rude. If she doesn't want to talk about it, she doesn't want to talk about it. It does sound pretty cool though." He turned to Talia, "Listen, you're standing inside the NSA. It's not like we don't keep everything secret anyway."

Talia shrugged. "It probably doesn't matter. They just always tell us not to talk about what we're up to. It's not that exciting, actually. I am working on a research project—"

"Wait, wait, wait," Knuckles said, almost speed-talking. "Let me guess. I'm good at this."

Cade laughed. "Here we go," he said as he shook his head. He glanced at Talia. "I hate to admit it, but he is pretty good at this."

"Good at what?" Talia asked.

Knuckles jumped up. "Condensed matter physics. So you're essentially a nuclear physicist. There's not many functions a nuclear physicist could perform for an agency like the Mossad."

"Oh, no?" Talia said as she started to smile at the kid.

"No," Knuckles replied. "Think about it objectively. It's the *Mossad,* that's the limiting factor. I mean, a nuclear physicist could do all kinds of different things if they worked in the private sector, or for a different type of government agency. But the Mossad? The interests of the Mossad are very singular. So, let me think. What would the Mossad need with a nuclear physicist?"

Knuckles stared at her and tapped a finger to his lips. "The Israeli government has had nukes for a long time, and even if they were developing more, it wouldn't be the Mossad that would do that. No, a spy agency would only be concerned with covert actions and intelligence gathering. Hmmm." He snapped his fingers. "I've got it!"

"Is that so?" Talia said.

Knuckles started. "We've been trying to get more funding for it too. I mean, we've got fairly robust systems in place at our shipping ports and airports. But there are lots of holes. And the Australians have done some amazing work as well, but their satellite systems are still experimental. Kind of glitchy, if you want to know the truth."

"Knuckles," Cade said. "What are you talking about?"

"She works on detection of SNM. It's the only answer," Knuckles replied.

Cade thought a moment. "Special nuclear material?" He looked at Talia. "Is that right?"

Talia grinned. "You're good, kid."

"So which system are you guys focused on?" he said. "Let me think. You've got enemies on all sides of you. You'd have to be concerned about a nuke being snuck in. I mean, why wouldn't you? We've got the same problem. Not the enemies on all sides part, but our borders are porous. We're always worried somebody will slip something on a container ship and smuggle it into the US.

He squinted his eyes. "You're working on a Cargo Advanced Automated Radiography System to detect high-density material based on the principle that it becomes less transparent to photons of higher energy? Or no, wait, how about nuclear resonance fluorescence imaging, where you can identify materials based on the spectrum of gamma rays a nucleus emits when struck by photons of a specific energy?"

"Knuckles," Cade said, "where do you get this stuff? Do you do nothing but read? Do you go out at all? You are such a PowerPoint Ranger."

"Very impressed," Talia said to Knuckles. "You know your nuclear physics."

Knuckles turned a shade of crimson. "Well, I try."

She then looked at Cade and laughed. "A PowerPoint Ranger?"

"Yeah," he replied as he said, "It's like a soldier who never goes out in the field but is instead tasked with building PowerPoint presentations."

Knuckles looked down. "Like you're a Meat Eater or something." He looked at Talia and as if to explain, said, "Special Forces soldiers."

She nodded. "We've got those technologies in place. But having a device slip across the border is only one of the nuclear threats we are building contingencies for."

Cade leaned up. "You're concerned about one being launched against you."

Talia nodded.

"Oh," Knuckles said. "You need to detect a device at a distance before it gets to your borders. Are you working on improving Australia's technology? The Optus D2 Comsat satellite may be experimental, but it can detect high-velocity spin-off particles from enriched uranium. We've used their satellites here."

"Not exactly, no," Talia said. "The Optus D2 is a good start, but like you said, not a specific science. We don't have the luxury of being *almost* right. We've got to be sure. My work involves technology that would stimulate fission in SNM."

Knuckles squinted a moment, then said, "Photonuclear? Cool. I didn't think that worked."

"What worked?" Cade asked.

Knuckles was again in his element. "A Photonuclear Inspection and Threat Assessment System would detect SNM up to, what, a kilometer away? Unlike other systems that operate at very close range, like our border detection systems or the Comsat satellite, this would beam high energy photons at a target to stimulate fission."

"And what would stimulating fission do?" Cade said.

Knuckles replied, "You never studied. If you stimulate fission, you would be producing the characteristic signatures that are needed for detection." He looked at Talia. "Did you make it work?" Talia didn't answer. "Well, at least tell me this, what platform would you use for your detection equipment?"

"Drones, presumably," Talia replied.

"Right," Knuckles said. "Makes sense. A large enough drone, like say a General Atomics Avenger, would provide the perfect base."

Talia said, "I'm working to make Israel a safer place." She smiled and then stared at the ground. "It's what I've wanted to do my whole life." She looked at the two of them. "My parents, you see? They were killed when I was very young. A bomb."

"Hezbollah?" Cade asked.

A lump formed in Talia's throat but she shook it off. "When I was done living with the anger, I decided to do something with all that energy. I wanted to find a way to stop it."

"Yeah, *I'd* say," Cade said. "If you could detect a nuke that's near your borders, you'd be saving a lot of lives."

28

"Bill," Jana said as she tracked him down. "We can't just leave her like this."

"I hear you, but my hands are tied. Without a threat to the sovereignty of the United States, I can't commit resources. Look, you saw the intel. It's a detail of some hair-brained plan to steal a weapon from us back in the 60's. Kind of pisses me off, if you want to know the truth. They're our allies, for God's sake."

"What am I supposed to do, go back and tell her, sorry we can't help, here's a bus ticket and some spending money?"

"Of course not." His voice reminded Jana of her grandfather's. He took her by the shoulders. "You've known me a long time, Jana. Did you really think I would send a young woman out into danger? It's just that I can't put government resources on it, and you know it."

"So what are you suggesting?"

"Look, she needs someone uniquely qualified to help her with two things, finding out who is trying to kill her, and protection. You and I know just such a person."

Jana paused a moment. "You aren't suggesting—"

Bill nodded. "He's perfect for the role, and you know it."

Jana's shoulders slumped. "I have a hard enough time being around one ex-boyfriend. Now you want me to bring in another?"

Uncle Bill grinned. "I enjoy seeing you squirm. Besides, you're a professional. You just need to brief him on the situation. After that, he and Talia are on their own. In the meantime, we'll see if the lab can recover anything else off that microfilm, but that's all."

Uncle Bill started to walk away, but Jana stopped him in his tracks. "There's more to this than you're letting on."

Bill said. "What makes you say that?"

"I don't know." She studied his eyes a moment. "Something about the way you questioned that island. What does a microscopic place like Kitadaitō have to do with anything?"

"You're imagining things."

Jana crossed her arms.

Bill exhaled. "Just set it up. Get him here. That will make me feel better."

29

John Stone's phone buzzed in his back pocket, and he pulled it out. He looked at the screen and immediately recognized the caller.

"Are you kidding me?" he said before answering. "This is Stone."

On the other end of the line, Special Agent Jana Baker said, "You know damn well who's calling, Johnny."

Stone grinned. "Hello, babe."

"When are you going to stop calling me that?"

"Dammit, Jana. Why are you always so hostile? I apologized already, many times, in fact. If you're going to talk to me like this, why are you calling?"

"Kind of over-reacting, aren't we?"

Stone rubbed his temples and let out a long exhale. "I'm sorry, I don't mean to snap at you. I guess I'm a little on edge lately."

"Are you working?" she asked.

"No."

"Well, that's your problem. You were never much for sitting still. If you didn't have some enemy combatant or drug cartel or terrorist in your sights, you were never happy."

"Is this a social call?"

"No," Jana replied. "I've got something for you. Well, maybe. Depends on if you're interested."

"Would I have to work with you?" Stone said, half joking.

"No."

"I'm in."

"Nice."

"No, seriously. What?"

"Protective detail. I don't want to talk about it over the phone. Can you meet me?"

"Protection is not exactly my specialty."

"Yeah, it doesn't involve blowing something up. It's work, Stone. Would it make you feel better if I told you someone is trying to kill her?"

"Her?" Stone said as he smiled. "Is she my type?"

"Men," Jana muttered. "Just meet me at The Fort. Can you come?"

Stone glanced at his wristwatch and yawned. "All right, Baker. See you there." He hung up, then pushed his sandy blond hair out of his eyes. His thoughts drifted back to his undercover assignment on the island of Antigua where he'd first met Jana. "I really screwed up that relationship," he said.

He got up and started throwing his things into a duffel. Any chance to see Jana was better than no chance at all.

30

NSA Command Center

STONE WENT into the sprawling command center with his identification card clipped to his t-shirt and walked over to where Jana and Talia were waiting. Jana turned to him. "You look like a beach bum," she said. "Has nothing changed since Antigua?"

"Nice to see you, Baker."

Referring to the multiple security checkpoints at NSA, Jana said, "Have any trouble getting in?"

"Just that one female guard," he replied. "She always gives me such a hard time."

"You have that effect on women," Jana said. She turned to Talia. "Talia Stiel, meet John Stone. *Mister* Stone is a contractor. He's done a lot of work with us in the past."

Stone shook Talia's hand.

"Nice to meet you," Talia said as she glanced him up and down. "I was expecting someone," she paused, "bigger."

"Yeah," Stone said as he frowned. "I get that a lot."

Talia looked between Jana and Stone. "You two know each other?"

Jana blew past the question. "Mr. Stone has a background in special military operations. Black ops mostly, the kind that don't end up on the evening news. He's been on quite a few missions. You'll find he's not only good at protective services, he's good at investigations as well." She turned to Talia. "The US government is picking up the tab for Mr. Stone's services. But I suggest you two get started. I don't know how long that will last."

"You're not coming with us?" Talia said to Jana.

"Afraid not."

"Pity," Stone jabbed.

Jana flicked her eyes at him. "I've got to get back to the field office. Call me if you need anything. Let me have a word with you."

The two of them walked into a conference room.

Stone's hands found the pockets of his tattered jeans. "Couldn't stand to be away from me, could you?"

Jana shook her head. "Same old Stone."

"Hey, I'm kidding. Man, I didn't think we left on such bad terms. Where is all this hostility coming from?"

"There *is* no hostility," Jana said with a little more intensity than she had intended. She crossed her arms, and her suit jacket tightened against her. "I know protective detail isn't your cup of tea, but she needs help. Uncle Bill has cleared you for full operational knowledge, but I want you to be careful. We know practically nothing about the danger she's in. She'll give you all the details, but if half of what she's saying is true, the asset that is after her is going to take another crack at it. She's Mossad, Johnny. She circulates at high levels, and in my opinion, the Mossad has got a mole."

"Meaning?"

"Someone is helping the assassin from the inside. They want her out of the picture."

"Maybe the assassin *is* Mossad."

"Maybe," Jana replied. "Talia can give you his full description. She was face to face with him. A man meeting the same description murdered her grandfather two days ago and then went after her." Jana looked into the depth of Stone's blue eyes, and her shoulders loosened. "I'm sorry," she said, "I didn't mean to snap at you. It's been a long time, and I should just let the past stay in the past."

"Do you ever think about me, Baker? Think about us?"

An awkward silence ensued, and Jana's eyes found the tops of her heels. "There's something else. Uncle Bill isn't being completely forthcoming. He's keeping something close to the vest. I cornered him about it, but he was evasive."

Referring to their past relationship, Stone said, "I take that as a no." He exhaled. "I've never known Bill to hold back."

Jana swallowed. "Be careful out there, Johnny. This isn't a game."

She walked out.

31

Stone waved Talia over. "Why don't we sit down a minute and talk about your situation."

Talia, however, picked up her backpack and headed toward the elevators. "I can brief you in the car."

"The car?" he said. "We're not going anywhere. Now, come sit down so we can discuss—" But she was already in the hallway.

"We're going to the Naval Academy," she said as he caught up to her.

"The what?" Stone said. "We're not going anywhere." But Talia continued walking. He caught up to her again as she boarded the elevator. "Where do you think you're going?"

She keyed the elevator button to the main floor, and the doors wafted shut. "There's nothing more for us to do here," she said. "We've got to go dig up a grave."

"Dig up a grave?" he said. "Look, lady. I appreciate your situation, but while you're with me, I'm in charge."

"Is that so?" Talia said as the elevator doors reopened on the lobby floor. She walked into the sprawling area and toward the front exit. "I'm the one they're after. I'm the one whose life is on the line. And I can tell you one thing, they're after me because they're afraid of something." She pushed through the glass security doors and walked into the bright sunlight.

"Yeah," Stone said, "I'm afraid of something too. That I've just signed on to a protectee with a death wish." He reached out and stopped her.

"If you expect me to help you, in fact, if you expect to be alive tomorrow morning, you're going have to accept the fact that in the field, it's *my* show."

"It's *my* life."

Stone flung his arms into the air, and his volume escalated. "You aren't even field personnel!" He lowered his voice after several people turned to look. "This is my domain. While you were sitting in a classroom or lab studying nuclear *whatever*, I was up to my eyeballs in covert ops, war zones, firefights, people shooting at me, stuff exploding. I've worked numerous covert investigations and been in undercover roles you wouldn't believe. I've been places you don't even want to think about. My life has been spent dealing with situations like this, and I won't tolerate a loose cannon."

She exhaled. "Fine, but I'm not wasting another minute. We're going to Annapolis. And I don't know what you're so worried about. Right now, no one knows where I am. Did you think they're tracking me, here, at NSA headquarters?"

They began walking across the parking area through a huge section of parked cars.

"We're not going to some Navy-boy graveyard."

"Hey!" she snapped. "That's my great uncle you're talking about."

"Fine, your great uncle, whatever. Look, we're going to lay low. If for no other reason than I don't know what I don't know. I'm not walking into an ambush because I didn't have the correct intel. I've seen that happen too many times." Stone said, "Let me see your cell phone."

"What for?"

"Give it to me," Stone said with his hand out.

She started to argue but thought better of it. She fished into a side pocket on her backpack. "See?" she said as she handed it to him. "It's powered off. They can't track me."

Stone inspected the phone as they walked into the parking area reserved for visitors, then over to his vehicle.

"This is what you drive?" she said as they walked to a tattered, two-door Toyota Land Cruiser. The box-shaped SUV was pock-marked with tiny dents down one side, and a long scrape down the other. Rust had taken hold where the paint was missing. She smirked. "It's just lovely."

"Now you have a problem with my ride?" he said as walked to the right side of the car and opened the front door. "I bought this in Kandahar. It's armored."

Talia shook her head and followed. "Wait. First, you act like an asshole, and now you're holding the door open for me?" But as she walked up behind him and looked in, she caught sight of the steering wheel. "This thing is right-hand drive?"

"I can tell already this detail is going to be like pulling teeth." He turned to her. "Your seat is over there. This isn't a limousine service, Miss Stiel, and I'm not your servant. Yes, this is my POV. Yes, it's right-hand drive. Yes, it's really armored. And no, I'm not being an asshole." He thumbed toward the other side of the vehicle. "The passenger door isn't going to open itself."

"Fine." Talia walked around to the left side of the SUV and got in. Stone sat in the driver's seat then reached in front of her and popped open the glove box. He began fishing around inside it. "POV?" she said.

"Privately-owned vehicle."

"In Israel, we call them *cars,*" her emphasis on the word made it sound like she was talking to a two-year-old.

"Never should have signed up for this," he half-muttered as he continued digging in the glove box.

"What are you looking for?"

"You ask too many questions." He pulled out a small metal paper clip. "This," he said. He bent the clip to expose one end, then inserted it into a tiny pinhole on the side of Talia's phone.

"You trying to break my phone?"

"First rule of protective detail. Don't be tracked. I'm removing the SIM card." He inserted the end of the paper clip then pushed. The tiny SIM tray popped out. He handed the phone and SIM tray back to Talia. "Here, stow that in your gear. I feel better knowing the SIM isn't in the phone." He started the engine then reached under the seat and withdrew a Glock and tucked it in his back.

Talia bristled at the sight. The last time she saw one of those, she was looking at the business end.

"You don't trust me," she said, her tone leaning to the accusatory.

Stone flicked a glance but otherwise said nothing.

"How do you think they're going to track a phone that's turned off?"

He started the engine. "Look, lady. I've seen a lot of weird shit on what one would have thought to be the simplest of operations." He pulled out of the parking spot and turned in the direction of the security gates.

"You can't track a phone that's been powered down."

"Is that what your years of field experience and knowledge of surveillance and digital circuitry tell you?"

"It doesn't take a nuclear physicist to tell you that you can't track a powered-down iPhone."

He applied the brakes just hard enough to rock the truck to a stop. "But apparently it does take a nuclear physicist to annoy the hell out of you. And it only took two minutes to do it." He began to drive again.

Talia crossed her arms. "I live in a male-dominated society and workplace. I get sick of being told what's going to happen when and where."

As Stone drove up behind a short queue of vehicles exiting past security officers, he said, "No, that's not it."

"What's that supposed to mean?" she said.

"Christ," he said as if talking to himself. "It's like having a conversation with Jana."

32

Visitor Parking Lot, NSA Headquarters, Ft. Meade, Maryland.

TALIA GLANCED at Stone as they drove and said, "You two were together, weren't you?"

They passed the guard gates and onto Canine Road, Stone got in the right lane to fork onto Maryland Route 32, an east-west artery known as the Patuxent Freeway.

He ignored the question. "I don't know how I get into these situations."

"You don't want to tell me about you and Jana? *You're* the one who's being evasive."

"It's not that you don't like being told what to do, it's that you don't like being told what to do by a man."

Talia's mouth opened as if to react, but she stopped and composed her thoughts. "I've spent my whole career being stepped over for promotions so a man could get the job, and putting up with the other male-dominated crap. I don't know what it's like here, but in the Mossad, women have to fight for everything they get."

"All right, all right," Stone said as he steered the vehicle around the circular on-ramp and headed east. "I've got no problem with women in leadership roles or even combat. Christ, can we have a cease-fire?"

Talia looked onto the freeway. "I still don't get why you bought a car with right-hand drive. You Americans drive on the right side of the road like we do."

"So?"

"Like I said, you're the one being evasive. What are you doing with a right-side drive vehicle?"

"Do you always ask this many questions? Or are you just trying to annoy me?"

"I'll ignore that," she said. "You learn things about me; I learn things about you. It's called a civil conversation, Agent Stone."

"I'm not an agent. Never have been."

She raised an eyebrow at him.

"I used to be an *operator*. Just call me Stone. Everyone else does."

"The car?" she said.

"I spent so much time overseas, I got used to right-hand drive."

"There, that wasn't so hard," she said.

"Now, tell me the whole story, the background and how it came to be that people started shooting at you out of the blue. Not that I blame them, mind you."

"Hysterical," she replied, sarcasm lacing her tone. "I'll tell you my story if you give me your phone."

"Why would I give you my phone?" Stone accelerated to bring the SUV up to highway speeds. "You want to pop out my SIM card to get back at me?"

"No, but I should. My godfather is going to be worried sick. I need to let him know I'm okay."

"No can do," Stone replied.

"Give me your damn phone!" Talia said as she held out her hand.

"How do you know your godfather's phone isn't being monitored by the people trying to kill you. Did you ever think of that?"

"He's a director at the Mossad. Believe me, nobody is listening in. Security is so tight, it would be like someone eavesdropping on a call to the president of the United States." When she could tell Stone wasn't convinced, she continued. "Do you know anything about secure comms?"

"Do I know anything about secure comms? Lady, I've got a top secret security clearance. My life is on the line every time I deploy to one shit-hole country or another. We go through a lot of training."

"Then you know what data-in-transit and data-at-rest encryption are. You're familiar with SUITE B cryptography, and FIPS 140-2 validated keystrokes. *No one* is going to intercept this call."

"How do you know so much about . . . I thought you were a nuclear . . ." Stone searched for the words, "something-or-other. If you know so much about secure comms, how come your phone isn't encrypted?"

She shifted her voice to imitate his. "Because I'm a *nuclear something-or-other*. My work is in the lab, not in the field. I've got no need."

She glanced at her watch but remembered it was broken. "What time is it? Moshe will be at home at this hour. All his calls route through Mossad HQ. There's no way to eavesdrop." She looked at him. "Stone, you're being paranoid."

"What does he do for the Mossad?"

"*Ëlohim Adirim*!"

"No need to get testy about it," Stone said as he laughed.

"You don't even know what I said."

"Even if I didn't, your tone speaks volumes. But what you said was *great God*, but I think the English equivalent would be *good Lord*."

She stared at him. "You know Hebrew?"

"I've spent a lot of time in the Middle East, Dr. Stiel. You'll find I know a great many things."

"I'm not a doctor," she said, allowing herself to relax just a bit. "Now, would you give me the phone?"

He shook his head and muttered. "I was right. This is going to be like working with Jana." He went on, "I suppose since no one knows where you are, and no one knows me, it couldn't hurt. But don't mention anything about your location." He pulled the phone from his back pocket and handed it to her.

"Stone, Moshe is my godfather. He raised me. After the shooting at the Mossad, he was so worried I thought he was going to pass out." She glanced at the phone. When her eyes landed on an app labeled *Securesmart,* she glared at him. "You knew the whole time that your phone is secure, and you still gave me crap about wanting to use it? With Securesmart, even your NSA couldn't track this phone."

Stone smiled as he continued driving. "Ah, the pleasures of field work."

"Unbelievable," she said as she tapped Moshe's number into the keypad. "It's no wonder Jana dumped you."

"You don't know anything about me."

She glanced at her digital watch, its face still badly scratched, and tapped it several times. Although it was now broken, she smiled as she thought back to when Moshe had given it to her several months prior. "It'll be like two in the morning there, but I guarantee he'll be wide awake. The poor man." Talia put the phone to her ear.

As per protocols, the phone rang twice then was picked up by an automated system. Talia heard the familiar digital sounds as the system flushed the line for intrusions. When it was forwarded to Moshe's mobile, he picked up on the first ring.

Moshe's voice sounded weary yet laced with desperation. "Moshe Himmelreich," he said.

Talia's throat tightened. "Aba, it's me."

"Talia?" he almost yelled.

Talia heard something that sounded as if Moshe had jumped up, then knocked into a table. "I'm all right," she said.

"Oh, thank God! My dear, I've been so worried."

"I'm sorry, Aba, I had to disappear. I couldn't risk calling you until now."

Talia listened and could hear the rapidity of Moshe's breathing. To her, it sounded as though he had covered his mouth. She could just picture it. "I've been, oh, it's just so good to hear your voice. You're not hurt?"

"No, I'm fine. And you don't have to worry about me. I'll be okay."

"Darling, someone is trying to kill you. How can you say it will be okay?"

She glanced at Stone. "I've got . . . protection."

"Someone is with you? But wait, how do you know you can trust him, or her, or, oh, I'm just so relieved. Where are you?"

"I'd better not say. Mr. Paranoid over here would go nuts if I did."

"Who is with you? There was no caller ID. You're calling from a secure line, aren't you?"

"Yes," she replied. "Listen, I just wanted to call to let you know I was all right. Have you been able to find out anything internally? Aba, we both know someone had to have helped that man get into Mossad HQ."

"I know, I know. But so far, my dear, we haven't been able to identify him. We took the surveillance footage and ran it through facial recognition, but nothing."

"Okay, just keep trying." Talia rubbed the face of her watch, an attempt to wipe off the scratches. "It's good to hear your voice."

"Oh, Talia, I've been so worried. What are you going to do?"

She squelched the lump in her throat. "Right now, we're going to just debrief. This person I'm with, he doesn't have the details."

"Can you trust him?"

"He's . . ." Talia glanced at Stone. "I'll tell you about him later." She rubbed her eyes. "I need some sleep. This has taken more of a toll on me than I realized."

"You do that, my darling. And don't do anything foolish. Just lay low until we get to the bottom of this from our side. We don't know what we're dealing with."

"I know." As the road converted from the highway into Forest Drive, a three-laner, Stone slowed as they approached a red light. "Aba, I have to go now. I'll stay in touch."

"How can I reach you?"

"For now, let me call you."

Moshe paused. "That's a good idea. But please, do call me."

"Goodbye, Aba. *Ani ohevet ot'h'a.*"

"I love you too, my dear."

Talia hung up and tried to hide the fact that a tear was threatening to roll down her cheek. "How much time do we have?" she said.

"It's about five more minutes over to my apartment."

"We're going to your place?"

"Sure. Like we said earlier. No one knows about me, other than the NSA, that is."

"All right, but after we debrief, I want to go straight to this Naval Academy of yours."

"What is with you and the Naval Academy?"

Stone turned left onto Forest Hills Avenue and entered a quiet, tree-lined suburban neighborhood. Talia looked at the houses, mostly two-story Cape Cods. "You live here? It's pretty."

"A few blocks over. An apartment. Or do you call them flats? I don't remember."

"Makes sense. A guy like you."

"A guy like me?"

"To have an apartment instead of a house. I don't exactly picture you as the sensitive, settled down type. Little house with a yard and a white picket fence. Isn't that what you Americans think about?" Stone shook his head, and Talia continued. "A little wife, two point something kids, and what, a Beagle? Lab? What are the most popular dogs here?"

"You are infuriating, you know that?" Stone then muttered, "Remind me, the next time Jana calls and asks for a favor, the answer is no." They drove past a small, 1970's era church, then further down, into his apartment complex. The sign out front read *Laurel Ridge Apartments*.

Talia looked around. The grounds were modestly kept, but the buildings, three-story, 1980's-style brick and plank siding, were showing their age. Talia said, "Not exactly a . . ." she thought a moment, "how do you guys put it? A babe magnet?"

"Oh, and I suppose you live in a palatial mansion in, where, Tel Aviv? Yeah, I've been there. Not exactly a resort town, is it?"

Stone drove to the third building on the left then parked on the end. He cut the engine. "Grab your ruck. We're upstairs."

"My what?" Talia said as she opened the door and grabbed her backpack.

"Your pack," he said as he motioned to her backpack then walked under the awning toward the exterior staircase.

As she followed, she said, "What, you're not going to carry it for me?"

As Stone went up the steps, he turned. "You've already got me pegged as the not-so-sensitive type with the little wife and two-point-something kids. Carry it yourself."

Talia scowled as she watched the back of his head. "Men."

33

Stone approached the door of his apartment, but instead of putting the key in the door handle, he knelt down and squinted into the bolt lock.

"What are you doing?" Talia said.

Stone plucked a blond hair out of the keyhole and showed it to her. "Just being careful," he said. He dropped the hair and unlocked the bolt.

"What are you talking about?"

As they entered the Spartan apartment, he closed the door and locked it. "This is a third-floor apartment. Not likely someone would try to break in through one of the windows."

"Would you speak plain English?"

"Christ, you've really never been in the field before, have you? Look, it's simple. I put one of my hairs into the bolt lock when I leave. If someone tried to pick the lock or entered with a key, the hair would get crushed into the keyhole or would fall free. As long as that hair is there when I get back, I know no one has been in here."

"My God, you are so paranoid. What kind of life is this?"

He threw his keys onto the countertop. "Mine."

Talia shook her head and walked to the small kitchen. To Talia, it didn't look like it had been used since 1984. The white Formica counters were chipped and swollen at the seams where water had penetrated. The cabinets, also white, were dingy and two of the doors hung slightly askew. But Talia's eyes stopped at the hideously patterned linoleum floor. "You know what a mop is?"

"Hey, it may look like shit, but I clean regularly. I'm military, remember? Or, ex-military, anyway."

She walked into the small living area and looked at the barren walls. "No pictures, paintings, nothing? I don't know how you men survive sometimes."

"I get along just fine, thank you very much." He sat at a small round kitchen table. The plastic seat covers had cracked long ago and foam cushioning pushed through. "Have a seat. We need to talk about what brought you to have someone shooting at you."

Talia tossed her backpack on the second-hand couch. "Hey, that's not funny." She glanced around. "Where are the *shirutim*?"

Stone frowned. "The services? Oh, I forget that's what you Israelis call the restroom. Sure, right over there."

When Talia returned, she said. "I still don't get why Americans put a toilet in the same room as your tub."

"Yeah, yeah, yeah, our cultures are different in so many ways. Israeli restrooms always separate the two. And there's other things. You people talk to your bosses the same way you talk to your annoying little brothers, you see no difference in how you should address them. And when Israeli's talk, they spit it right out. Your culture is written all over your face. When Americans talk, we prefer to soften the edges, sugar-coat things."

"And why do you do that?"

"We still get our point across," Stone said, "we just don't see the need to be assholes about it."

"You're calling me an asshole?"

"Can we dispense with the cultural differences speech? Come on, sit down. Tell me what happened."

Talia flopped onto the chair.

"Jana didn't give me too much background. Just the highlights. She did say your grandfather told you some wild story, and when you investigated it, you'd tripped across some information?"

"You speak of her fondly." She glanced at the apartment. "Did you have her up here to your bachelor pad?"

Stone relented. "We dated when we were both on Antigua. Why? You jealous?"

"Not likely," Talia replied.

"Can we get back to business?"

"My grandfather, who I'd thought was dead since I was a little girl, told me he had been involved in a Mossad operation in the '60s. His assignment was to steal a nuclear device from a US warship."

"Yeah, like those Navy pukes would let him walk off with one of those. Go on."

"Why do you hate the Navy so much?"

"It's just an Army-Navy thing."

"At any rate, the operation failed. But his brother was on board the aircraft carrier and knew about the operation. He murdered him to keep him quiet."

"That's what Jana mentioned, the supposed accident where the pilot, plane, and bomb were dumped overboard?"

"Yes. Anyway, my grandfather wanted to unburden his guilt over killing his brother. In the hospital, after I left, he was murdered. But I think he would have died fairly soon anyway. He was close."

"And the murderer's description was the same as the man who came after you. Middle Eastern, tall, thin, scar down his face?"

Talia's eyes drifted off like she was seeing the face again. "The eyes," she said. "They were almost dead looking."

"Back to your grandfather. Jana told me how he originally wanted the brother's casket shipped to Israel, but it got sent here instead. And he wanted you to have the grave exhumed? That was his real intention?"

"Yes," Talia said as she thought back to the intensive care unit. For just a moment she could almost smell the sterility. "I didn't believe his story at the time. I mean, growing up, Moshe always said grandpa was a *Meschugener*. What do you call it here?"

"A nut-job," he said. "But you *did* end up investigating his story, didn't you?"

"I searched the Mossad personnel files and found my grandfather in the system. And I found reference to an old operation called *Red Scorpion*. But then, when I turned back to the computer screen, it was gone."

"What was gone?"

"*Red Scorpion*. I was looking at it on my monitor, and the next thing I knew, the screen had blanked out. It said it had been redacted, like somebody erased the file."

"Is this when you went to the storage area to find the actual records, and someone started shooting at you?"

"Almost," Talia said. Her lower lip trembled.

"What?"

"That's when I was told my grandfather had been murdered." She wiped a tear before it could drop then cleared her throat. "Yes," she continued, her voice now devoid of emotion, "the next day, I went to the records room and found the case files."

"Files, plural?"

"Things get a little hazy here."

"Well un-hazy them."

Talia squinted at him. "*Shmendrik*," she said.

"I'm not a jerk. You just get on my nerves."

"I don't know *what* Jana saw in you. I found the original *Red Scorpion* case files, yes. But it was sitting in the active section, which made no sense since it happened fifty years ago. But right next to it was another operational case file, this one codenamed *Absolution*. It was apparently joined to *Red Scorpion*, and not nearly as old. Maybe it was a continuation of operation *Red Scorpion* somehow? I don't know. Anyway—"

Stone cut her off with a grin. "Treadstone upgrade?"

"Huh?"

Stone shook his head. "Never mind, Hollywood joke. Go on."

"Thank you," she said, "I think I will. I read what I could, ended up finding that microfilm, and then some psychopath started shooting at me. The same guy that murdered my grandfather, then came after me, and I don't know why."

"It seems obvious he's trying to stop you from finding something out."

"Yeah, like what's in that case file. And, what's in that casket."

Stone placed his face into his hands. "Here we go again with that damn casket."

"We're going to Annapolis, to the cemetery."

"That takes us out into the open."

She stood. "*Ya Allah*," she said as her hands found her hips. "It's our only lead."

"Lead on what?" Stone replied. "What do you think is in there anyway?"

"I have no idea," she said, "but we've got to find out."

"You realize your great uncle's body isn't in there, right?"

"I have a Ph.D. in condensed matter physics. I'm not an idiot. I get the fact that when his plane was purposely dumped overboard, they never recovered his body. My grandfather said they put his personals in the casket."

"And you think a footlocker full of undershirts, deodorant, a pocket knife, and some old copies of *Playboy* magazine is going to crack the case for us?"

"What's *Playboy* magazine?" Talia asked.

"Not important."

"I don't know, maybe there's something in there that would give us our next clue."

"Clue? This isn't a game. If that scar-faced guy is what I think he is, he'll stop at nothing to kill you. We can't take unnecessary risks."

"I agree he's some kind of assassin," Talia said as she rubbed her sore wrist and unstrapped her wristwatch. "But nobody knows where we are. We're safe." She put the watch on the table and continued rubbing.

"Your grandfather was murdered right after you left him. Hasn't it occurred to you the psycho might have learned what your grandfather told you to go do? The cemetery is the one spot on the face of the earth that we'd be expected to go."

"So you *do* believe there's something in that casket."

Stone searched for the words as if he didn't want to get caught agreeing with her. "Maybe," he finally said.

"So can we go?"

Stone looked out the window at the darkening sky. "Too late to go on campus at this hour. Hey, what's with the wrist?"

"I think I twisted it when I ran from those Mossad agents."

Stone picked up the scuffed digital watch. "Banged the hell out of what looks like a brand new watch." He tapped it. "Broken?"

"Guess so. It's upsetting too. Aba gave me that watch a couple of months ago, on the anniversary of . . ."

Stone studied her face. "Of?"

"Of my parents' deaths." Her voice took on a distant quality. "Aba always wanted me to remember the good things about them, the happy times. He didn't want that day to be . . . he would always have us remember them on that day, but then he'd turn it into a day of fun, with gifts and everything."

Stone nodded then turned his attention to the watch. He flipped it over to inspect it. "What's this thing on the band? This stick-on strip."

"Oh, something Moshe insisted on. I work in the lab a lot. It's kind of a safety thing, like a piece of litmus paper. It's nothing."

"Looks like the button on the side of the watch is jammed." He removed a small pocketknife and opened it, then pushed the point of the blade into the button. "It might still work if I can get it to pop free." He fiddled with it a moment, and when it dislodged, he looked at the face, and the watch screen came to life. He handed it back to Talia.

"Thanks."

"See? I'm not such an asshole."

"Don't push it," she said, though the slightest edge of a grin formed on her mouth. Talia rubbed her eyes. "I'm exhausted."

"Bedroom's in there," he said.

"Just one?"

"I'll bunk on the couch."

"Are the sheets clean?" she said before picking up her backpack.

"Does the Pope shit in the woods?"

She turned. "I'm Jewish. What is that supposed to mean?"

"Never mind. Sheets are clean. Food's in the reefer. Make yourself at home. And just sleep till whenever."

"Reefer?"

"Sorry, we called it a reefer in the service. Refrigerator."

She walked to the bedroom but stopped. "How long of a trip is it to get to the Naval Academy?"

"About four minutes."

"Four . . . you mean to tell me—"

"Yeah, it's two miles up the road," he said as he pointed. "You'll be up to your eyeballs in Navy boys."

She pointed a sharp finger. "You know I've been wanting to go there this whole time, and you're just now telling me it's two miles away? You are so infuriating!"

"Growing on you, huh? Yeah, happened the same way with Jana."

"Oh!" she said, then walked into the bedroom and slammed the door.

"Got a real way with the ladies," Stone said to himself as he laughed.

34

Laurel Ridge Apartments

DEEP IN THE NIGHT, as Stone slept on the couch, what had started as a dream melted into the etchings of a nightmare. As the terrors began, his body thrashed on the narrow couch until the sheet he had draped over himself flipped onto the floor.

In the dream, he relived something from his past, a horror that had occurred at a remote bunker at Incirlik Air Base in Turkey. It was the same scene Stone had never been able to get out of his mind. In it, his partner and best friend, Charlie Ochoa, was in the midst of a mental breakdown. Their operation had gone wrong, very wrong. It had been an assassination order targeted at a high-priority terrorist subject, and through his sniper rifle, Ochoa had accidentally shot a woman holding a baby.

Ochoa screamed, "Stay out of this, Stone! You are the *last* person I want to see!"

Stone's eyes locked onto the detonator in Ochoa's hand and he knew the immediacy of the situation—Ochoa was going to kill himself. Stone repeated the words he had said that fateful day, "Charlie, come on man. What are you doing? You don't want to do this." Only this time, it was as if Stone was watching himself from above.

"What would you know about it?" Ochoa belted back as tears began to flow. "You weren't the one who was eyes-on, looking through the reticle. All zoomed up in the scope till it looked like you were standing right there. You didn't see the pink!" Ochoa cried as he yelled. "You didn't see the gray matter all over the sidewalk, and that little teeny skull, all torn to shit. She was holding a little baby, man!"

"It was my call, and you know it. I gave the order to fire. We went over this," Stone's dream-self pleaded. "It's not your fault."

On the couch, Stone's chest heaved up and down as his breathing became labored.

"I was the one that tapped her out," Ochoa yelled, "not you! My trigger, my kill!" Ochoa's crying erupted. "I can't take it anymore. I can't take it! It's all over me, man. I can't get it off. Get it off of me!" Ochoa swiped at his sleeve over and over.

"Get what off?"

"I can't get these brains off of my arm." Then he swatted at the air again. "And the pink! It's everywhere. I can't breathe!"

The nightmare roiled forward. "I'm coming in," Stone said. He stepped into the doorway and Ochoa depressed the button on the detonator. The sound of the explosion was cacophonous. Stone's body was blown backward and slammed into the wall behind him.

At the same time, his dream-self started to regain consciousness, Stone thrashed on the couch. His breathing became muffled as if someone was choking him. Stone felt as if something was being pressed into his face and mouth and held there.

His body convulsed and gasped for air.

In the dream, the pressing continued until finally, Stone yanked a wet object off his face. He held it out at arm's length and looked in horror. It was the bloody skin from the dead baby's face.

"No! No! No!" Stone screamed as he woke up on the couch. He flung himself off and crashed onto the coffee table, cracking it to pieces. He then scrambled to his feet. "Get it off!" he yelled as he plucked and yanked at his face. "Get it off!" He tripped on a piece of broken wood from the table and crashed into the wall.

Talia, having been awakened in all the noise, yanked open the door of the bedroom and felt across the wall in the darkness until her hand landed on the light switch. "What? What?" she yelled.

But Stone kept pulling at his face and looking at his hands. "Get it off!"

She went to him. "Get what off? Stone, wake up!" She shook his shoulders, but he pushed her back, then looked at his hands again.

"It's stuck to me!" he blurted, but when he could tell there was no blood on his hands, his emotions began to settle. After a few moments, he leaned his hands on his knees and crushed his eyes closed.

"Are you all right?" she said.

He gasped at the air, trying to catch his breath. "Oh God," he said as he stood upright and wiped his eyes. He fought back any additional emotion and continued looking at his hands, flipping them over.

"A nightmare?"

"Yes," he said, acknowledging her presence for the first time. Stone's breathing began to settle.

"Do you want to talk about it?" Her voice was soft this time, warm.

Stone tried to regain his composure.

Now that things had quieted, Talia's eyes ran across his bare chest.

Stone looked at her as if trying to replace the horrifying images from the nightmare with something else. A moment later he realized he was staring and glanced away. In his peripheral vision, though, his eyes picked up every detail: the snug, sleeveless tank top, and the painfully obvious fact that she was not wearing a bra.

Both of them became suddenly aware they were practically naked and turned from one other, each crossing their arms in the process. "I'm all right," he said. "I'm sorry if I scared you."

"You broke that coffee table to pieces. Are you hurt?" she asked sneaking a peek at his chiseled body.

Stone looked for injury on his stomach and legs. "I'm fine."

"If you need to talk, we can, I mean, I can go put on some clothes and—"

"No," he said, "it's the middle of the night. Go back to sleep."

Talia walked to the bedroom.

Though he tried not to, Stone's eyes were pulled to the beautiful curves of her backside as though magnetized. After she closed the door, he shook his head. "Don't mix business with pleasure, John." Though he knew, that's exactly what had happened with the beautiful Agent Jana Baker.

35

NSA Headquarters

Uncle Bill walked into the command center after having delivered another threat assessment to the Secretary of Defense. A few of the analysts looked up. The haggard expression they could see on his face was a trademark of his years of service. To them, his dedication was what made Uncle Bill, Uncle Bill.

It was already 9:00 a.m. and Knuckles, who had been at his desk since before first light said, “How was it, sir?”

“Same old cheery outlook. Terrorists can be real assholes.”

“Any new priorities?”

“None,” Bill said as he pulled off his glasses and rubbed his eyes. “We’ll have more decryption packages coming in.”

“Chatter from that North African terror cell?”

“Our current flavor-of-the-day.” Bill smiled. “Where’s Cade?”

“Oh,” the kid replied. “I think he went to the lab to check on Agent Stiel’s microfilm.”

“She’s not an agent, son.”

“Right. I keep forgetting.”

As Cade walked in, Bill said, “Any luck?”

“Well,” Cade replied, “sort of. The lab was able to pull a few sections of the degraded microfilm into a readable state. They said there’s a lot more work to recover the rest. In fact, they're not sure they'll be able to, but they asked if they could keep trying."

"Certainly," Uncle Bill replied. "It may not be a priority, but I've earned the right to a few transgressions. What did we get so far?"

Cade said, "I uploaded the new data to Knuckle's shared drive."

Knuckles swiveled his chair to face Cade. "Why did you upload it to *my* shared drive? It was *your* assignment."

Cade grinned. "Because you were going to stick your nose into my business anyway. I figured I'd just facilitate the process."

"Some of us like to be thorough," Knuckles said as he spun back around to his laptop.

"Teacher's pet," Cade jabbed.

"Rube," Knuckles replied.

"Boys, boys," Bill said as he placed his glasses back on his face. "A little professionalism." He shook his head. "I'm getting too old for this." He turned to Knuckles. "Pull up the new data on screen six, son."

Knuckles tapped at his keyboard until a .jpeg file displayed on the overhead monitor. The three looked up as Knuckles slowly scrolled down the image.

Uncle Bill squinted at the screen. "Well, I don't suppose I should have expected much after just one day of work. I can barely read that."

The three of them turned as Special Agent Baker walked in and placed her bag on the desk. "Hello, Jana," Bill said. "What brings the FBI in this morning?"

"Morning, Uncle Bill," she said with a smile. "I'm still working that North African terror cell. Came over to see what the decryption said."

Knuckles thumbed to Cade. "Genius-man over there hasn't decrypted it yet."

Cade scowled. "I've been a little busy. Sorry, we got distracted by the microfilm."

"From Talia?" Jana said. "Is that it?"

"Yep," Bill said. "The lab's first pass anyway. We were just about to take a gander. Son," he said to Knuckles, "Proceed."

"Yes, sir."

Cade's eyes flicked across Jana's figure, but only for a moment. He pointed at the monitor. "That piece looks legible. Zoom in, Knuckles." As the monitor re-centered and zoomed closer, the three stared and found a new series of encrypted characters had been exposed from a previously illegible section. "This section looks different from the after-action report. The font, I mean."

"Very observant, professor," Knuckles replied. "This font is an early Helvetica whereas the after-action was Times New Roman. You've just about cracked the case." Their friendly interoffice rivalry lived on.

"Run it through," Uncle Bill said as he crossed his arms. "Let's see what Mother has to say."

Jana said, "Mother?"

Bill whispered back. "The computer system. Got that one from the movie *Alien*."

Jana laughed. "Thought you'd bring them a little culture, did you?"

Within a few moments, the computer had transcribed the shapes on the image into text, then decrypted it using the crypto variable from the previous day's decryption. Cade read:

OPERATION RED SCORPION
11 DECEMBER 1965

"BASED on the earlier data from the microfilm, they were planning on a rendezvous on 16 December, right?" Knuckles said.

"Correct," Bill replied.

Cade continued.

CONTINGENCY PLAN BRAVO has failed. My attempts at recruiting SUBJECT were in progression, but after several days of active engagement, SUBJECT responded in the negative. I have instructed ECLIPSE to initiate communication re: cancellation of rendezvous plans for 16 DECEMBER at pre-arranged rally point. SUBJECT has now made overt threats that put the mission in a state of imminent compromise.
NEW COURSE OF ACTION: neutralize SUBJECT.

CADE LOOKED AT BILL. "I'm assuming that *Subject* is the brother, the A-4 Skyhawk pilot?"

"Holy shit," Knuckles said. "They're going to kill him."

"Did kill him." Uncle Bill's fingers descended into the enormity of his gray beard. "This after-action aligns with what Ms. Stiel's grandfather told her, that on board the *Ticonderoga*, after his attempts to convince his brother to go along with the mission failed, he murdered him."

"Neutralize," Jana added. "Such a nice, sanitary way to put it."

"And Eclipse is mentioned again," Knuckles said. "What's that?"

"Someone else working the mission with the grandfather," Bill replied. "Again, I'm not seeing anything here that would necessitate us committing resources. This is all 1965 stuff." Bill's eyes narrowed. "Still . . . " he said as his words trailed off.

"What?" Jana said.

Bill said nothing.

"Bill," she pressed, "you're still thinking about something, something you alluded to yesterday."

He shut his eyes and rubbed his forehead. "My question is: if this was an Israeli operation, why was the rally point on a US-held island?"

Silence pervaded for several moments.

"I never thought of that," Knuckles said.

Jana stared at Bill. "*That's* what you were getting at."

Knuckles jumped up and began to pace.

Uncle Bill smiled and leaned to Jana. "Watch this."

Knuckles loved this part. He was in his element now. "Okay," he said as his pointer finger went into the air, "let's think about this. The year was 1965. So what was going on in Israel in 1965?" He continued as though he were having a two-way conversation. "Well, I'm glad you asked that. That was around seventeen years *after* the country was first founded. And as we all know, controversy surrounding the formation of Israel was enormous. If measured, it would be roughly equivalent of how large Cade thinks his brain is."

"Stay on point," Bill said.

Knuckles went on as he paced the floor, "With enemies on all borders, Israel believed they were in imminent danger of being invaded. At the time, they were involved in a global, and not-so-subtle, quest for a nuclear weapon to defend themselves."

Knuckles rubbed the peach fuzz on his chin. "Even the United

States wanted to help, but we couldn't. I mean, after all, it was against the Partition Plan." He flicked a glance at Cade. "And as we all know, the UN Partition Plan for Palestine, under Resolution 181, recommended the creation of independent Arab and Jewish States."

Cade rolled his eyes. "Do you ever go out? Or do you just sit in that apartment studying things to impress people?"

"So," Knuckles went on, "we have a situation where Israel is asking different countries for a nuke, but none of them can give it to them due to the treaty. But like I said, the US wanted to help." Knuckles looked up at Uncle Bill and snapped his fingers. "That's it! That's the connection."

"Wait," Cade said, "what?"

Jana's mouth opened and hung there a moment. "No, it can't be. You don't actually think—"

"Think what?" Cade said.

She turned to Bill. "So *that's* what's been bothering you, the Kitadaitō Island connection? Since it was under US control, you actually believe the US was involved in the original plot?"

"To steal a weapon from itself?" Cade blurted. "That's insane."

"But wait," Jana said. "What if we did help? What if that's the only way we could assist the Israelis, to somehow sneak one to them. If the weapon were ever discovered by other countries as something that originated from us, we could say it was stolen."

Cade sat down. "Bullshit. You're saying we would murder one of our own pilots, a decorated service member, so we could steal a weapon from ourselves and smuggle it to the Israelis?"

Knuckles looked at him. "Think about your history, Cade. What was going on in the late 1930's in this country?"

"We're talking about the 1960's." Cade leaned his head into his hands. "I don't think I want to hear this."

Knuckles said, "No, you're missing the point. Roosevelt was in his third term as president and started his fourth in 1940. The war in Europe was raging, and he wanted to help England, but Congress and US law wasn't going to let him. Most Americans at the time didn't want to see us dragged into a foreign war. So FDR created the Lend-Lease program as a way to get around all that. We sent tons of military equipment and supplies to Great Britain."

Cade snapped back, "But we didn't *murder* one of our own people to do it!"

Jana kept staring at Bill. "Bill?"

Bill walked a few steps then turned to face them all. His eyes, however, did not leave the floor. “I looked it up.” He exhaled. “November 1965. I found an order. An operative codenamed *Eclypse* had been dispatched to the Philippines, Subic Bay.”

“That’s where the *Ticonderoga* departed from, just before the incident.” Knuckles said.

“Bill,” Jana said as she walked to him. “Are you saying?” She paused a moment. “Where did the order originate? Who did Eclipse work for?”

His eyes met hers. “The Central Intelligence Agency.”

36

Morning light pierced through the window blind in Stone's apartment as though it were made of translucent plastic. Talia squinted. She got out of bed and stretched. It had taken her quite a while to fall back to sleep after Stone had awoken her with his screaming nightmare.

She reached into her backpack and pulled out a change of clothes, a pair of snug-fitting jeans and top, then tiptoed out the door. She glanced at the couch. Stone was asleep with the blanket covering him from the waist down. She couldn't help but glance at the musculature of his naked chest. She went into the restroom and showered.

By the time she was done though, the smell of freshly brewed coffee penetrated the door. She ran a brush through her wet hair and stepped out to find Stone sitting at the small round table. He looked over the top of a coffee mug and said, "Good morning. I made coffee."

"Yeah, I can smell it." She closed her eyes and drew in the aroma. "Reminds me of . . ."

"Of what?" he said as he put down his mug.

"No, it's nothing."

"How personal can a cup of coffee get?" he said almost laughing. "Are you always this private with people?"

She picked up a coffee mug Stone had apparently set out for her and poured. "When I was a little girl, Aba and I would go to his cabin on Dalton Lake. It's way up in the north country. He had what must have been the only drip coffee maker in Israel."

"Oh, that's right. You people use instant coffee. What's that electric water heater thing called?"

"A koom-koom?"

"Yeah, that's it."

"Instant coffee is not that bad."

"Not that bad? Cafe Nes, or what's that other brand? Elite?" Stone shook his head. "Instant coffee hasn't been a thing here since the '70s."

"Yes," Talia replied as she took a seat and held the coffee under her nose a moment. "And I suppose we should homogenize the world with your Starbucks."

"It would be a start."

"When are we going to the cemetery?"

"You're relentless, aren't you?"

"I don't get you Americans. Why don't you just say what you mean, do what you know you need to do?"

"Yes, I know. You Israelis are far more direct."

But her tone changed when she tasted the coffee. "Oh my God, that's so good."

"See?"

"Okay, you're right. There, I said it. John Stone was right about something."

He shook his head.

"Stone," Talia said, "what was that last night?"

Stone sat up straighter. The expression on his face made it look like he was searching for words. "It was . . . nothing."

"In Israel, people are under stress. It's not like here. We've got terrorists on our borders. We go through bad periods of bombings. We all have to serve in the military. What I'm saying is, this is common. Having nightmares, PTSD, whatever you want to call it, it's not something to be ashamed of."

He stood, and his words came out with the sharpness of a razor. "I do *not* have PTSD."

"I'm here one night, and you wake up screaming? What would I have found if I'd been here every night for the past month?"

"I don't want to talk about it." He walked into the kitchen and Talia studied the tightness in his shoulders. "What do you eat for breakfast?"

"Changing the subject. Hmmm," she said. "I don't eat breakfast. Can we go? After I finish this cup of coffee, that is?"

The lightness of her voice seemed to make him relax again. "Relentless." He looked at his watch. "Okay, those Navy pukes will be awake by now."

"If they're anything like our military academies, they've been up since 4:30 a.m."

Several minutes later, they were out the door. They hopped into Stone's SUV, and as he cranked the engine, he glanced at her. The morning sun had cracked through the leaves of the trees and illuminated the outer edges of her dark hair.

Talia glanced over. "Why are you looking at me like that?"

He cleared his throat. "Nothing." He backed out and headed toward the exit of the apartment complex.

"I'm still mad at you," she said.

"For what?"

"For not telling me we were only two miles away from the cemetery."

"Well," Stone said, "I was hungry."

"Men," Talia replied. "They're always thinking with their stomachs, or their . . . " She stopped herself.

As Stone turned right and accelerated onto Bay Ridge Avenue, he said, "What's that? Cat got your tongue? I thought you Israelis always spoke your mind." He laughed.

"Just get us there."

After a short drive Stone turned left on the two-laned 6th Avenue and drove across the small bridge that spanned a waterway. There were boats docked on both sides.

Talia said, "There must be a hundred boats. What do you people do to earn all this money?"

"Hey, don't look at me."

They crossed the bridge, drove past a few apartment complexes then Annapolis Elementary School. Talia glanced back as they passed the three-story brick building. "Everything matches here. I mean, all the buildings, it's so uniform. And look at that." She read the words painted on a cute, two-story brick building abutting the sidewalk. It looked like an old house. "Annapolis Summer Garden Theater. Culture and everything." She turned to Stone. "You could use a little culture."

"How do you know I don't frequent the theater, spend hours in the library, or take in an opera now and then?"

"And all these people are out. What are they doing?"

Stone thumbed to their right. "We're right here at Annapolis Harbor.

There's a boat show at the yacht club this week." At a traffic circle, they kept to the right and merged onto Randall Street. Stone added, "This is the little town square."

"So this is what you people call *New England*."

"A lot of the architecture looks just like this. Some of these buildings have been here since the 1700's."

After they crossed Prince George Street, Talia said of the two-story houses on either side of the narrow road, "I like the porches. We don't have much of that in Tel Aviv."

"Yeah, I guess not. Sitting outside in the middle of the blazing desert isn't high on a lot of people's priority lists."

"We aren't just sitting in the middle of the desert. It's a modern city, Stone."

"Yeah, been there."

They drove a few more blocks. The houses on the right melted into the whitewashed, six-foot brick wall of the United States Naval Academy. Talia glanced at the signage. *Founded 1845*. There was an open walkway in the wall protected by cement posts to prevent vehicles from entering. Several people, some in civilian attire, some in Service Khaki uniforms, and a few in crisp Service Dress Blue, walked in various directions.

"I'll give them this," Talia said. "They have good looking uniforms."

At the intersection, Randall Street came to an end where a matching brick wall separated the grounds of the Naval Academy. Stone stopped the SUV and glanced to the right at the steel entrance gates; they were closed.

"Shit. I was afraid of this," Stone said.

"It's closed?" Talia said. "We can't get in?"

The gates were flanked by four heavily armed Marine Corp guards. Stone turned the vehicle toward the gates as one of the Marines approached the driver's side. "Happens a lot," Stone said. "If there's a security threat, they lock the campus down. Didn't you see the guards checking IDs back there?"

Stone rolled down his window as the guard approached. "The Yard is closed to visitors today, sir. I'm afraid I'm going to have to ask you to turn around."

"DOD," Stone said as he pulled out a set of credentials from his back pocket and handed them to the soldier.

The guard read them a moment. "Yes, sir." He waved to the other guards and handed the identification back. The mechanical gates began to swing open. "If you can pull your vehicle through the gate and over to the Lance Corporal, they'll conduct a vehicle search, and you can be on your way."

Stone edged the SUV forward and stopped about fifty feet down. He and Talia got out while two Marine guards inspected the interior. A third held an inspection mirror on a long pole and ran it underneath the car.

"You're free to proceed, sir," the young Marine said. Stone and Talia hopped back in, and they drove into the main campus.

"The Yard?" Talia said.

"That's just what the squids call the Naval Academy."

Talia almost laughed. "Squids?"

"Yeah," Stone replied, "Navy pukes."

Talia shook her head. "Aren't you all on the same side?"

"Sure. In fact, I like Navy boys. They've been kind enough to give me a ride whenever I needed to go into an LZ." Stone glanced at her. "What? Oh, come on. Like Israeli soldiers don't have rivalries with other units. We just like to use colorful names for each other, that's all. We've got a lot of names for Navy boys. Squids, Swabbies, Bubbleheads. But you know, those Jarheads aren't that bad, really. Met some damn tough Jarheads."

"Again, can you speak plain English?"

"Jarheads are Marines."

"And Bubbleheads?"

"Navy submariners. They've given me a ride on quite a few occasions too. Get some pretty good chow on board a sub, actually."

They drove a tree-lined street with houses down one side. The homes were large, stately, and perfectly manicured. Most had matching striped awnings overhanging one or more sets of first-floor windows. To Talia, it looked like something out of one of the Norman Rockwell paintings she'd seen. "But," Talia said, "we're in a neighborhood again? Who lives in those houses?"

"Probably brass. Oh, sorry, officers."

Stone took a couple of turns as they drove past large red-brick buildings. They passed a rotunda building and a large green space called Radford Terrace, and as he turned from Maryland Avenue onto Decatur, Talia said, "You know where the cemetery is?"

"Sure, just across the water up here."

"How do you know so much about this place?"

Stone exhaled. "Been here many times. Briefings and whatnot."

They drove across a two-lane bridge that spanned the inlet. On the other side, they turned right then onto Ramsey Drive. It curved along the water until the cemetery came into view. A few hundred headstones were neatly arranged on a gentle tree-covered hillside.

Stone pulled the car to the side and into an open parking space. They got out, and Stone said, "It's your show now."

Several cadets on their way to Sherman Field, adjacent to the cemetery, were walking past and Talia called to one of them, a female with her hair in a tight bun. "Excuse me," Talia said, "do you know how we locate a particular grave?"

"Sure," the young woman said, "what year was your loved one interred?"

"Around 1965."

"Let's see, Vietnam era, that should be over in section nine. It's just over the hill there. You'll find the headstones are arranged in date order."

Talia glanced at the hill then back to the cadet. "How do you know so much about the cemetery?"

The woman squinted in the bright light, "My grandfather and father are there."

"Thank you," Talia said as the cadet walked off.

She and Stone began walking up the hill in between headstones. In some sections, headstones were uniform in size and shape, in others, various dimensions and designs were intermixed. As they crested the low rise, Stone said, "Lead the way."

They walked through the rows, reading dates on the stones. "1970," Talia said as she crossed over two more rows, "1967, and this one is 1966. He's got to be close."

"What was his date of death?"

"5 December 1965," Talia said as she continued walking past headstones. "These are from '65. Yes, see, 30 December, this one, 11 December." They walked past a space where a thick tarp had been stretched tightly across the ground, then on to the next. "Here's one from 2 December. But wait, this one is 27 November. I don't understand, these are earlier. We should have passed it already." She continued walking but found the further she went, the earlier the dates became.

Stone said, "You sure about the date?"

"Well sure I'm sure."

"And you're sure he's buried here, in this cemetery?"

"Of course I am. I looked it up." She backtracked to the headstone whose date of death was marked as 2 December 1965, then to the one past it which was marked 11 December. But then she looked at the rubberized tarp stretched across the ground between them. She pointed at it. "You don't think . . . "

Stone got on one knee and pulled up on the tarp. The material was tightly stretched and so strong, a person could walk across it without it breaking. He peered underneath. "Freshly turned soil," he said. He lifted harder until he could see a gaping hole in the ground where a grave and tombstone should be. He looked up. "It's gone."

The olive color of Talia's face washed pale. "It can't be."

Stone stood and wiped his hands together. "And look at this," he said as he pointed at the grass where they stood. "These impressions look like a piece of heavy equipment has been here." He looked over his shoulder toward a building in the distance. "A grave site has definitely been disinterred here. Come on. We can ask inside."

37

NSA Command Center

Upon hearing confirmation that the United States, had, in fact, been involved in the 1965 operation which resulted in the murder of a decorated Naval aviator, the group stood silent.

After a few moments, Uncle Bill asked, "What else is visible on the microfilm?"

Knuckles sat in his chair and tapped a few keys then used his mouse to scroll down the distorted image. But further down, it took on a different quality. Instead of being heavily yellowed, in this section, the microfilm was more bronze-colored.

"Looks like this section is newer," Knuckles said. He scrolled the image up and down with the mouse. "See? It's been spliced together with the older piece of microfilm above." When he scrolled to a section that appeared to be legible, he took a screen capture. "Okay, let's see what Mother has to say about this."

Cade studied the characters on the screen. "Doesn't that look like a different cipher?"

"It sure does," Bill said. "And a hell of a lot more modern."

"Still," Knuckles said, "won't take Mother any time to crack it."

"Kind of weird, isn't it?" Jana said. "One strip of microfilm, yet from two different time frames?"

After a few minutes, Knuckles sat upright. "She's got it! Okay, let's take a look." He put the deciphered text onto the screen.

As they studied it, Jana said, "Most of this is still gibberish. You sure *Mother* has decoded this correctly?" She smirked at Bill.

Knuckles answered as though quoting a mantra. "Mother is good, Mother is wise, Mother is all knowing. I think the degradation of the microfilm is at play here. She's doing her best to read the symbols but can't see many of them clearly. This is her best guess. But some of these areas of the microfilm are in good enough condition, so confidence is high."

"How high?" Uncle Bill asked.

Knuckles glances at his laptop. "Ninety-four percent." He looked up at the monitor above. "Okay, this first section is just boilerplate."

UNAUTHORIZED ACCESS PROHIBITED
UTILIZATION OF THIS SYSTEM IS GOVERNED BY THE PROTECTION OF PRIVACY LAW
CODE SECTION 5741-2984
DATABASE CLASSIFICATION: HIGH SECURITY
BREACH NOTIFICATION: UNAUTHORIZED ACCESS WILL BE PROSECUTED
LEVEL: HIGH TREASON
AUTHORITY: ISRAELI LAW, INFORMATION AND TECHNOLOGY AUTHORITY (ILITA)

"YADDA, YADDA, YADDA," he said as he scrolled down. "Now, the good stuff."

CODE NAME OR DESIGNATION: ABSOLUTION
CROSS REFERENCE: RED SCORPION
INSTANTIATION: 5 AUG 1996
VISIBILITY: EYES ONLY
CASE NO: 380987
DATE CLOSED OR TERMINATED: 11 MAR 1998

"Wow," Jana said. "Look how much more recent that was."

"*Operation Absolution*. Cross-referenced with the 1965 operation, *Red Scorpion*," Knuckles said.

"But look," Jana said as she pointed, "this says *Absolution* was terminated in 1998. I thought Talia said the file was in the active section."

"She did," Knuckles replied. "Perhaps it was terminated, but then reopened later?"

Cade added, "Or it was terminated, and they forgot to move the file out of the active section. I'll give them this though, they know how to come up with cool code names."

Bill raised an eyebrow at Cade and said, "Let's stay on point, people,"

Knuckles looked up and was about to read further but saw how garbled the next section of text was. "Oh, a couple of things. Just so you know, whenever Mother can't decipher a letter, she inserts an X in its place. Man, it looks like it gets worse the further it goes down the microfilm."

INTENDED OUTCOMX - STAXILIZE ISRAELX SECURITY:ELIXINATE XXMBIXGX
EXCUXPATXXY OVERVIEW - NEUTRALXXE XXXAXSE XETXEXXXTS TO PXEVENT XXXXOLLAX / XXMAX AXTAXXX.
PHASE AXPFA - INSERTION: XXVEXX INSERXXON OF THE XEXXON INSIDE XEXANXX.
PHAXE BXAVX - DETECTION: PRODUCE EVIDENCX OF THE THREAT.
XXASE CHXXLIX - OCXXXXTXXX: XXLL XXXLE XXXASIXN.

"Shit," Uncle Bill said. "Is that the best Mother can do?"

"Sorry, sir," Knuckles replied. "It's not Mother, its the fact that the microfilm was so degraded. Mother can't see the letters. Perhaps if the lab is able to further enhance the degradation—"

Jana stepped up. "For now, let's just see if we can decipher any of this." She looked up at the monitor. "Okay, first line is something like

Intended outcome, stabilize Israel, or *Israeli*, I guess, *security*, umm, *elixinate*?"

"Eliminate," Cade said.

"*Eliminate*," Jana said, then stalled on the last word. "Hell, I don't know what that means. Eliminate something."

Bill peered over the tops of his glasses. "When covert organizations write about eliminating things, you know, whatever it is, it's not good. Proceed."

Jana said, "The next line is complete gibberish. I guess that says *exculpatory overview*? *Neutralize* . . . something *to prevent* . . . something." She shook her head. "Then, I guess the next three lines are phase, what is that, *Alpha*? Then *Bravo*?"

"Yeah," Knuckles added. "And that last one could spell out *Charlie*."

Jana continued. "*Phase Alpha, insertion*, something, *insertion of the* something inside . . . somewhere. Again, pretty worthless. But Phase Bravo is almost totally clear. *Detection: produce evidence of the threat*. Then Phase Charlie. Christ, that's pretty much a waste of time."

Bill pulled off his glasses and rubbed his eyes again. "I'm sorry, but we can't spend more time on this project. I'm pulling the plug."

"But Bill," Jana said, "what about the lab? If they can enhance the rest of this microfilm, we might be able to read the whole thing."

"Agent Baker," he said with a more formal tone than usual, "we've got a North African terror cell forming which is a far higher priority than a piece of microfilm that's essentially revealing ancient history to us. This does not involve the sovereignty of the United States."

But Jana wasn't finished. "If we stop now, Talia will never find out who is trying to kill her and why. She'll have to go into hiding for the rest of her life."

"I'm sorry, Jana." Uncle Bill started to walk off, but Jana stopped him mid-stride.

"Bill, please. I'm asking you this as a favor."

He looked at Knuckles. "Is there any more of it, son? Or is the rest illegible as well?"

Knuckles scrolled the grainy image further down. "Looks like most of it isn't just illegible, it's nonexistent. The lab mentioned this to me. Said this whole lower section was too degraded. But they said there was one other little part that was legible. Hold on, let me find it." He used the mouse to continue scrolling down. After scrolling past blurred sections of microfilm, the legible section appeared. There, in nearly-clear text, they all read in silence.

FINAL ENTRY:
EXCULPATORY OVERVIEW: PROJECT HAS SUFFERED CRITICAL OPERATIONAL LEAKAGE
PROJECT ACTION: ABORT WITH EXTREME PREJUDICE
PROJECT IS TERMINATED.

OPERATIONAL DIRECTIVE [REVISED]

ASSET(S):
STIEL, YOSEF HAREL
DIRECTIVE: LIQUIDATE

COLLATERAL:
STIEL, YOEL DORON
DIRECTIVE: LIQUIDATE

COLLATERAL:
STIEL, GAVRIELLA MIZRAH
DIRECTIVE: LIQUIDATE

AUTHORITY:
EXECUTIVE ORDER: 9978307
SIGNATORY: CODENAME VIPERA

JANA WAS the first to speak. "Wait just a minute. Is this saying what I think it's saying?"

Cade said, "I think so. Yosef Harel Stiel, Yoel Doron Stiel, Gavriella Mizrah Stiel."

"Liquidation," Knuckles whispered. "They killed them all?"

"But," Jana continued, "that's Talia's grandfather, and," she hesitated a moment, "her parents."

"I was afraid we'd find something like this," Uncle Bill said as he looked at the three of them. "Covering their tracks."

"What do her *parents* have to do with anything?" Jana asked.

"Yeah," Knuckles added, "I thought she said they ran a bakery."

"I don't have a clue what her parents had to do with it," Cade said, "but that definitely confirms the grandfather was involved. I don't get it though. This section of microfilm was dated from 1998, right? If the original operation to steal the nuclear device was in 1965, and they're covering their tracks by killing off the assets, why did they wait thirty-three years to do it?"

"Jana," Knuckles said, "didn't Talia say her parents died when she was a child?"

"Yeah," Jana said as she sat. "She said they died in a bombing. One of those cross-border Hezbollah rocket attacks from Lebanon. Or Hamas, I don't know which."

"Go ahead, son," Bill said to Knuckles. "Look it up."

Knuckles pulled a browser into view and ran a Google search, but filtered it to news articles from Israel in 1998 that included the name of Talia's father, Yoel Doron Stiel.

"Here's one," he said. He clicked the first link. When the page loaded, their eyes were drawn to a photo of the scene, a city street torn to shreds by what could have only been a large bomb.

"Big crater," Jana said. Several mangled cars in various states of destruction and chunks of cement, dirt, and metal were strewn about. The article was written in English.

Knuckles read the caption. "Hezbollah rocket attack kills three." Then further down, "Yup, Yosef Stiel, Yoel Stiel, Gavriella Stiel. All killed. And here's the bakery." He pointed as the others read in silence.

A neighborhood bakery, *Sweet Nosh*, was leveled early this morning in an apparent rocket attack, the latest in a string of Hezbollah terrorist bombings that have rocked the city of Nahariyya. The attack took the lives of the bakery's owners, Yosef and Gavriella Stiel, who had opened it ten years prior. Also killed in the blast was a relative, Yosef Stiel, who was said to be working there.

JANA CROSSED HER ARMS. "This news article is crap. I mean, the microfilm makes it pretty clear the Israeli government wanted to eliminate her parents and grandfather."

"I'd have to agree," Uncle Bill said. "It wouldn't be too far afield to believe a covert agency would neutralize a target by making it look like something else."

Jana said. "I feel so bad. What's it going to do to Talia when she finds out her parents weren't just the victims of a random terror bombing? That they were murdered by her own government."

Uncle Bill lowered his eyes. "It's going to eat her up inside, that's what it's going to do."

"Bill," Jana said, "we can't drop this investigation."

"This isn't something I take lightly, Jana," he said. "I'm charged with deploying assets for critical cases. This is a top team, and I can't let personal feelings cloud my judgment."

But the disappointment in her eyes made Uncle Bill's shoulders slump. He lowered his voice. "I suggest you bring her in and let her see her this with her own eyes. We owe her that much. But as of right now, I want this team full-time on that North African terror cell."

Cade stepped up. "What if we work on this after hours?"

Jana turned to him. "You'd do that?"

Cade looked at Bill. "That means the team would be full time on the terror case. We wouldn't touch this one until after hours. What do you say?"

Bill rubbed his neck. "All of you?" When they nodded their ascent, he said, "So now I've got a crew who wants to work after hours." He exhaled. "Fine. But I'm going to regret this."

38

When Talia and Stone walked into the small glass and brick building on the edge of the cemetery, a Naval officer wearing service khakis stood from behind a small desk. "Sir, Ma'am," he said. "How can I help you?"

It was Talia who spoke first. "I'm looking for my uncle. He was interred here."

"Certainly, ma'am," the officer said as he sat. "What was his name and date of passing?"

"Golan Stiel, 5 December 1965."

With his fingers hovering above a keyboard, he stopped and glared at her. "Ma'am?"

"I said his name was—"

He stood. "Did you say Golan Stiel?"

Talia seemed to have lost her words.

Stone said, "Yes, Golan Stiel. 5 December 1965. Is there a problem?"

The officer said, "I'm sorry. Lieutenant Stiel's remains were disinterred. I was just looking at the paperwork."

"When did this happen?" Stone asked.

"Last night, sir."

"But . . ." Talia said, "why, how?"

He sat in front of the computer again and tapped at the keys. "Lieutenant Golan Stiel. I've got the orders right here. But to be honest, I've never seen it happen like this before."

"Like what?" Stone asked.

"I've never seen a disinterment happen so quickly. Normally, the process takes months."

Talia cleared her throat, and her words came out clipped, quiet. "And how long did it take this time?"

"One day," he replied. "But," he said as he rubbed his temples and stared at the monitor, "I still can't wrap my head around it. The order to disinter was fulfilled late last night. I just cross-checked it with the switch log."

Stone cocked his head toward Talia. "Each sentry standing post at a through-point keeps a security log of all comings and goings. What did it say?" Stone asked.

The officer let his finger trace the monitor. "Heavy equipment rolled in at twenty-three hundred, forty-one hours. It left at zero one seventeen."

Talia's hand found her stomach. "Why would a casket be removed in the middle of the night?"

"Not only that," the officer said, "all of this occurred during a Threatcon Bravo."

Stone said to Talia, "Heightened state of security when a predictable threat of terrorist activity exists." He looked back at the officer. "So the remains, casket, headstone, everything, have been removed, in the middle of the night, all after a one-day request? How is that possible?"

The officer studied the computer monitor a moment then snapped his fingers. "Looks like the order originated from top brass."

Stone started to interpret the term for Talia, but she held up a hand. "I got that one." She then said to the officer, "This makes no sense. The grave has been in the ground for over fifty years, and all of a sudden, it's dug up in the middle of the night?"

Stone said, "I need to know who signed that order."

"I'm sorry, sir. I can't divulge that information."

Stone pulled out his Department of Defense credentials and flipped them open. "This isn't a casual request."

After a moment of inspecting the credentials, the officer said, "Again, sir, I'm sorry. I'm not at liberty to disclose. If you had a warrant or if I was notified through channels that this office needed to cooperate in an investigation—"

"Yeah, yeah," Stone said, interrupting the man. And in a tone laced with sarcasm said, "It's a grave from 1965. Probably high on the security threat assessment list."

The officer just looked at him.

Talia swallowed. "Where are the remains now?"

"It doesn't give me that information, ma'am. In the extremely rare instances where an order to disinter is received by our office, once processed, it would be out of our hands."

Stone crossed his arms. "This cemetery isn't that big. There are what, a couple of thousand grave sites here? How many disinter orders do you receive in a year? Or *are you not at liberty to say*?"

"Twenty-four hundred, forty-eight niches to be exact. But as far as the number of orders to disinter? This is the first one I've ever heard of."

Talia said. "I can't believe this. It's gone? It's just gone?"

"Come on," Stone said, "this changes things. We've got to see if Uncle Bill has found out anything else. There's something going on here. We have to find out what it is."

They started to walk out, but the officer said, "Ma'am?" As Talia and Stone turned to him he pointed at the monitor, "the remains have been removed, but the headstone is still here."

Talia froze. It was almost as if her legs had momentarily stopped working.

"Where?" Stone said.

"It's out back. Would you like to see it?"

Talia covered her mouth. All she could do was nod.

The pair followed the officer out a rear entrance and over to a small brick storage building with a garage-style door on it. He pulled up on the door until it rolled open. The building had no windows and was only about fifteen feet deep.

He flicked a wall switch, and a single fluorescent light flickered to life. The cement floor was empty lest a single wooden pallet that sat to one side. On the pallet lay a headstone. Talia walked to it, her hands gripping her midsection. Stone followed.

The headstone read:

GOLAN DAVID STIEL
LIEUTENANT
UNITED STATES NAVY
FEBRUARY 6, 1936 – ISRAEL
DECEMBER 5, 1965 - EAST CHINA SEA

THEY STOOD in silence for a few minutes, staring at the aged stone.

"It's him," Talia finally whispered. "I never even knew he existed until a few days ago." She shook her head. "I don't know why I'm so . . ." Her words trailed off as she fought back tears before they could surface. She turned to face Stone. "What's happening to me?" This time she began to cry, and Stone put his arms around her. "First, my grandfather is murdered. Then people are shooting at me. The Customs people scaring me to death at the airport, now this?" She pushed away as if suddenly aware she'd let herself become vulnerable in front of him. "I'm sorry," she said as she wiped a tear.

"It's okay."

"Stone, where's my uncle's casket?"

"Don't worry. We're going to figure this thing out, together. Come on," he said.

39

With traffic as heavy as it was, the forty-five-minute drive from Annapolis to NSA Headquarters at Ft. Meade turned into an hour and twenty-minute slog. Stone glanced at Talia. Her face looked as white as the sheets on his bed.

"Hey," he said, "you still with us over there?"

"What?" she replied. "Oh, sure. Yes, I'm here."

"You haven't said a word in over an hour." He pulled the truck into a parking space in the visitor section in front of the NSA main entrance. "And not that it's any consolation, but I'm sorry about all this."

As he shut off the engine, Talia stared out the windshield. "I know I don't show it, but I am grateful for your help." A flicker of a smile appeared. "I'm usually not such a bitch."

"You're not a—"

"No, I haven't been myself lately. So much has happened, and it's dredging up feelings I've tried to bury."

"You've been through a lot."

For the first time, Talia looked at him and noticed tenderness in his eyes. It caught her off guard.

"Don't blame yourself. I haven't exactly been Mister Nice Guy."

"It wasn't your fault. I know it sounds like an excuse, but I haven't been able to think straight. And back there, I took one look at that headstone, and it all became so *real*. I mean, I barely believed my grandfather's story, but now . . . now I'm feeling things I haven't felt in a long time. My parents died when I was so little. I think after that, I kind of just shut down."

"You don't have to explain anything to me," he said. "Come on. If anyone can find out where that casket is, it's Uncle Bill."

They hopped out of the truck, walked through the massive span of glass double doors at the entrance of NSA Headquarters and made their way through security. Once they were down in the command center, they quickly found Knuckles. He was seated at his desk, so engrossed in his work, he didn't notice them approaching.

"Ahem," Stone said.

"What? Oh," the kid said as he looked up. "Ah, Agent Stiel, Agent Stone. We were just going to call you."

"I'm not an agent, Knuckles," Stone said, "and neither is she."

"Oh, yeah, sorry."

To Talia, the expression on the boy's face made it look like he was staring at two ghosts.

"Are you okay?" she said.

"Huh?" he replied. "Oh, no, sure, I'm fine." He diverted his eyes and studied the laces on his black Converse high top All-Stars.

"We came because we need help," Stone said as he studied the boy. "Yeah, what's with you? You guys find something on the microfilm?"

"The microfilm?" Knuckles replied as he shuffled his feet from side to side.

Talia frowned. "Yes, you remember the microfilm, don't you?"

"Um, yeah," Knuckles said, as he squirmed. "Yeah, we, ah . . . "

Stone studied the boy's body language. "Kid, can I give you some advice?" he said as a smile eased onto his face. "Never go into field work. You might fold under questioning."

Knuckles stood. "Will you excuse me a moment?" and walked off.

"What's with him?" Talia said.

"I don't know," Stone replied. But as Uncle Bill, Jana, and Cade walked out from a conference room with Knuckles in tow, he said, "It looks like we're going to find out." A half-dozen analysts walked out behind them and filtered their way across the room to their cubicles.

Talia felt a flutter in her gut. *This doesn't look good*, she thought. Uncle Bill smiled and took her hand, cupping it with his other. Talia looked at him. The look in Bill's eye was the same look she had seen in Moshe's when he told her that her parents had been killed all those years ago. The feeling tightened her throat. She pulled her hand free as if the act alone would spare her from whatever bad news he had.

"Talia," he said, "welcome." He motioned with one hand. "Why don't we come over here, away from all these people." He walked her toward a small conference room while the others followed.

Talia looked at them. "Is something wrong?" She took special notice that Jana would not make eye contact.

As they entered the room, Bill said, "Why don't you have a seat?"

"I think I'd rather stand," she said as she crossed her arms. "What is it? What's wrong?"

Bill looked down. He started to speak, but his voice cracked.

"Bill?" Jana said. "Why don't you let me." She stood in front of Talia. "We found something on the microfilm, something . . . important."

"Why is everyone looking at me like that?"

"There's no easy way to—" Jana said, stopping herself midway. Talia's breath froze, and Jana continued. "There were additional entries on the microfilm, but these were much more recent than the others. They were entered in 1998."

"1998?" Talia said, "but the operation was in 1965."

"Yes," Jana said, her voice softening. "Anyway, apparently the original project was renewed, under a new codename. We found some garbled text we can't yet read. It's a detail of whatever the newer operation was about. But we found . . ." She glanced at Uncle Bill and Stone. "I'm just going to say it." Jana swallowed. "We found the names of your parents in the file."

"My parents?" Talia blurted as she took a half-step back.

"Now, we don't know why," Jana said, "but your parents were, they were . . ." Jana finally spit it out, "It was a termination order."

"What?" Talia said as a quick pulse of light flashed in her eyes and her heart rate accelerated. No one said anything until Talia had had a moment to sit with the information. "My parents' names were in the microfilm, and it says they were terminated?"

Jana took her by the arm and guided her into a chair.

"It's not possible," Talia said as she placed a hand on her stomach and leaned into it. "Ima and Aba were bakers. They had a little bakery. They died when a Hezbollah rocket . . . why would anyone kill them?"

"We don't know," Uncle Bill said, "but somehow, there's a connection."

Talia's face paled. "I don't feel so good," she said as she started rocking her torso back and forth.

Bill said, "Knuckles?"

Knuckles grabbed a wastebasket and placed it next to Talia in case she was sick.

Jana knelt down. "I know. It's a lot to take in."

Talia's eyes flared. "I, this, this can't be happening. I don't believe you! They were bakers. I remember it vividly. Ima and I would roll dough together, I'd be covered in flour. Aba would give me the first Krantz to come out of the oven. We'd finger-paint flour onto each other's faces. I didn't imagine it! Those are the best memories I have, and I'll not have you ruin them with wild stories about things that aren't true!"

Jana turned to the others. "Why don't you give me a few minutes alone with her." After the others walked out and the glass door wafted shut behind them, Jana turned to find Talia pacing the floor. "You've got to believe me. I'm telling you the truth."

"How can I possibly believe such a story?" Talia said as she flung her arms out. Her wrist accidentally slammed into the back of a chair, and she recoiled.

Jana could see a tear well in Talia's eye. "I've been right where you are," Jana said. "I know exactly what you're going through."

Talia quieted as she rubbed her wrist. "How could you possibly know what I'm going through?"

"My father, he wasn't who I thought he was either. I didn't find out until about two years ago. The knowledge of it was overwhelming — like nothing else I've ever experienced."

"You are trying to tell me my parents weren't who I *know* they were?" Talia removed her watch and lay it on the table, then continued rubbing the sore wrist.

"I don't know who your parents were. What I do know is their names are on that microfilm. Them, along with your grandfather. It's a kill order, Talia. For whatever reason, the Israeli government issued a kill order on them all."

40

Talia choked back tears in an internal battle to maintain emotional control. "No, it isn't possible. The Israeli government would never hurt their own people. I can't even imagine it."

Jana said, "Our governments are not like rational thinking people, they're entities with a mission, a mission to stay alive. They'll do whatever it takes, and they don't have a conscience. I've seen it."

"Look, I'm never going to believe this." But then Talia's mind flashed back to just a few days prior when Mossad agents had shown up at her apartment.

"Then it's time to see it with your own eyes."

Talia wiped her cheek and walked out of the room with Jana and over to Knuckle's desk where the others had gathered. "Show me," she said as she crossed her arms.

Knuckles looked at Bill who nodded his ascent. Once the same image appeared on the monitor above, Knuckles scrolled down so Talia could read the text they'd all seen previously. When it got down to the section with the kill order, Knuckles paused it.

Talia's jaw clenched. Her eyes traced and retraced the names of her mother, father, and grandfather. But it took her a moment to register the magnitude of what she was reading. It was plainly obvious to her that this did, in fact, constitute a kill order.

Thoughts swirled in her mind. Her grandfather she could possibly understand. After all, he had been involved in the failed plot in the first place. Perhaps the Mossad needed to cover its tracks. But she thought, *Why would the Mossad issue a kill order on Ima and Abba? What could they have done?*

Memories from the bakery popped into her mind. They came to her in bits and pieces, separated by time. Her father, her dearest Aba, propping her on his hip and holding her with one arm while holding a hot, fresh Krantz pastry in the other.

"My little Talia. You have the first one," he'd say as she opened her mouth to devour the chocolatey baked goodness. But he would then tickle her ribs causing her to giggle so hard, she couldn't eat it. "But come on, we worked hard to bake this," he'd say. "Don't you want to eat it?" Tiny Talia would lean back in, but he'd tickle her again until Talia would laugh and laugh. "Aba, you're tickling me!"

"No, my dear, you must be mistaken." And the tickling would continue.

But today, standing in the center of one or the largest intelligence gathering organizations in the world took her back to the present. Silence played out as Talia stared at the monitor. After a few moments, Uncle Bill said, "Would you like to talk about it?"

Talia replied, "About why my parents' names are encrypted onto some operational report? All I want to know is why."

"We can tell you what we think," Bill said. "Son," he put his hand on Knuckle's shoulder, "scroll up a bit." When Knuckles had scrolled the image to where Bill wanted, Bill said, "Right there. This part here, we think it means a second operation was opened, somehow based on the first."

CODE NAME OR DESIGNATION: ABSOLUTION
CROSS REFERENCE: RED SCORPION
INSTANTIATION: 5 AUG 1996
VISIBILITY: EYES ONLY
CASE NO: 380987
DATE CLOSED OR TERMINATED: 11 MAR 1998

"It is apparent this new op, *Operation Absolution*, was a continuation of

Red Scorpion. We know *Red Scorpion* was an attempt to steal a nuclear device, but we don't know what *Absolution* is."

Talia's voice came out dry, almost arid as if she was talking to herself. "Absolution. Freeing from blame. A release from consequences, penalties."

"Yes," Uncle Bill responded. He nodded, and Knuckles scrolled further down. "This next part is highly garbled, but it defines the op as being designed to stabilize Israeli security, by somehow producing evidence of what it calls *the threat*. We don't know what threat they are referring to." Bill rubbed his neck. "Something obviously caused the project to be aborted. And it appears the reason is that knowledge of the operation was leaked in some manner. They were apparently so concerned about it they decided to . . ." Bill stopped.

"How do you Americans put it?" Talia said. "Tie off loose ends?"

Jana spoke up. "Your parents may have had nothing to do with anything. But maybe, through connection to your grandfather, they found something they weren't supposed to find."

Talia whispered, "And the Mossad murdered them for it." She shook her head. "The operation must have been a complete failure. Or things must have gone all, what's that other term you use?"

"Sideways," Knuckles said.

"Yes, sideways." Talia hesitated a moment. "Scroll back down to my parents' names." Knuckles complied. "This," she said as she pointed to the very last entry:

AUTHORITY:
EXECUTIVE ORDER: 9978307
SIGNATORY: CODENAME VIPERA

"An executive order," she said, trying to keep her voice from cracking.

Uncle Bill said, "In the United States, it takes an executive order to authorize such an action. It would be no different in Israel."

"Vipera," she said as her mind scrambled for answers. "Who is that?"

"No telling," Stone said from behind. "I've seen things like this before though, in briefings." The others turned to him. "Sometimes we'd get briefed just before we'd go on an op. They always wanted us to see the operation had exec signoff, so we'd know it was authorized. But there were never any real names used. None of the top brass wanted hard evidence that they had been the signatory. Blowback."

Talia's eyes tracked back and forth across the floor as though she was thinking.

Jana said, "Does Vipera mean something to you?"

Talia replied, "No," though as she looked Jana in the eye, she wasn't so sure Jana believed her.

41

The Raven pressed the Call button on his phone and held the device to his ear. The phone rang on the other end. A deep Israeli voice answered. "Identify," the voice said.

"Raven."

"Challenge: Enigma."

"Response: Swallow."

"Authenticate please."

The Raven flipped to a different app on his phone, one used to digitally verify his identity. He held the phone's camera close to his eye and waited while the app used the phone's camera to scan his retina. Then the app sent a series of encrypted codes across the ether.

"Authentication verified," the voice said. "Secure line. How can I direct your call?"

"Connect me to codename *Vipera*," The Raven replied.

He heard a few clicks, then a digital pulse, and the call was forwarded. The phone rang a few more times before being answered.

"You are no doubt calling to inform me of the success of your mission."

The Raven hesitated. "It is not that simple."

"It is exactly that simple!" Vipera said, his voice almost exploding into the phone.

"There are . . . complications."

"What *complications*?" The word rolled off Vipera's tongue as though it tasted of the bitter herbs of a Passover Seder. "Have you not even been able to locate her? How hard could it be? She's a single female, and she's wearing a tracker!"

"The target has assistance."

This time Vipera paused. "What type of assistance?"

"Heavy," came the reply. And referring to John Stone's background as a covert assassin and military operator, said, "A clipper. I'm sending you the dossier on him now. The stakes are far higher than you first imagined."

"How does she know a—" Vipera paused. "Never mind. This needs to happen."

The Raven clenched the phone tighter. "I am aware of the importance of my assignment."

"Then you know time is short. I don't care what the risks are, she is to be neutralized, immediately."

"*I* am the one on foreign soil. *I* am the one who will be disavowed should anything go wrong." The Raven hesitated, waiting for a sharp reply. When none came, he continued. "Not only are we dealing with an asset who is a clipper, they have made visits to the National Security Agency, the headquarters at Fort Meade, Maryland."

"I *know* where it is!" Vipera barked. The Raven heard a heavy exhale across the phone. "*Ya Allah!* She's just a researcher. How does she have contacts with American intelligence? What are her movements?"

"She was picked up at US Customs when she entered the country. They held her for questioning. She was released to parties unknown. Then she went to the NSA where she later departed with the asset."

"Protective detail. She has gone out of our control."

"You were the one who wanted to use her to have the grave exhumed."

Vipera's voice on the other end exploded again. "You will not speak to me in that manner! I know it was my idea. As it turned out, we had to execute a contingency plan to have the grave exhumed urgently. That was a risky move, far riskier than having her make the request herself."

"They went to his flat where she stayed the night. But then they went *there*."

"The cemetery?"

"Yes," The Raven replied.

"Dammit! Now they know the exhumation has already taken place. Why didn't you neutralize her then?"

"The cemetery is deep within the grounds of their US Naval Academy. It's a secure facility and was on some kind of heightened state of alert. Had I made attempts to enter, I would have drawn attention, and you know it. And what would have been the point? Neutralization of the target at a place like that would have been suicide. The grounds would have gone on lockdown, and I would have been trapped."

"I am not concerned with your problems. My focus is very singular. Now that their government is involved, we must do anything in our power to protect our secret. That coffin's transit must not be stopped." The Raven's jaw crunched hard enough to crack a tooth. The man continued. "Where is she now?"

"Back at the headquarters of the National Security Agency."

In a tone consistent with an officer issuing orders, Vipera said, "Don't *take* that tone with me. You will execute your orders, and you will not fail. Once she departs NSA, follow the ping. It's a dead giveaway of her physical location." His next words came out as though he was speaking to a two-year-old. "You can follow a ping, right?"

The line went dead. The Raven glared at the phone and nearly crushed it in his hand. "Can I follow a ping?" he said in a mocking tone. *"Khara!"*

42

NSA Headquarters

"Uncle Bill," Stone said, "we need some help."

"What is it?"

"We just came from the Annapolis cemetery. We found the grave site."

"And?"

"It had been dug up."

Bill looked over the tops of his glasses.

Talia said, "They wouldn't tell us who ordered it, but apparently the exhumation occurred in the middle of the night."

"When?" Jana asked.

Stone answered. "Late last night. They wouldn't share much information with us. Said the exhumation order came from the top."

Knuckles stood. "Why would anyone dig up a grave in the middle of the night?"

"That's what we want to know," Stone said. "Bill, something's going on. It may have been dug up in the middle of the night, but it isn't as if it was stolen, it was authorized through the chain of command. Can you locate that casket?"

Uncle Bill removed his glasses and cleaned them using his knit tie. "We've devoted far too many resources to this. I've spoken with my crew.

Out of respect for Miss Stiel and the Mossad, we've gone this far, but without evidence of any threat, I'm afraid we—"

"But," Knuckles said, "you told us it was okay if we wanted to work on it after hours."

"I did," Uncle Bill said.

The kid continued. "I'll work late. And after all, we've already finished most of the sweep on that North African terror cell."

Bill exhaled. "Fine, look it up. Start with the Bureau of Veterans Affairs. They control all the military burial grounds in the country. Their system can probably tell Miss Stiel here where the casket has been moved. If the exhumation orders did, in fact, come through channels, it will be under honor guard conditions. One or more soldiers will be with it at all times."

"Hurry, Knuckles," Jana said, "before he changes his mind." She turned to Bill. "I knew you had a heart."

Knuckles sat and spun his swivel chair into place, then began pecking away at his keyboard.

"I'm going to regret this," Bill said. He turned to Talia. "Miss Stiel, I've spoken with our people. As your life is in danger in your homeland, the United States can offer you political asylum."

Talia said, "Asylum? Live here, permanently? Israel is my home. My life is there, my work. Someone will have to take care of Moshe when he's older."

"It's your decision," Bill said, "but if I were you, not only would I request asylum, but I'd give strong consideration to entering our witness protection program. If elements inside the Mossad are after you, you'll need help to disappear. A new identity. We can take care of that."

Talia's mouth hung open a moment as if to speak. Then she said, "A new identity? I can't believe this. If I have *nothing*, I have myself, who I am. I can't just up and disappear on Moshe, on my work. That sweet old man needs me. And what I've discovered in the lab, the ability to detect nuclear material at great distances, it's not just some theory, I've made it work. But it needs testing, further development. The security of Israel is partly in my hands."

"Yes, ma'am," Uncle Bill replied, "but it wouldn't do anyone any good if you got killed before you could finish that work." He looked over the tops of his glasses again. "Something to think about," then walked toward his office.

Jana looked at Talia. "Bill has good intentions. He's a good man. He just wants you to be safe."

Stone added, "I'd listen to him."

"Yeah," Jana added. "That wasn't a plastic bullet we extracted from your backpack."

Knuckles continued to tap away at the keyboard.

"So you all think I should just give up? Disappear into, what do you call it, the Heartland?" She started to pace the floor. "I could never leave Moshe. And besides, he'll get to the bottom of this. He's been high up in the Mossad since I was a little girl. If anyone can figure this out from the inside, it's him."

"You've got to be kidding me," Knuckles blurted as he stared at his monitor.

Everyone turned.

"What?" Jana said as they gathered around the boy.

"I found your casket."

"Where is it?" Talia asked.

Knuckles answered with a long exhale. "About one hundred and twenty-seven nautical miles off the coast of Spain. Pontevedra, Spain, to be exact." He turned around. "It's onboard El Al Airlines, flight 1187. Departed JFK at 2:30 a.m. Eastern. Arrives at Ben Gurion in Tel Aviv at 8:20 p.m. That's local time."

No one said a word. Talia rubbed her wrist and said, "I can't believe this. It's already gone?"

Stone walked up beside her and placed a gentle hand on her shoulder. Jana studied his body language as if taking mental notes.

"I really thought I'd be the one to have the casket exhumed. I mean, he was *my* uncle."

Knuckles looked at the others as if waiting for permission to speak. "But I thought his remains weren't in the casket."

"They're not," Talia said. "But whatever is in there must be pretty valuable, otherwise why all the rush? And why are people shooting at me over it?"

Stone shook his head. "Who could have a fifty-year-old grave exhumed in the middle of the night, and have it on an international flight an hour later? This is insane."

Talia turned to him. "Come with me."

"What?" he replied.

"Come with me, to Israel. I've got to see this through."

"I can't just go traipsing off to Israel." Jana smirked, and he turned to her. "Something funny?"

"No," she said, almost cracking a smile. "It's just that I have a hard time picturing your calendar to be full."

"Nice," he said. He looked at Talia. "Flying back to your own country? Sounds like a suicide mission. You can't go back to Israel, probably ever."

"Take up a new identity, here, in the US? Is that what you suggest? I have no intention of leaving my old self behind. I need your help. I've got to find out what's going on. I've got to get my life back. Besides, you'll be there to protect me. Come on, you're still being paid, right?"

"It's suicide," he said.

Talia squared off in front of him, her eyes locked on his. "I'm going, with or without you."

Stone's shoulders slumped. "Dammit, why are all women in my life so hard-headed?"

Jana said, "We're not hard-headed. We're strong."

Stone's eyes traced the ceiling. "Knuckles, can you find us a couple of seats on the next flight out?" Talia smiled at him then he said, "I don't know *why* I'm agreeing to this."

43

NSA Command Center

JANA PULLED STONE ASIDE.

He took one look at her and could tell she had something to say. It was just her way.

"Already?" she said as she crossed her arms.

"Already what?"

"You've known her for what, two days? I see how you look at her."

"Baker," Stone said, "what are you talking about?"

"It's not like you and I are still dating. It's okay."

"You think I'm interested in Talia?"

"It's so obvious," Jana replied. "I can see why. She's beautiful. The long hair, and just your body type."

"Back up for just a minute there. I mean, sure, she's attractive, but I'm not—"

"We dated for a year, John. I know you. I know you through and through. It's me your talking to."

Stone studied Jana's face then turned to look across the room at Talia. "I don't know what you're talking about."

Jana smirked at him. It was a look he'd seen a thousand times. But then, her facial expression lowered. "I miss you."

Stone's eyes met hers. "Then you shouldn't have left me."

"I didn't leave you."

"Well, you backed off. I don't know, Babe, I thought we had something there."

"Antigua was a blur. It feels like a thousand years ago. I don't know why I left."

"You know exactly why you left. You left because you wanted to go back to your life, back to the Bureau. You finally listened to all those voices telling you to. It's just," he said as his hands found his pockets, "I was hoping we would stay together. I was . . ."

"What?" Jana said.

"I was in love with you."

Jana's mouth dropped open. "I think I was in love with you, too."

"But still, you chose your career over me."

"What did you expect me to do? You could have come with me."

"And what, see you in between your assignments and my ops? We had our chance. But that time has passed."

Jana let a little grin show. "Yeah, now that you're in love with the hot Israeli girl."

Stone allowed himself to smile. "She's not hot. Besides, are you jealous?"

"Of course, she's hot. I don't even like women, but look at her," Jana said.

"You saying you'd switch teams?"

"John!" Jana said almost laughing. But then her tone sharpened. "When you two go to Israel to track down this coffin, you keep your eyes open. We've still got nothing for you to go on, and you'll be on your own out there."

"I can handle myself."

"That's exactly what I'm afraid of."

Jana walked away, and Stone watched her. He shook his head. "These women are going to be the end of me."

44

Laurel Ridge Apartments, Annapolis, Maryland

PICKING the lock had been a breeze. The Raven closed the apartment door behind him and locked the bolt from the inside. He glanced again at an app on his phone that showed the location of the tracking device. "Still at Ft. Meade," he said. "Plenty of time." He walked to the back bedroom and began his search there, but was careful not to disturb anything. He didn't want his presence to be detected.

The bed was neatly made, and Talia's backpack lay on top. He unzipped the main compartment and carefully pulled items out. But after discovering only clothing, he replaced the items and moved to the other zippers. But again, found nothing out of the ordinary.

He moved to the closet doors. They were of the louvered bi-fold variety. A cheap hollow core type. He slid them open. Inside Stone's closet, he found typical items. Shirts and pants hanging neatly on wire hangers. Everything neat and orderly.

"Precision. Evidence of a long military career, Mr. Stone," he said. Instead of shifting the clothing items to the side, however, he thought it better to not touch them. It would be difficult to put them back in their exact spot.

But when he glanced down at the carpeting, a frayed spot caught his eye. He knelt down and pulled on it. A rectangular section of carpeting, about four feet long, pulled back and revealed a thin piece of perfectly cut plywood underneath. The plywood had three hinges screwed onto the far side. It was a false floor. "Well, Mr. Stone, hiding our firearms, are we?" he said with a smirk.

He opened the plywood door and leaned it against the back wall of the closet. It revealed another door underneath, this one metal. It was a gun safe, the type with cylindrical locks that utilized a tubular key to open it. He shook his head. "Surely, Mr. Stone, you could do better than this."

The Raven pulled out a thin, wallet-like case from his back pocket and opened it. Inside, tucked neatly into little slots, were various sizes of metal lockpicks. But one was of particular note. It was a tubular key, a universal, used by locksmiths to gain entry into vending machines and the like. He inserted it into the cylinder. The lock turned with ease. He pulled the door open and leaned it against the other.

He noted the weapons inside. "Ah, very nice, Mr. Stone." He placed his hands on the body of a SOCOM Mk-13 sniper rifle and lifted it from its cradle. "I may have to change my opinion of you. Remington 700 Long Action, Lilja Precision 26.5 inch barrel, McMillan A-2 Tactical Stock with saddle-type cheek-piece. Nightforce NXS scope. And chambered in .300 Winchester Magnum. This must have come in handy on many occasions."

He lay the rifle back down and picked up the next. "But this is my personal favorite. The Heckler and Koch M4. Ah, yes, a very nice piece of hardware indeed. And this one with the eleven-inch barre. 5.56mm, and a tool-less gas regulator. Must make it nice for mounting a suppressor when you want to maintain quiet. This must have been with you on many a long night."

The Raven thought a moment. "Looks strikingly like the configuration favored by operators of the United States Army's Delta Force. Hmmm, I do wonder about you, Mr. Stone. Perhaps I've underestimated you." He continued inspecting the weapon. "Very nice indeed. Though, in my opinion, not as nice as the new 416 model."

The Raven stared out the window into the trees. He thought about how fun it would be to kill Stone and the beautiful Talia Stiel with one of Stone's own weapons. He smiled, and a tingling sensation rode his spine. He glanced back into the gun safe and caught sight of the suppressor, an eight-inch long tubular device used to silence the weapon.

"Yes, and wouldn't it be fun to kill you with it, then force the muzzle under Miss Stiel's neck, and pull the trigger?" He laughed at the thought. "Make it look like a murder-suicide. Authorities will think you've gotten into a lover's quarrel. Ah, I do enjoy my work."

He screwed the suppressor onto the end of the M4's barrel until it snugged. "There, not too tight. Wouldn't want to strip the threads. And where do we store our ammunition, Mr. Stone? Ah, here it is," he said as he pulled out a thick, heavy box of 5.56mm ammo and two empty magazines. He set the weapon down, opened the ammunition box, picked up one of the mags, then closed his eyes.

Mechanically, as if he'd done it countless times, he began sliding loose rounds into the mag. *Click*, sounded the first round. *Click*, sounded the second. He continued until the magazine was full, then picked up the next and repeated the process. When both mags were loaded, and with his eyes still closed, he picked up the weapon and slid the full magazine into the magazine well, then grabbed the charging handle and rocked it back. The snapping action sent a live round into the chamber.

The Raven opened his eyes, and he shouldered the weapon. He looked down the sights as if aiming at a target. "You are mine now."

With one last glance at the tracking app on his phone to verify Stone and Talia were still at NSA headquarters, he lay the weapon on the bed, and waited.

45

NSA Command Center

Stone walked up behind Knuckles who was hunched over his laptop. "You working on getting us a flight?"

"Huh? What, are you kidding? I'm playing Fortnite."

"No, you're not."

"No, I'm not." Knuckles swiveled his chair toward Stone. "I could have put you on the 6:00 p.m. El Al, flight LY 2, JFK to Tel Aviv, which would touch down at Ben Gurion International at 11:50 a.m. tomorrow. First class tickets, the works."

"And why didn't you?"

"Because you told me not to." The kid grinned. "You're on an Air Force C-17 Globemaster out of Joint Base Andrews. Departs around the same time."

"Twenty-four hours in a jumpseat." Stone grinned. "Just like old times. All the luxuries of home. Talia's going to just love this. Thanks, Kid," Stone said. He turned to Talia. "We've got to go. That doesn't give us much time to pack."

"How far is the base?" Talia said.

"About an hour," Stone replied.

"Knuckles, you've been such a big help," she said. "I couldn't have found out half of what I now know without you." The boy smiled and his face flushed into a shade of crimson. "I can't go without thanking Uncle Bill and Jana."

"They're in his office," Stone said. "Come on."

The pair walked over to Bill's office, and Talia stood in the open doorway. Bill looked over the tops of his glasses at her. "Headed home, Miss Stiel?"

They walked in, and Talia said, "I couldn't leave without saying goodbye, and thanking both of you." She shook Jana's hand. As Uncle Bill stood, he walked around the desk and shook hers as well. "Bill, I know you've done so much for me already, but will you let me know if you find anything else from the microfilm?"

"I've already told my team I've authorized the lab to keep trying. And, each team member has decided to continue working after hours to see if they can find out anything else. I'm sorry I had to cancel the project. But you know how it is, priorities and all."

"I understand," Talia said. "What you've done for me means a lot. Thank you, and I hope I see you both again."

Stone and Talia walked out of the Command Center. Neither really said anything as they made their way out of the building and into the stark sunlight.

46

As they left NSA Headquarters, Stone pulled the truck onto the freeway and headed toward home. "We'll just have time to throw a few things together before we need to head to Joint Base Andrews."

"You've been there before?" Talia asked.

"Many times."

"I take it this isn't going to be the most comfortable flight?"

"If you consider jump-seats and shoulder harnesses comfortable, sure. Oh, and it's not exactly a temperature controlled environment either. Might get a bit chilly up there."

"Why didn't Knuckles just put us on a commercial flight? Trying to save money?"

"Hardly," Stone replied. "I asked him to do it this way. Security. I was concerned we'd be sitting ducks. I mean, if someone inside an intelligence agency as capable as the Mossad wants us dead, arriving on a commercial flight at Ben Gurion International would be the last thing we ever did. This way, we depart from, and arrive at, a US air base."

"Customs?"

"No Customs," Stone said.

Stone drove through town and made the final turn into his apartment complex. He pulled the SUV into a space in front of his building, and they got out. They ascended the exterior staircase and Talia glanced at her wrist then said, "Oh, I forgot my watch back there. How much time do we have?"

"Not enough. We need to be AIC in ten."

"AIC?"

"Ass in car."

Talia shook her head as they climbed to the third floor. "*Ass in car*? Why do men have to speak in code all the time?"

"We don't," Stone replied. At the top of the third-floor landing, he stopped and laughed. "I got sick of telling someone that we need to leave at say, 5:00 p.m. to then find out she'd. . . .," he stopped mid-sentence and looked at Talia as though he hadn't meant to identify the person, ". . .be finishing her makeup or grabbing a purse or something. By the time we got in the car, it would be five after and we'd be late."

"You and Jana were serious, weren't you?" Talia said.

"What makes you think I'm talking about . . . oh, never mind." He turned to put the key into the deadbolt but stopped, almost as if he had frozen.

Talia said, "What?"

He turned with abruptness and shoved her to the side, away from the door, until she was against the exterior banister railing. "Someone's been inside while we were gone," he said as he pulled the Glock from his back.

The sight of the gun caused Talia's eyes to flare. "Are you sure?" She held a hand over her mouth.

He whispered this time. "Sure I'm sure. The hair I inserted into the bolt lock is gone." He pulled out his phone and popped on the LED flashlight, then knelt in front of the lock. He held the light to it and squinted inside the keyhole. "Yup," he said, "it's crushed inside there."

"Well, what if it was just the apartment manager or something, doing maintenance, and he's still in there?"

"Then he's about to get the scare of his life. Besides, what if it *wasn't*?"

"You're not going in there, are you?"

"Stay down. I'm going to clear the apartment. If you hear shooting, get the hell out of here." He detached the key to the apartment and slipped the key ring to her. "Get in the truck and don't look back."

"Shooting?" she said as her breathing began to quicken.

He slid the key into the bolt lock so slowly it was almost silent. He then turned it until the bolt slipped free of the strike plate. "Be right back," he said.

From his crouched position he slipped the door open and slid inside.

"Stone!" Talia whispered. But it was too late, he was already in. She stayed down and leaned her head into the open doorway and watched as Stone remained low. He opened one of the lower kitchen cabinet doors and pulled something out. To Talia, it looked like a small, olive-drab colored canister. She heard a faint sound from the back of the apartment. Stone pointed the Glock in that direction. He looked right, then left as if he was ensuring the front room was clear. Talia pulled her head out of the doorway and cupped both hands over her mouth.

Her breathing accelerated, and she found her knees had begun knocking together. She knelt forward as that familiar feeling of nausea began to take hold. "No, no," she said to herself. She drew in several deep breaths, an attempt to thwart the impending bout of Vertigo.

As hard as she tried, she couldn't hear another sound coming from inside the apartment. Even the sounds of her own breathing, of cars on the roadway out front, dropped into clipped silence. Her heart rate accelerated and her chest began to heave, an effort to vacuum in enough oxygen.

Then, with a sudden ferocity, Talia heard a violent shuffling sound, and a single gunshot ruptured the eerie quiet. It was followed by Stone's booming voice, "Talia, move!"

She tried to stand, but her legs wouldn't cooperate. It was as if they were fused together. A muffled series of sounds erupted, like rapid-fire thumping. Splinters of drywall and wood blasted from the wall above her as bullets ripped through. It was automatic gunfire.

More loud single shots rang out, then a cacophonous bang. The sound was louder than anything in Talia's experience, so loud, all she was left with was a piercing ringing sound. She felt the percussion and wrapped her arms over her head. It was her only defense.

The explosion was followed by several loud gunshots, then she heard the distinct sound of shattered glass intertwined with the ripping down of a metallic window blind. Stone called to her. "Talia? Talia?" He ran through the open doorway. Talia was clutched into a ball. Shards of splintered wood and drywall peppered across her hair, back, and arms. "Are you all right?" Stone said as he pulled at her.

Talia looked up through eyes of terror. Her mouth opened but nothing came out. Stone ran his free hand across her back, searching for an entry wound, but when he found none, he dropped the near-empty magazine from his Glock and charged it with a fresh one. "Get in," he said as he grabbed her up and shuffled her inside. "Stay down. There was just one of them, and he jumped through the window."

Talia blurted across choked vocal cords, "You're leaving?"

"I'll be right back. Lock the door behind me!" He was out the door and down the stairs before she could utter another word.

Talia bolt-locked the door and then ran to the bedroom where the intruder had apparently been hiding. She crouched in front of the shattered window and looked down. On the grass lawn below lay a morass of shattered shards of glass interspersed with broken wood and a mangled window blind.

Talia looked to her left and saw a woman peeking from her apartment window. Apparently she'd heard the gunfire. Then, out of the corner of her eye, Talia saw motion. On the ground, about fifty feet away, she watched as a man leapt up a ten-foot chain link fence that bordered the property. He scaled it with the speed of a leopard and flipped over the top. As his feet hit the ground on the other side, he turned and looked at Talia, and their eyes met.

Talia looked him straight in the face, and her mouth dropped open. A sickening, crooked smile appeared on his face, then he disappeared beyond the hedges. He was gone.

47

NSA Command Center

Uncle Bill walked out of the war room followed by a dozen senior military leaders, all dressed in Class A uniforms. Bill walked toward Cade and Knuckles as the men, all members of the Joint Chiefs of Staff, departed.

Knuckles looked up from his laptop. Something about the expression on Uncle Bill's normally stoic face gave him pause. "Sir?" Knuckles said. "Is everything okay?"

Cade swiveled his chair around. Bill's eyes were locked onto the ground in front of him. He crossed his arms, then one hand began rubbing his chin which was buried somewhere underneath his cavernous gray beard.

Knuckles flicked a glance at Cade, then said, "Sir?"

Bill removed his glasses and rubbed his bloodshot eyes. "I'm getting too old for this shit," he muttered. He looked from Cade to Knuckles then said, "You know how I told you I couldn't assign any priority to Miss Stiel's case?"

"Yes, sir," Knuckles said. "But you said we could work on it after hours. I mean, that's still all right, isn't it?" The boy squirmed in his chair. "We're not using any government resources to do it. We're just—"

"It's all right, son," Bill said. "In fact, it's more than all right."

Cade nodded toward the war room. "Something happen in the security briefing?"

"Yeah, you might say that," Bill replied. "You two have been working on that North African terror cell, so you've been a little out of the loop with regard to the Middle East. There have been some . . . developments." He used his knit tie, a style throwback from the 1980's, to wipe his glasses clean. "We're picking up a surprising amount of chatter. And it's coming out of Israeli channels."

Cade and Knuckles looked at one another.

Bill continued. "Military chatter. Lots of it. As you well know, chatter only escalates when a large scale operation, or at least a military exercise, is about to take place. But that's not the half of it."

"What?" Knuckles said.

Bill put his glasses back on. "CIA says their people on the ground are reporting an influx of Israeli troops, massing at the border."

"Which border?" Cade asked.

"Northern Israel," Bill replied. "The one with Lebanon. We're talking about tens of thousands of troops."

Knuckles sat more upright. "Heavy armor?"

Bill nodded. "The Sec Def is on the horn with the Israelis at the moment. He's pressing them on it. If they are preparing for an invasion of Lebanon, the world needs to know why. Now, I don't believe this has anything to do with Talia's case. But I've got a bad feeling inside, and I'm not going to look back on this with regret. I want every stone overturned.

"From this moment forward, I want you two on it. I've got an entire team already listening in on Israeli chatter, and satellite imagery is in the pipe. But you two," he said as he pointed at them both, "start working down Talia's case. I want to know what's on the rest of that degraded microfilm, and I want to know right now."

48

"Talia!" Stone yelled as he leapt the railing of the first-floor staircase landing, "get down!" He ran across the lawn and up to the fence with his weapon forward. But after he realized the intruder was gone, he turned and walked back until he was underneath the window. He looked up at Talia. "You okay?"

Talia's hand was covering her mouth as the adrenaline surge took its toll. She nodded, but it was all she could do to fight back the forming tears. *Keep it together*, she thought. She shook her head, hard, an effort to further thwart nausea and dizziness.

"You're sure you're not hit?"

"I'm sure," she said across choked vocal cords.

Stone knelt at the spot where the intruder had landed on the lawn. He picked at the larger pieces of broken glass as though looking for evidence. "Blood," he said. "Either from the broken glass or . . ."

When he appeared to be about finished, he flipped a piece of wooden window frame over, then picked something up and looked at it. From her vantage point, Talia couldn't tell what it was.

In the distance, the faint sound of a police siren became audible, and Stone and Talia both looked in that direction. Stone stood, wiped his knee, then jogged to the stairs and went up. Talia unbolted the front door and Stone came inside. "We've got to go, right now." He went straight to the bedroom. "Grab your ruck, throw everything into it. We leave this apartment in thirty seconds."

Stone picked up a heavy backpack of his own, one he apparently kept pre-packed, and threw it onto the bed. He reached down and picked up the H&K M4 assault weapon. "I think I hit him," he said as Talia came in and grabbed her backpack. "Damn good thing he dropped this."

Stone let the magazine fall from the weapon and yanked back on the charging handle. The snapping action caused a live cartridge to fling out of the breach. He took hold of the stock and twisted the butt end until it popped open. He shook it, and a small tool fell into his hand. He used the tool as a push-lever to remove the rear pin. The rifle separated into two roughly equal length parts. He stuffed them into his pack.

He then went to the closet and flipped the door of the gun safe closed, turned the key to lock it, and flipped the carpeting over the top of it. "Come on, we're going."

Talia darted into the restroom and grabbed a few things, jammed them into her pack, and slung it over her shoulder. They were out the door and onto the staircase seconds later.

The sound of the police siren had escalated in volume and had been joined by at least two others. "Why are we running from the police?" Talia said as they jumped into the truck. "Wouldn't they be able to help us?"

"That was no petty burglar. That was a professional hit, and we nearly walked right into it." Stone flicked a glance at an apartment window in front of them. Two faces were looking out, framed by window curtains. He started the engine, dropped the transmission into reverse and the tires barked as he jammed his foot on the gas. The siren was nearly upon them now. He accelerated and wove his way out of the apartment complex. Just as he turned right, a police cruiser screeched into a turn to enter.

As they got clear of the complex, two more police cruisers sailed past. "I barely got a look at the guy. All I remember was a flash of his face, a scar, and those eyes. I don't know, almost like an albino's eyes, like those of a jackrabbit. Then the shit started."

Talia's voice came out stilted as she stared straight ahead. "It was him. I'm sure of it."

"Him who?"

"The same man that tried to kill me at Mossad headquarters. I'd recognize those eyes anywhere."

49

Stone hammered a closed fist onto the top of the steering wheel. "Dammit! I just can't figure out how they found us. We've been so careful. Yet we walked right into that." He pulled something out of his pocket. "Here. He must have dropped it when he hit the ground. What's on the screen?"

Talia took the object, a mobile phone with a freshly cracked screen. She blew on the screen to remove tiny shards of loose glass. She pressed the button, and the screen blinked to life. "God," she said, "you can barely see anything on this. The screen is too shattered. But," she squinted at it, "it's unlocked. The app is a map of some type. Hmmm, not one of the normal street map apps though."

Stone headed north on Forest Drive as Talia studied the phone. "What's it a map of?" Stone said.

"Well, it's like a satellite view of, well, it's Ft. Meade."

"NSA?"

Talia used two fingers to zoom the map closer. "Ouch," she said as she blew a tiny shard of broken glass off her thumb. "Yes. There's a little dot on the map right on top of NSA headquarters."

"A dot? You mean like when you drop a pin onto Google Maps?"

"No," Talia replied as she studied the screen. "It's a dot, and it's, I don't know, what's the word? Pulsing?"

They glanced at one another. Stone forked left and followed the signs for US-301. "I don't like this," he said. "We come home and surprise a hired gun, and the guy's got a map of where we just were." He shook his head. "We've got to get rid of that phone."

"Why?" Talia said. "This could be evidence. It might have clues on it. We don't even know what this mapping app is."

"That phone could be used to track us. We damn sure can't drive right out to Joint Base Andrews and telepath our location." He pulled the car into a large retail shopping area and wove his way to a Holiday Inn Express hotel in the back. "We're dropping that off. I'll call Uncle Bill and have him pick it up. They can analyze it further. We can't take the risk."

After Stone pulled up to the hotel, he hopped out and went inside. A few moments later, he was back in the driver's seat. "All right. I left the phone at the front desk. Bill's sending a courier to pick it up right now."

"Really? Just like that? He didn't seem that willing to help earlier."

Stone pulled out. "Maybe he changed his mind."

"So the guy just jumped out of the window?" Talia said.

"Not exactly. I kind of threw him."

"You threw him out the window?"

"We surprised him. It was like he wasn't expecting us to show up. When I first saw him, he was sitting on the bed, putting the phone back in his shirt pocket, like he had just been looking at it. But when he saw me, it was as though I'd caught him completely off guard. I didn't see he had my M4 laying next to him. He went for it, and the shooting started."

Talia thought back to the terror of those events. "So he was firing your own weapon at you?"

"I'm pretty sure he took a round in the shoulder because the M4 hit the ground. Anyway, I jumped on him before he could grab it again. But all of a sudden he had this damn ice pick in his hand. Came out of nowhere. I locked up his arm as he tried to stab me with it. Then I spun my weight into him. His body crashed through the window."

"How come it wasn't loud?"

"The glass breaking?"

"No, all that gunfire," she said. "I mean, that was an automatic weapon, right? It was so muffled-sounding."

"He'd attached my suppressor."

"Why do you have a suppressor?"

"You don't want to know."

"And now that weapon is in your backpack? You're just going to board a plane with it?"

"Done it a thousand times. This is no commercial flight. We used to deploy from Andrews all the time. And we'd have a lot more on us than just small arms."

Talia nodded. "And you keep a backpack laying around, fully packed?"

"Habit," Stone said as he got onto John Hanson Highway, also known as US-50. "Never knew when orders would come through. There's no time to pack. Even now, I still get called for things, like when nuclear physicists from the Israeli Mossad show up and need help."

"Very funny," Talia said. "But back to how he found us, what do you think?"

"Well, if it's true someone inside the Mossad is behind this, they could have easily found out when you crossed US Customs. But it would have been impossible to track you after that. Your phone was off, you were escorted to NSA HQ, and no one would have known that. Then a wetboy just shows up at my apartment? I don't get it."

"A wet *boy*?" Talia said, almost laughing.

"An assassin. No matter how they found us, one thing is for sure. Someone doesn't want you to find that casket."

"It's got to be more than that, doesn't it? I mean, they know I've found out something, and they want me silenced."

"Let's take it one step at a time. We'll get on this transport and track down that casket."

"Maybe NSA will be able to decrypt the rest of the microfilm."

"And," Stone added, "figure out what's on that assassin's phone." He looked back at her. "What?"

She had been staring at him. "Nothing," she said as heat flushed her cheeks. "It's just, I guess what I'm trying to say . . . what you did back there was . . . thank you."

50

Within moments of leaping the fence at John Stone's apartment, the Raven crossed the road and jumped onto a city bus. He made his way to a seat at the rear. His escape had been lucky, and he knew it. And the fact that the bus was almost empty worked to his advantage as well. Yet now that he'd gotten away, his real trouble was just beginning.

He applied pressure to his left shoulder. The entrance wound from the .9 mm round that struck him wasn't so bad, but the exit wound was another story. Blood pulsed from the back of his shoulder with impunity—the bullet had apparently clipped an artery. He knew time was short. If he didn't find medical help fast, he would bleed out.

The fact that he was wearing such a dark colored shirt played to his advantage. It served to hide the blood fairly well. But in broad daylight, he knew it wouldn't take long for a bystander to see the volume of blood rolling down his back. He removed his thin outer jacket and draped it over the wounded shoulder. It served to further cover the blood stains.

He kept his right hand underneath the jacket and pressed his fingers into the exit wound. At the same time, he pressed his shoulder back into the seat. The extra pressure further prevented blood loss. But the more pressure he applied, the more pain rocked through him.

I can't go to a hospital, the Raven thought. *Gunshots always draw the police. No, I must get help elsewhere.* And he knew exactly the type of place he'd need. He glanced at his watch. *If I can just get to one*, he thought.

He found his left arm to still be somewhat functional. It caused him great pain to use it, but at least it worked. He fumbled in his shirt pocket for his phone but soon realized the phone was gone. His mind exploded into a whirlwind of thoughts. *What if the phone is discovered? The tracking app, the encrypted communications app. The operation could be compromised.* But the more he worried over the jeopardy of the mission, the more he realized he had to concentrate on the immediate priority.

A woman seated across the row from him stood and held the overhead safety bar in preparation to get off at the next stop. "Excuse me," he said, his accent heavy of the Middle East, "isn't there a veterinarian's office nearby?"

"Uh, let me think. There's not a regular office, but there's a vet attached to the back of that big pet store up here. Can't remember what it's called. I'm pretty sure anyway. It's in that shopping center," she said as she pointed.

"Thank you," he said, then gritted his teeth against a wave of pain.

The bus came to a stop in an area covered in retail shops. As he held as much pressure as possible on the wound, he got off and crossed the street, walking toward the stores. When he spotted the PetDepot, he headed straight for it.

As he entered the front doors, he glanced at the store hours. The store was open until 9:00 p.m. But the veterinary office was another story. It was only open until 6:00. *Perfect,* he thought. *They would be closing about now.* The sign read:

Veterinarian on Duty
Roger Murdock, DVM

He walked to the back of the store where the veterinary office was located. As he approached the door to the small waiting area, a woman stepped out, a purse in one hand, her lightweight coat in the other. "Oh, I'm sorry, we're just closing."

He smiled despite the pain coursing his shoulder. "Not to worry," he said, almost as if to laugh, "Roger and I were college roommates."

"Oh, wow," she said with a smile. "Have fun." She walked off.

The Raven let the glass door close behind him, turned the knob on the bolt lock, then flipped the hanging sign around so that it read "Closed." He let his blood-covered right hand out from underneath his coat and removed a pistol, a polymer-framed Jericho 941 variant, chambered in 9 mm. He held it forward and walked to the back.

51

PetDepot Veterinarian's Office

Blood pulsed down the Raven's back, and a new wave of pain came with it. He braced against its intensity, then walked to the back of the office.

The veterinarian, a man of about thirty years of age, was removing his blue office scrubs. But when he looked up, the sight of the gun and bright red blood caused him to freeze in place. "We don't have any drugs here," the vet said.

"I'm not looking for drugs. I've been shot, and you are going to help me."

"I'm a veterinarian. I can't—"

The Raven pulled back the hammer with his thumb. "You will help me right now."

"Okay, okay," the vet said as he put his palms forward. "Um, okay, sit on the exam table. Let's have a look at you."

As the Raven slid onto the table, the vet slowly pulled back the coat covering the shoulder. "Wow, you've lost a lot of blood. You need a hospital. Can't I call an ambulance for you?" But the look the Raven gave him spoke volumes. "No hospital, okay. I'm going to cut this shirt off of you."

The vet picked up a pair of medical-grade scissors and cut the shirt away. "Oh man," he said as he looked at the exit wound. "It's hit an artery. We've got to stem the bleeding. Ah, here, put that thing down. Apply pressure to this while I get my equipment." The Raven glared back. "Really, it's okay. I'm not going to try anything. Just put the gun down, you need to apply pressure, quickly."

The Raven tucked the gun into his belt and used his right hand to stem the bleeding. "I will kill you without hesitation. I'll only remind you of that fact once."

"No problem," the vet said as he opened a cabinet and withdrew a syringe and vial of medication. "I'm just going to give you something for the pain." The vial was labeled:

Diazepam Injection
5 mg/ml

THE VET DREW a bolus of the medication into the syringe and walked back. "I'm going to have to get inside that wound. This is a general anesthetic. It will take the edge off, then I'll numb up the wound itself." The Raven nodded his ascent, and the vet administered the injection.

Within seconds, the Raven felt a warm flush across his face, but then his eyes became droopy, and he started to waver. "What have you done?" he said as he fumbled for the firearm. But it was too late. His eyelids shut, and everything went black.

* * *

SOMETIME LATER, the Raven awakened. His eyes flared opened, and he found himself still in the vet's procedure room. He was face down on the cold steel table. When he looked out the window, he could see it was now dark outside. As his thinking cleared, he realized he had been knocked unconscious. Adrenaline-infused anger pulsed into his veins. He sat up and began a frantic search for the gun.

"Looking for this?" the vet said as he walked back in the room. He held the gun with his thumb and forefinger as though it were contaminated. "It's okay," he said. "You're safe." He set the firearm on the counter and picked up a medical chart. "I'm sorry I had to put you under. The truth is, you would have never made it to the hospital. And there was no way I could have operated on you with just a local anesthetic."

The Raven's eyes locked onto the pistol.

The vet wrote on the chart while talking at the same time. "Well, that's one procedure I've never done before, not on a human, anyway. The bullet clipped the brachial artery just above the anterior humeral circumflex. You're lucky to be alive. You'd have bled out within minutes. It also clipped the bone structure of the subclavius. That's your clavicle. You'll be in a sling for a while. I know you said no hospitals, and I get it, but you're going to have to." He continued scribbling on the chart. "I've stopped the bleeding, but you'll need a vascular surgeon to take a look at that."

The vet stopped writing just long enough to look up. He found the Raven standing in front of him, the gun in his hand.

"Wait," the vet said, "I saved your ass, and I didn't call the cops. You're safe."

The Raven pulled the trigger. The bullet struck the man in the forehead, just above the left eye. He was dead before he hit the ground. "And I thank you. However," he said as he admired the dark red blood as it spread across the sterile floor, "I can afford no witnesses."

52

The Raven leaned over the dead body and rifled through the man's pockets. He removed a wallet, pulled out the cash, then dropped the wallet to the ground. "Stolen cash, stolen drugs," he said. "They'll think it was a simple break-in that went wrong." He then picked up the phone receiver and dialed a number. On the other end, a male voice answered. "Identify," it said.

"Raven, unsecure" He heard several digital tones as the line was pinged for vulnerabilities.

"In the clear, affirm," the voice said. "Designator?"

"Designate sierra tango lima one one six."

"Designator and voice ident, affirmed. Destination?"

"Vipera."

"Hold, please."

The call was routed. When his contact picked up on the other end, the man's voice almost erupted. "What are you doing calling me on an unsecure line?"

The Raven replied, "There was a . . . problem."

"A problem? A problem?" the man screamed. He lowered his voice and then said, "I sent *you*. You and you alone. And why? Because you have never failed. Yet you've screwed up this operation again, haven't you?" There was silence across the line. "I give you simple orders. How hard is it to sanitize one rabbit?"

"I told you," the Raven barked back, "she is not alone. She has protection."

The Raven heard a long exhale on the other end. "What happened?"

"Something went wrong with the tracker. I was inside his flat watching the ping on the map. They were at NSA Headquarters for hours. I had just finished rechecking their location when all of a sudden, he was inside the apartment."

"You were caught off guard? A man in your position can *never* afford to be surprised. I am fast losing confidence in your skills."

"There is nothing wrong with my skills!" The Raven barked a little louder than he had intended. "I have carried out your assignments for years without fail."

"Until now. I assume you were seen? I cannot express the depths of my disappointment. You have been compromised, and certainly now, you could be identified."

"I will not fail."

The line went dead.

The Raven slammed the receiver down then slapped the phone off the desk. It crashed into the wall, and plastic pieces broke off of it. He gripped at the pain in his shoulder and his chest heaved up and down. The knowledge of just how unmitigated a failure this mission had become sent adrenaline coursing into his veins. "I *will* complete my mission," he said out loud. "I *will* complete it."

53

NSA Command Center

KNUCKLES SPEED-WALKED into Uncle Bill's office with his eyes glued to a printout. "Sir? The lab sent over something else. It's about the microfilm." He looked up. Bill was seated behind his desk, and a man wearing the uniform of a four-star general sat across from him. The general glanced at the kid. When his eyes landed on Knuckle's Converse high-tops, he raised an eyebrow.

"Ahem," Uncle Bill said. "Doesn't anyone knock anymore?"

"Oh, ah, sorry, sir, sirs. I didn't mean to interrupt."

"That's okay, son," Bill said as he dropped into a sarcastic tone, "What General Mears here had to tell me wasn't really that important." He looked at the general. "What was it, General? Something about a terrorist bomb going off at the Tunis-Carthage International Airport?" Bill looked over the tops of his glasses at Knuckles.

Knuckles slowly stepped back. When he got to the doorway, he said, "This, ah, this can wait," and walked back to his desk.

When he sat back down, Cade said, "Tail between your legs?"

"Not funny."

"Oh, don't worry about it. That's only the, what, tenth time you've waltzed into Uncle Bill's office when he was talking with one of the Joint Chiefs?"

"Lay off of him," Jana said from a desk near Cade.

"Thank you, Jana," Knuckles said. "She's the only one that gets me."

Cade smirked. "At least someone gets you."

Uncle Bill came out of his office and shook the general's hand, then walked over to them. "So, what is it that's so important?"

Knuckles squirmed. "Sorry about that, sir. This is another piece of Talia's microfilm. I printed it out for you. I'm afraid it doesn't tell us much more."

"In that case," Bill said as he took the sheet of paper, "I'm glad you interrupted then." He read the paper. "This is all they were able to decrypt?"

"Yes, sir," Knuckles said. "They got the first and fourth lines."

Bill read the newly decrypted text.

INTENDED OUTCOME - STABILIZE ISRAELI SECURITY:ELIMINATE BOMBINGS
EXCUXPATXXY OVERVIEW - NEUTRALXXE XXXAXSE XETX-EXXXTS TO PXEVENT XXXXOLLAX / XXMAX AXTAXXX.
PHASE AXPFA - INSERTION: XXVEXX INSERXXON OF THE XEXXON INSIDE XEXANXX.
PHASE BRAVO - DETECTION: PRODUCE EVIDENCE OF THE THREAT.
XXASE CHXXLIX - OCXXXXTXXX: XXLL XXXLE XXXASIXN.

"WELL, that just about cracks the case," Cade said.

Bill added, "So all we have right now is that this Israeli operation was meant to stabilize their security and that in Phase Alpha they were going to insert something into somewhere. Phase Bravo is to produce evidence of the threat, and I can only assume that last line is Phase Charlie, to do something, somewhere." Bill nodded. "Man, that's heavy. Think I should call the president?"

"But, sir," Knuckles said as he stood.

"I'm just playing around with you, son. The lab say they could get anything more?"

Knuckles sat back down. "Still working on it."

"Just let me know if they find something concrete." Bill walked off.

Cade said, "Did he just say *heavy*?"

54

Mashabim Air Base

TALIA WALKED up to Stone who was talking to the airman. "We're not staying here."

"What?" Stone said, "Airman First Class O'Malley here just got us squared away."

O'Malley eyes flicked down to Talia's trim figure but looked away quickly.

"We're going to Abba's."

"Hey, I was just kidding about all that stuff. It's not like we're bunking in the same room. Right, airman?"

"That's an affirm, sir," came O'Malley's reply.

Talia shook her head. "We're going to Moshe's. He'll be worried sick about me. And before you go and get all, what do you call it, Postal? Moshe's got armed guards around him all the time. It'll be as safe as sleeping here."

"It's one o'clock in the morning."

"Just check out a vehicle. Come on," she said as she slung her pack onto her shoulder, "it's not as if someone will be waiting to attack us outside the base. No one even knows we're here." She walked away.

Both Stone and the airman watched as she exited the building.

When Stone didn't move. The young airman said, "So, it'll just be the vehicle then?"

"Damn she's hard-headed."

The sergeant typed at a keyboard and didn't glance back up. "Women. Can't live with 'em, can't live *with* 'em. And I don't mean to step in another man's pond, sir. It's just that, there's a lot of spec-ops guys who come through here. Had one of them give me a piece of advice once."

Stone exhaled. "And what was that?"

"Never pass up a good thing."

Stone nodded. "Yeah, heard that one myself."

The airman handed him a set of keys and pointed. "Parking spot number sixteen. Motor pool is—"

"Over there. Yeah, been here. Hey, when did the Air Force start using keys?"

"A couple of keyless Hummers drove themselves off the base last year. Kind of pissed off the colonel."

"That would do it," Stone said as he shouldered his ruck and walked out. Once outside, Talia followed him to a fenced area where several dozen Humvees were parked in neat rows. When they got to their vehicle, they both threw their gear in the back and hopped in. Stone started the engine, and they drove toward the exit. He said, "What's the drive to Tel Aviv?"

"About one hundred fifty kilometers. Two hours. But when I used to come out to the nuclear research center, I'd do it in an hour and forty."

"Sounds great. Just what I need, to get arrested in a foreign country driving fifty kilometers over the speed limit."

They drove in silence much of the way. Talia looked out the Humvee's bullet-proof glass into the darkness. At this time of night, there wasn't much to see, and she knew what was out there anyway. In this part of the desert, there was nothing but parched soil and scrub brush. But the further northeast they went, headed toward Tel Aviv, the more the landscape changed.

The highway had been cut into a mélange of sedimentary rock formations and dusty mountains. Those were interrupted by dry river beds and deep craters. By the time they came into the lights of Tel Aviv, Talia shook off the sleep and gave Stone directions to Moshe's house.

The stately home was nestled in the back of a gated community, the type encircled by an ornate metal fence. As they drove through the guard gate, Stone peered at the homes. Although it was dark, the neighborhood was well lit with ensconced street lights. Most of the houses had exterior lighting to illuminate their grandeur as well.

"Your godfather must do pretty well," Stone said.

"*Do*?" Talia said, unsure of the translation.

"Yeah, he must earn a lot of money."

"Oh. Sure, I guess so. I never thought about it."

They approached a cul-de-sac at the end of the neighborhood. The home at the end sat in a space that could have held five. It was surrounded by a fence of its own, and dual entrance gates spanned the driveway. Talia nodded, "A guard will let us in. But they're not expecting a military vehicle to pull up in the middle of the night, so go slow."

Stone pulled the vehicle to the gate, and a guard dressed in a business suit came out still speaking into a hand-held radio.

"This is going to be awkward," Stone said. "Bulletproof windows on Humvees don't roll down." Stone flicked on the vehicle's interior lighting so the guard could see clearly.

"No worry," Talia said as she held up her ID. The guard looked at Stone but upon seeing Talia, nodded his recognition. He spoke into the radio, and the gate swung open. "You must come here a lot," Stone said.

"Of course. Most Sundays. Except when Moshe has to travel."

Stone parked at the end of the drive and they got out. "Your father has guards twenty-four hours a day? What does he do again?"

"Remember, he's not technically my father. He's my godfather. He was very close with my parents."

"Yeah, yeah. He raised you."

"He's Director of Political Action."

"And that requires armed guards because...?"

"He's number two in command of the most elite intelligence agency in the world."

"The most elite?" Stone smirked. "I don't know about that."

"You're not in the United States anymore, Stone. The Mossad Intelligence Services have a lot of enemies. It's not safe, even deep inside Tel Aviv. Over the years, there have been attempts. He's risked his life for his country. He's a patriot."

As they stood at the door, Stone glanced at a security camera mounted to the brick but then turned his attention to the heavy bronze knocker. It had been forged in the shape of a snake's head.

Talia inserted her key into the lock, but before she could turn it, a guard on the other side pulled the door wide. The man's face lit up like a person greeting an old friend. "Miss Talia, at last. We've been worried sick about you. Thank God you're all right."

Talia smiled and kissed the man on the cheek. "Shimon, this is John Stone." As they walked in, she said, "Shimon has been with us for . . . how long?"

"Oh heavens," Shimon said, "your Aba and I served together during the Six Day War, The War of Attrition, the Yom Kippur War," he said with a dismissive wave of the hand. "Ancient history! You don't want to hear that. You are well?"

"I'm fine," she said with a smile. "Is Aba asleep?"

"Talia!" Moshe said from the top of the grand staircase, his effeminate inflection in full swing. The man shuffled down the steps. "I can't believe it. I've been worried to death." Moshe hugged her. "They said you were at the front gate. Oh, my dear, let me look at you." He held her back as though inspecting her for damage.

Shimon said, "I'll give you your privacy." He shook Stone's hand. "It was nice to meet you," then walked off.

"I'm fine, really," Talia said with a smile wide enough to cramp her cheek muscles. "Aba, this is John Stone. He's the reason I'm fine."

Moshe shook hands with Stone. "Thank you. Oh, thank you." He turned to Talia. "We heard about the attack at Mr. Stone's flat, through diplomatic channels, of course. Are you sure you're all right?"

"Yes, yes, Aba."

"Please," Moshe said as he pointed to a set of plush couches, "come, sit. Tell Aba all about it." As they all sat, he went on, "All the resources of the Mossad at my fingertips and even I haven't been able to find my own Talia."

Talia said, "It was the same man, Aba. I'm sure of it."

Moshe's brow crunched. "The same man?"

"The same man that tried to kill me at Mossad HQ was there, at Stone's apartment. He was inside, just waiting."

Moshe sat forward on the couch. "I don't understand. I've redirected internal Mossad resources to try to locate you. And we haven't been able to turn up a thing, other than the fact that US Customs flagged your passport when you got there. And then, after the attack at the apartment, a friend at the US State Department was able to fill me in on what happened. But somehow this man found you? How is that possible? For this," Moshe searched for the word, "*assassin* to track you down when I couldn't?"

Stone interrupted. "Maybe that's your problem." Talia and Moshe looked at him. "You've got a mole."

Moshe's eyes traced the floor a moment. "Inside the Mossad? That's impossible."

"It's entirely possible," Stone said. "In fact, it makes perfect sense. You said it yourself. You've got assets within the Mossad that have been directed to search for Talia. Sounds to me like the mole is one of them. He found her, withheld the information, and communicated it to the wetboy."

"Excuse me?" Moshe said.

Talia said, "The Americans use the term wetboy to mean assassin. The man is Israeli, with a scar running one side of his face. But I don't know if you could see it in the surveillance videos. His eyes are pale blue, almost white."

Moshe glared at Stone. "A mole? Inside the Mossad? I assure you, Mr. Stone. The Mossad has no moles."

Stone raised an eyebrow but otherwise let the subject die.

Moshe took Talia's hand and spoke as though a lump had formed. "I'm just so glad you are safe."

"I'm fine, but we need your help."

"Of course, my dear. And I know where it is. The coffin of your dear departed great uncle, that is."

"That's great!" Talia replied as she clutched Moshe's hand. "It disappeared so quickly. The only thing we knew was it was on a plane bound for Israel."

"Never fear, my dear," Moshe said as he stood. "Your Aba is on the case." He smiled. "I had it seized when it arrived. It's in a holding area at Mossad HQ. In the morning," Moshe looked at his watch, "Oh my, look at the hour. In the morning we'll all go down there together." He turned to Stone. "You will join us, Mr. Stone, no?"

"Wouldn't miss it," Stone said as he stood and shook Moshe's hand.

"It's settled then. My dear, I think it's best you get some rest. Show Mr. Stone to one of the guest rooms. He should be quite comfortable, yes?"

Moshe ascended the first few stairs, then turned. "Oh, how could I have forgotten?" A smile widened on his face. "I guess I was just so relieved to see you were all right, it completely slipped my mind. My dear, I have the most wonderful news. Your project was given a green light! The first unit has already been deployed. Isn't that wonderful?"

Talia looked at him a moment, her face etched in confusion. "It's operationalized? But Aba, it's not ready."

"Of course it is, dear! Oh, you were always too hard on yourself. Your work is brilliant, and you should be proud. This is the first step in making The Land a safer place. It's been deployed using a drone. A really big one," he said with a smile. "It's patrolling our borders as we speak." He took a last look at her and clutched a hand to his mouth. "It's just so wonderful to have you home."

55

NSA Command Center

"FINALLY," Knuckles said as an internal NSA courier handed him a sealed manila envelope.

As the man walked off, Cade slid his chair over. "Your subscription to *Boy's Life* finally come in?"

"Very funny."

"*National Geographic Kids*? No? Ooo, wait, it's that correspondence course you ordered called *How to Talk to Girls*?"

Knuckles just stared at him. "This coming from a guy who hasn't had a date in a year."

Cade propped his feet onto Knuckles' desk. "At least I *had* a girlfriend." They both looked to the other side of the wide space at Jana who was busy on her laptop and stared at the beautiful woman.

Knuckles said, "At least I don't try to pick up chicks at a Trekkie convention."

Cade capitulated. "Okay, we could do this all day. Is that the results from the lab?"

"Yup," Knuckles said as he unwound the string that bound the envelope shut. "The final analysis of the microfilm. Let's just hope they were able to repair the degraded sections. Although, why they insisted on putting it on hard copy is beyond me. Don't they know they're killing trees?"

"Kind of a good point," Cade said. "In the three years I've worked here, I don't recall anything coming on paper."

Uncle Bill walked up behind them, his eyes locked onto the manila envelope. "Oh shit," he said.

"What?" Cade said as he looked up.

Uncle Bill waved at Jana until he caught her attention. He looked back down at the envelope. "This can't be good."

Jana approached. "What's up?" she said to Bill before spotting a crumb from an orange cracker caught on his knit tie. She shook her head then plucked it free.

Bill pointed to the envelope. "Lab results on the microfilm." He pushed his glasses against the bridge of his nose. "The only time NSA sends a hard copy is when the Eyes-Only status has escalated. Tear into it, son."

Knuckles pulled out the contents and his eyes chased across the words on the cover sheet. "Okay, yadda, yadda. Lab guys say this is the best they can do. Even if they wanted to, they can't recover any more data. And some of what they did repair had to be interpolated."

"Meaning?" Jana asked.

Knuckles' eyes lit up as he saw another chance to show off his extensive knowledge. "Interpolation takes a number of data points, obtained by sampling or experimentation, which represent the values of a function for a limited number of values of the independent variable."

"Uh huh," Jana replied.

"Good Lord," Cade said. "He means the degraded sections of the microfilm weren't totally readable, so the computer looked at the existing pixels and made its best guess."

"Sorry," the kid said. He held up the next sheet. It contained only two paragraphs. "Here's what it says." He read.

CODE NAME OR DESIGNATION: ABSOLUTION

CROSS REFERENCE: RED SCORPION

INSTANTIATION: 5 AUG 1996

VISIBILITY: EYES ONLY

CASE NO: 380987

DATE CLOSED OR TERMINATED: 11 MAR 1998

. . .

"We've seen that already," Knuckles said. "But this next part is the part we couldn't read at all."

INTENDED OUTCOME - STABILIZE ISRAELI SECURITY:ELIMINATE BOMBINGS

"Yeah," Cade said. "Understandable."

EXCULPATORY OVERVIEW - NEUTRALIZE LEBANESE SETTLEMENTS TO PREVENT HEZBOLLAH / HAMAS ATTACKS.

"Neutralize?" Uncle Bill said. "That's what it says?"

"Yes, sir," Knuckles replied as he continued.

PHASE ALPHA - INSERTION: COVERT INSERTION OF THE WEAPON INSIDE LEBANON.

Cade looked at Uncle Bill. "Insertion? What weapon?" He thought a moment then stood. "You don't think—"

But Bill held up a hand. "I don't want to go there."

Knuckles read further.

PHASE BRAVO - DETECTION: PRODUCE EVIDENCE OF THE THREAT.
PHASE CHARLIE -

Knuckles stopped mid-sentence, his eyes locked onto the next words.

When he read them, he sounded as one reading an obituary.

PHASE CHARLIE - FULL SCALE INVASION

Uncle Bill's normally tranquil eyes widened. He took the sheet from Knuckles, and his eyes traced it in repeated succession. "What's the lab's confidence assessment on the interpolation?"

"Eighty-seven percent," Knuckles replied.

Bill's jaw muscles clenched, though, underneath his beard, no one could tell. "Shit!" he blurted.

"But Bill," Jana said, "This is all history, right? I mean, this project was terminated in 1998. Why are you so upset?"

"Forty-five minutes ago, team two decoded a message from Tzahal, the Israeli Defense Forces. We're not supposed to be listening in on them, but given the current climate, it was deemed necessary. It was an encrypted communique from the Israeli Defense Minister to his Chief of General Staff. It specifically stated *Operation Absolution* was a go."

"Wait," Jana said, "this thing is real? It's active?"

"That's exactly what I'm saying. They're going to invade Lebanon." Bill walked toward his office.

Jana turned to Cade. "I've been out of the loop. What's going on?"

"Yesterday, we got reassigned to work Talia's case, high priority."

"I thought Bill wasn't going to commit resources to that," she said.

"That was before CIA alerted us to the fact that Israeli troops were massing at the border with Lebanon," Cade said. "Heavy armor."

Knuckles looked at her. "And not an hour ago, satellite recon shows they've redeployed a large contingent of their air force to bases in the north, closest to the Lebanese border. They're ramping up for something big."

56

An hour later, Jana walked into Uncle Bill's office. She stopped at the door to find Bill with the phone to his ear. He waved her in. "How are we supposed to know the difference?" he said into the phone. He waited for the reply, then said, "Leslie, that's not good enough. And you can tell him I said that. Goodbye." Bill slammed the phone's handset onto the base with just enough force to cause it to slide on his desk.

"Remind me to not talk to you on the phone," Jana said.

"That was the US embassy in Tel Aviv, Leslie Fineman. She's Deputy Chief of Mission." Bill rubbed his eyes. "We went to school together. She said the secretary of defense and the ambassador got on a call with the Israelis." Bill put his hands on his hips. "They say their military escalation is just a war game."

"And they believe that?"

"Hook, line, and sinker."

"What about you? Do you believe it?"

"I don't know. I just don't know anymore. It's like I told Leslie, there's no way for us to know the difference between a war game and preparations for an invasion. And if the damn Israelis aren't going to communicate this type of thing to us in advance, it pisses me off!"

Jana crossed her arms. "You know this isn't my area. Bureau rarely gets involved overseas."

"I know," Bill said as he shook his head. "I didn't mean to yell at you. But I just, I don't trust them anymore. The Mossad hasn't been exactly forthcoming lately. And I don't like that I just sent Stone and Miss Talia back there. I've got a bad feeling about this. I'm—"

"Getting too old for this shit?" she said with a smirk.

He laughed.

"Maybe it is war games. Maybe they're just flexing their muscles for Hezbollah and Hamas to see. You know, just trying to remind them of what's possible."

"I hope you're right," Bill said.

"And it could be that the interpolation of that microfilm was incorrect anyway."

"Yes, we could be wrong. The problem is, in our line of work, people die when we're wrong."

Jana walked back to her chair. But when she saw something on Knuckles desk, she couldn't help herself. "Is that a new watch, Knuckles? It's lovely. A little feminine for you, isn't it?"

"Huh?" he said. "Oh, the watch. Yeah, very funny. No, one of the interns just brought it over. Someone apparently left it in the conference room."

"Yeah," Cade said, "and the first person they thought of was you."

Knuckles shook his head.

"Hey," Jana said as she stood and picked it up, "isn't this Talia's watch?"

"Oh, yeah," Knuckles said, "I think you're right. She kept rubbing her wrist. She must have taken it off and forgot about it."

Jana studied it a moment. "This looks like hers, but I don't remember it having a two-toned watch band."

"What are you talking about?" Knuckles said as he took the watch from her.

"I remember looking at it," Jana said. "I only noticed it because it's an all-white watch, and set against her dark skin, it stood out. Why is one side of the watch band now pink?"

Knuckles studied the watch band. It was a normal band yet one side had a bright pink stick-on adhesive strip attached to it. His eyes traced the floor as though searching a memory.

"What?" Cade said as he stood.

"This is no fashion statement, it's a PRD." He looked at them and found blank expressions on their faces. "Didn't you ever study? A personal radiation detector. It's a dosimeter that instantly detects radiation exposure. It makes perfect sense. In her line of work, she'd have one of these on her person at all times."

Jana said, "It turns color when it detects radiation?"

"Yes," Knuckles said. "These things are great. They don't require batteries or calibration. They even function even after an electromagnetic pulse."

He started to go on, but Jana waved him off. She took a few steps forward, entranced in the thought. "I swear, this wasn't pink before." But then her eyes widened. It was as if she'd answered her own question. "Oh my God." She turned to them both. "Come on!"

57

Jana ran into Bill's office followed by Knuckles and Cade. "Bill!" she yelled.

Seated behind his desk, Bill startled. "Good Lord, child."

"Look at this!" She handed the watch to him. "It's a—"

"Personal radiation detector," he said as he stood from his chair.

Jana said, "It's Talia's. It's her watch. Bill, that strip wasn't bright pink the other day. I'm sure of it. But now it is. Talia has been exposed to radiation, and I think I know where."

Uncle Bill's eyes squinted as the thoughts played forward. "You don't think—"

"It has to be," she said.

"What?" Cade said.

"The gravesite," Jana said. "Think about it. The Israeli government has a grave exhumed in the middle of the night? We've said all along there had to be something of value in that coffin."

Knuckles said. "You mean?"

"That's exactly what I mean," Jana said. "The microfilm. The operation from 1965 to steal a nuclear device from the *USS Ticonderoga*. What if it succeeded? What if they actually did get that weapon into the coffin and it was shipped to the United States? Don't you get it?"

Uncle Bill shook his head. "That pilot, his plane. The whole thing dumped overboard. Everyone assumed the warhead was attached."

"But it wasn't," Jana said. "They stole it."

"But that coffin has just been shipped back to Israel," Knuckles said.

Jana covered her mouth. "Johnny," she said.

Bill pointed at Cade, "Call John Stone. Get him on the line, right now. Tell him he's walking into a big bear trap. Hurry, son." Cade ran, and Bill yelled after him, "And tell him to get to the embassy! That's the only place they'll be safe in that country." He put his hands on his hips and began pacing the floor, entranced in thought.

As Jana watched him, she couldn't help but notice the similarity in mannerisms between he and Knuckles.

Bill began speaking as if talking to himself. "They steal a weapon in 1965, from us." He mumbled a few things, then said, "Once that coffin was sealed, it would never have been opened again. Then it gets laid to rest at Annapolis. No wonder the Israelis couldn't get to it. That must be why Talia's grandfather told her she had to go to the US and have it exhumed, and sent to Israel."

Jana tried interrupting him. "As a family member, she'd have the legal right to make the request."

But Bill was too deep in concentration.

"They know the weapon is in there," he continued as his arms gestured into the air, "Then, out of the blue, fifty years later, the thing is dug up in the middle of the night?" He stopped and pointed at Knuckles.

"Yes, sir?"

"Get a hazmat team over to the cemetery. I want to know if its safe, and I want to know what nuclear materials, if any, they can detect."

Knuckles ran off.

"There are two pieces missing to this puzzle," Bill said. "One," he held a finger and continued pacing, "the Israelis have plenty of nukes in their arsenal. There must be a specific reason they need that weapon, that particular one. And two, someone had to make the request to exhume. Someone in authority." He looked at Jana. "I've got to make a call."

58

Estate of Moshe Himmelreich

IT WAS the middle of the night. Talia felt her heart pound harder as she watched her bedroom door swing open. She knew who had opened it. Although darkness pervaded everything, a dim light from the hallway illuminated Stone's V-shaped silhouette. He walked in. Neither said a word. The closer he came, the harder her heart pounded. His shirt was off, and she found herself tracing the lines of his torso. He put his arm around her waist and pulled her tight. His hold on her was firm, confident, and she found herself staring at his lips.

As their lips touched, she awoke abruptly and sat bolt upright in bed. It had all been a dream. Morning light streamed in, and she looked around the room, disoriented, but it only took a few moments for her brain to catch up. She knew exactly where she was, her own bedroom, a place she'd slept countless times.

Her breathing rate slowed from its previous pace as she lay her head back on the pillow and put a hand to her heart. She shook her head at how hard it was pounding, then placed the back of her hand on her neck. It was moist with warm heat. "God," she said as she threw the covers off, "where did *that* come from?"

She got up and stretched her hands to the ceiling. As she looked at herself in the full-length mirror, her mind flickered back to the dream, but she shook it off. With all of the events of the last crazy days, she felt out of sorts, as though she had been living someone else's life.

Forty minutes later, she walked down the stairs and into the kitchen. She found Stone sitting at the breakfast table, reading from *Yedioth Tel Aviv*, a local newspaper. Without realizing it, she stopped. Stone looked up and when he noticed her staring said, "What?" He looked at his shirt. "Did I spill something?"

The same wave of heat rose across Talia's neck. "No, nothing." But her feet still didn't move.

"You sure you're okay?" Stone said as Talia dislodged visions of the dream from her mind's eye.

She walked to the refrigerator, a Bompani brand built-in that she recalled had cost Moshe a small fortune. "Fine," she said. She opened the left side door and used it to shield herself from view. Her mind scrambled to come up with a plausible diversion. "You can read Hebrew?" she said.

"What?" He glanced at the paper. "Oh, well, kind of. I wouldn't try to pass the Defense Language Proficiency Test, but I can get by."

Talia pulled out a Tamara yogurt, grabbed a spoon and sat across from him. She peeled the top and took a spoonful. "Military operator, language skills. Any other surprises, how do you say it, up your sleeve?"

Stone's eyes continued tracing words on the page. "Yeah, I also cook."

"Really?" she said.

"Is that so surprising?"

"Is that how you started with Jana? Did you two meet on the beach on Antigua, and you cooked her a romantic meal?"

He folded the paper down so he could see her. "What?"

"Nothing. Um, you didn't get yourself some coffee?"

"I didn't know how to use that thing."

"The koom-koom?" she said, almost laughing. "Stone, it just heats water. There's a button." She pressed the button on the device to turn it on. "Hot water in seconds."

"Hot water to make instant coffee." He shook his head.

Talia unscrewed the lid on a jar with Hebrew writing on it. "Elite Instant isn't that bad. It's what Israelis do in the morning."

"I know, I know. You don't want us to homogenize Israel with a Starbucks on every corner." Stone folded the paper neatly and laid it down.

"I don't think it's safe to go to Mossad HQ. There's a mole. You know it; I know it."

"Agreed."

Stone sat a little more upright. "Well, that's a first."

"But we're still going. I hear what you are saying, but between you and Moshe, and with all the increased security around the place, I don't think anyone is going to come after me."

Stone thought a moment as Talia scooped a heaping spoon of instant coffee into two cups, then began pouring the steaming water onto it. "I have to admit, it's safer that the casket is at Mossad HQ than in some outside holding facility."

"They may not yet know the identity of the man that tried to kill me, but they know what he looks like. There's no way he'd make it in there again."

Moshe walked into the kitchen. He was wearing a three-piece suit and bow tie, a bit of an oddity in Israel, but it suited him. "Ah, my dear, you are up. I'm so glad. I was going to let you sleep." He gave her a hug then made himself a cup of instant.

"My internal time clock is off," Talia replied.

"Well," Moshe said, "you've had something to eat? Both of you? When we're done with our morning cup, we'll go see what secrets are inside that casket. Kind of exciting, don't you think?" But when he saw the look in Talia's eye, he stopped. "Oh, I'm so sorry, my dear. How insensitive of me." He patted her forearm. "Your poor great uncle. Such a tragedy. To be killed at such an early age? A heroic fighter pilot, from what they say."

"It's okay, Aba," she replied. "Let's go. I want to get this over with."

Moshe tossed back his remaining coffee. "You are welcome to ride with me."

"No need, Mr. Himmelreich," Stone said. "We can just meet you inside."

"Please. Moshe. Call me Moshe."

Stone nodded. "But there is one more thing, sir?" Stone said. "As you're certainly aware, the United States government has taken an interest in the security of Miss Stiel. As assigned protective detail, it is my directive to stay with her at all times. If you could make sure I'm cleared into Mossad HQ, that would be most appreciated."

"It would be my pleasure," Moshe said, his tone almost giddy. "But it's hardly necessary. Anyone that comes through security with me is cleared."

"But probably not anyone carrying a concealed weapon."

Moshe's face flattened. "Oh. A very good point you raise. Yes, I'll take care of it. We are ready, no?" He set his coffee on the counter and was out the door.

Talia smiled as she watched him.

"Kind of happy, isn't he?" Stone asked.

"All my life."

59

Mossad Headquarters, Tel Aviv, Israel

ALTHOUGH IT HAD TAKEN several minutes to clear the security checkpoint, Moshe, Talia, and Stone finally walked through and continued down a corridor.

"Well, that was fun," Talia said, referring to the grilling Stone had received about his concealed firearm.

"Serves them right," Stone replied. "Moshe told them to expect me, that I was an armed contractor. But they still had to give me grief."

"It's over now," Talia said. "Aba, where are we going?"

"Secure storage area three. A lovely place. Have you not been?"

"No," Talia said, "I didn't know we had secure storage areas."

"Not to worry, my dear," Moshe said as he turned and almost speed-walked toward a set of elevators. Once there, he set his chin onto a small tray and waited as a digital light scanned his retina. A moment later, the doors wafted open.

As the three boarded the elevator, Talia half-kidded with him. "How come I don't have access to anywhere that requires a retinal scan?"

Moshe swiped his identity card across a reader and the doors closed. "All in good time, my dear. All in good time."

The elevator descended several floors. When the doors re-opened, they were in a large, dimly lit underground storage facility. The area was subdivided into bays with tall chain link fencing securing each. Talia took note that even the ceilings of each bay were enclosed in fence material.

"Here we are," Moshe said as he walked them down a long aisle. "Underground storage facility three. Isn't it wonderful?"

"Charming," Stone said as he looked around.

Moshe led them deeper down the row. "We house all kinds of things. Most of them, temporarily, of course. But one never knows what secrets are hidden in these crates." He smiled at Talia. "You'll notice there's no access to this level from the outside. We are four floors below ground. All of this is brought down on freight elevators." He glanced at the small metal signs denoting each bay. "308, 309. Ah yes, here we are. Bay 310."

Talia placed a hand on his arm. "This is it?"

"Yes, my dear," Moshe replied.

And referring to the Judaic week-long period of mourning she said, "He's alone? No one is sitting *shiva*?"

Moshe said, "But his body, he's not here, my dear."

"I know that, Aba. But this is all we have left of him." She un-tucked the right side of her shirt and began yanking at the seam with both hands. She wrenched at it until it tore, a symbolic act known in Jewish circles as the first step in the acceptance of grief.

He inserted a key into a standard padlock and unlocked it, then pushed the chain link door open. When he did so, it sounded like metal on unlubricated metal. The bay was about twelve feet wide and equally as deep. Even though the lighting was poor, it was obvious the bay contained but a single item, a long coffin-shaped crate, covered in a heavy canvas tarp.

Talia stared at it. For just a moment, her breathing stopped. Her uncle had perished off the East China Sea. His casket, empty of anything other than his footlocker, had traveled first to the Philippines, then to the United States, a journey of 7,500 miles. And yet here it was, sitting in the heart of Israel after a 5,800-mile journey from the US Naval Academy.

Her mood darkened. Gone was the earlier smile on her face. Gone was the feeling of excitement at what she might discover. And gone was the sound of their earlier footsteps, echoing on the cement floor.

Suddenly, Talia felt very alone, as though she was about to meet her uncle for the first time, a glimpse into a past she had never known.

Moshe stood with his hands joined and waited.

The three walked in, and Talia stood next to the tarp. It was drab tan in color and in the poor lighting, it looked like a death shroud. Talia shivered.

She spoke, and her voice came out clipped, quiet. "Won't it be," her voice had cracked, and she cleared her throat. ". . . degraded?"

Moshe answered. "The casket itself was protected by a cement burial vault. The outside, at least, is very well preserved."

Stone opened his mouth as if to say something, but then stopped.

Talia turned to Moshe. "You've seen it?"

Moshe hesitated then said, "When I learned it was in transit to Israel, I ordered the Flag of Israel be affixed around it. It has remained sealed since the passing of your uncle."

She nodded.

"May I?" Moshe said as he motioned to Stone. The two men walked to either side of the tarp and waited for Talia. When she nodded, they gently lifted the tarp and set it behind. The casket was indeed, covered in a blue and white Israeli burial flag fitted to wrap the entire surface.

Talia stared a moment, and her eyes became glassy. In her vision, the casket itself stayed in sharp focus, but everything around it, including Stone and Moshe, faded into a blur. Her eyes traced the edges.

"Why did you order the Flag of Israel placed on it?" she said, her eyes never leaving the large Star of David on top.

"I'm sorry?" Moshe replied.

"He was an officer of the United States Navy," she said, almost whispering.

Moshe seemed to stumble for words. "Oh, well, the American flag is underneath."

Stone narrowed his eyes at Moshe a moment.

"Go ahead," she said, whispering. "Take it off."

Stone and Moshe knelt down at their respective ends and pulled back the Israeli flag. They held it by the corners and walked toward one another. Stone took the ends from Moshe and folded the flag, then set it aside. Beneath the Israeli flag lay an American flag. The colors of the flag were faded to a point that one had to stand just above it to make out the stars and stripes.

Stone said, "This would have been the original flag, draped over the casket at his service. He was buried with full military honors." He looked at her. "Normally, the flag is removed though and given to the family."

Talia nodded, and a single tear rolled off her cheek. "He had no family in America." The men picked up the American flag and Stone folded it into a neat triangle, then tucked the end tightly.

"Why do you do that?" Talia said. "Fold it that way?"

Stone said, "Each of the thirteen folds has significance. The triangular shape represents a tri-cornered hat, symbolic of those worn by colonial soldiers during our war for independence. The stripes are wrapped until they cover the blue, representing the light of day vanishing into the darkness of night."

"That's beautiful," Talia said. Her throat tightened, and another tear fell. "This is ridiculous," she said as she wiped it. "I didn't even know him."

Neither man spoke.

Talia cleared her throat. "Please."

"Are you sure, my dear?" Moshe offered.

Talia nodded.

Moshe said to Stone, "I asked them to leave a pry bar here."

Stone reached behind the casket and picked a heavy metal bar off the floor. He came around to the front and knelt down and inspected the seam closer. After a moment, he inserted the flat end of the prybar, then applied pressure. The lid of the casket popped open with little fight. Though Talia's eyes were mesmerized by the opening of the lid, she couldn't help but notice Stone turn to her with a confused look. He opened the lid fully and let it lean in the upright position.

Talia stepped closer and peered inside. The padded, silk lining had turned brown and fallen from the sides of the interior. Some had been reduced to nothing but dust.

She looked at the only object inside, a footlocker about three and a half feet long. It was made of sturdy plywood which at one time had been painted black. The corners and edges were covered in metal stripping and what had once been leather handles protruded from both sides. Though the paint had chipped and flaked badly, the name of her great uncle was still visible across the top. It had been spray-painted in white sixty years prior.

Talia read the words.

STIEL, GOLAN DAVID
LIEUTENANT, J.G. 0-1684920

SHE STOOD a moment then ran the backs of her fingers across the name. Suddenly, everything had become very real.

60

US Embassy, Tel Aviv, Israel

Talia and Stone followed the two SEALs onto an elevator and down to the sub-basement level. They walked down a long corridor. At the end of the hall were two Marine guards standing post outside a steel door.

As they walked in, the first SEAL said, "This is the Situation Room. Authorized personnel only."

Talia hesitated a moment as if to wait outside.

"Oh, no, ma'am. We need you, too," the SEAL said.

Inside were several embassy employees along with Leslie Fineman, the US Embassy's Deputy Chief of Mission. They were on a video conference call and watching a large monitor at the front of the windowless room. On the monitor was a view into the NSA's war room where Uncle Bill and several men in uniform were gathered around an oblong conference table.

"I know that," Fineman said, apparently speaking to Uncle Bill Tarleton, "but the ambassador says there's no way they're going to back down. The Israelis believe there's a threat, and that the threat is headed straight to their northern border."

"Leslie," Bill said, "they've massed tens of thousands of troops along the northern border, and their air force has deployed the bulk of its fighters, fighter-bombers, and long-range bombers there as well. We estimate they've deployed over eighty percent of their military strike capacity onto the border with Lebanon."

"We know that. But they've detected a threat, and the ambassador says—"

Bill stood from the head of the table in the war room. "Consider the timing. The Israeli military mobilized days ago, before this supposed nuclear threat was detected. Think about that for a minute. How did Israel detect a nuclear weapon deep within Lebanon before they detected it? Something stinks here. The timing doesn't add up. They geared up for a full-scale invasion of Lebanon, and now they're using the nuclear threat as an excuse."

Leslie Fineman leaned back in her chair. To Talia, she looked as though she was thinking over what Bill had said. "The Israelis told the ambassador they had been conducting war games."

Bill walked closer to the video camera on his side.

"Leslie, we go back a long ways. I know you. Your bullshit detector is even more sensitive than mine. I've got a bad feeling. Israel and Lebanon have been at odds for decades. It's no secret the Israelis would like to wipe out Hezbollah and Hamas to secure their northern border. In the past, they've conducted extensive bombing campaigns into Lebanon to combat terrorist rocket attacks, but if ground forces invade," he said as he shook his head, "it will be a wholesale slaughter. Women, children, grandmothers. We've got to do something." Bill waited a moment as he watched Fineman's response. "Leslie," he said as he looked into the camera. "Have I *ever* steered you wrong?"

Fineman looked at the monitor a moment. "What about that Bayesian Statistics lab?" She was trying to make light of a tense situation and Bill knew it. Before he could speak, she held up a hand. "You've convinced me. I'll call the ambassador. But even if he presses them, the Israelis are not easily swayed. We need a contingency plan."

"What we need," Bill said, "is to be able to prove conclusively the weapon they're tracking is ours. You combine direct evidence that it's our nuclear weapon and tie it to their covert operation to steal it in the first place—"

Fineman snapped her fingers and pointed at the monitor. "Exactly. If we could do that, the Israelis would call off the invasion."

"We've got to find that weapon," Bill said.

From the back of the room, Talia said, "I can find it."

Everyone turned and looked.

Talia walked forward. "I can track it. It's my technology that's being used to track this device in the first place. If I can get back into Mossad headquarters, I can track it." She turned to the two Navy SEALs. "And direct you where to go."

"That could work," Bill said. From within the NSA war room, he turned to the table of uniformed men. "Admiral Mears? What assets are in the area?"

Mears replied, "We can't just send in the Teams on a whim. I agree on the strike priority, but I'm not sending men into a big bear trap. This has got to be planned."

One of the SEALs spoke, "All due respect, Admiral. We live, eat, and breathe under the philosophy *no plan survives first contact*. We're out of time. If we wait, it will be too late."

The admiral looked down and appeared to be pondering the statement. He nodded. "God help us all. The *Abraham Lincoln* is off Cyprus. About one hundred nautical miles from the coast of Lebanon. You'll get your tasking shortly."

"We'll take it from here, Leslie," Bill said, "but get the ambassador on board. We're talking about sending a team into Lebanon. If the Israelis move, the first thing they'll look to do is take out that device. I don't want our people in harm's way any more than they have to be."

One of the SEALs spoke, "All in a day's pay, sir."

"It's settled," Fineman said. She then turned to the two SEALs. "If you succeed, you'll be saving tens of thousands of lives, maybe more."

"If you'll excuse us, ma'am? Got an MH-60 Seahawk heating up on the roof."

They started to walk out, but Fineman stopped them, "Gentlemen?"

They turned back.

"Godspeed."

61

NSA Command Center

CADE DIALED Stone's phone number for the seventh time. "Uncle Bill, all it says is the caller is out of the service area, then it goes to voicemail."

"Well, keep trying son," Bill replied. "Knuckles, did you get anything off that recovered cell phone?"

Knuckles sat at his desk with a hand on the mouse and staring at the monitor. "Yes, sir." The phone Stone found at the scene of the shooting incident at his apartment lay on the desk. Knuckles had disassembled the broken phone, and three wires were now connected to various internal components. "This is, this is bad," the boy said.

"Spit it out son," Bill said as he pressed his glasses to his face. But upon seeing the phone and its various parts splayed across the desk added, "Jesus, I didn't look at it when it came in. Is that what I think it is?"

Knuckles replied, "Yes, sir. A Boeing Black."

Cade slid closer. "It's a smartphone. What's the big deal?"

Knuckles was almost incredulous. "What's the big deal? This phone was developed by Boeing Corporation in collaboration with Blackberry and the Defense Information Systems Agency. Along with the secure mobile solution they developed, it's almost impenetrable. There's no data that lives on these devices. The only people that can buy them are governments or the military. The system works by using the handset to access a remote server on the JWICS network."

"Ah, professor?" Cade said.

But Knuckles was unabated. "Dual SIM cards enable it to access multiple cell networks, and the thing can be configured to connect with biometric sensors and satellites. The phone itself is just a keyboard that sends signals to the server where all the real data is stored." He clicked the mouse a few times. "That off-the-shelf commercial piece of crap you carry has an enormous attack surface. Those phones are vulnerable as hell. But Boeing and the DOD came together to create this system. They started with a heavily stripped-down version of Android to avoid unneeded security risks. For example, this thing doesn't support MMS and can't connect to those stupid Bluetooth earbud things you use to listen to Brittany Spears with. The encryption keys are generated automatically on the device in a random pattern. It's a beautiful piece of work."

Cade smirked. "Brittany Spears? I still don't see what the big deal—"

But Uncle Bill removed his own cell phone from the front pocket of his cavernous slacks, a pair he'd probably owned since 1985. He held it up for Cade to see. It too was a Boeing Black.

Oh," Cade said. He looked at Knuckles. "Know-it-all."

"All right, boys," Bill said.

"Sorry, sir," Cade said. "But, if the device itself doesn't store any data, then what are you trying to get off of it?"

"Not trying," Knuckles said, "doing. I had to replace the Tegra chip because it was damaged."

"Where did you get one of those?" Uncle Bill asked.

"Got a buddy from Georgetown that works at Nvidia."

Bill nodded.

"I've obfuscated the phone's broken screen onto my laptop. I'm tapped into the JWICS server, so we're seeing the decrypted version. It's what the phone would see."

Uncle Bill and Cade looked closer. Knuckles scrolled his mouse across the monitor through a series of secure text communications on the phone's messaging application.

They read through a conversation between the assassin and a contact codenamed "Vipera" which detailed the various movements of the assassin's apparent target, Talia Stiel. Bill shook his head. "Christ, that doesn't leave much to the imagination. These phones are only available to our intelligence services and a few of our allies. Who the hell does this guy work for?"

Special Agent Jana Baker walked up and leaned over the monitor. "A little light reading, gentlemen?" But as her eyes traced the string of messages, a set of encrypted communications between the assassin assigned to kill Talia and his handler, her demeanor shifted.

Knuckles scrolled to the last few messages. "The conversation string we've just read was sent before the attack at Stone's apartment. But the time stamp on these next few incoming messages indicates they were sent after that time."

Jana said, "Which means the assassin never got them, correct?"

"That's right," Knuckles said. "He apparently lost the phone when he jumped through a third story window. This first one," the boy said as he pointed at the monitor, "was sent just after the firefight."

VIPERA:
Status?

"AND THESE WERE SENT the following day." Knuckles read them aloud.

VIPERA:
Rabbit is out of pocket.

"WHEN THERE WAS NO RESPONSE, he sends:"

VIPERA:
Rabbit in Tel Aviv.

JANA SAID TO UNCLE BILL. "I've heard you guys use the term Rabbit before."

Bill replied, "In covert parlance, it's slang for 'target.'"

"Again, because the asset doesn't have his phone anymore," Knuckles continued, "the handler is still getting no response."

"But how does the handler know she's in Tel Aviv?" Jana added. "Nobody knows she's in Tel Aviv."

The next message read:

VIPERA:
New clipper assigned.

"WHOA," Bill said as his eyes perked.

"Clipper?" Jana said.

It was Knuckles who answered. "Assassin. Since the handler is getting no response, he's assigned a new assassin to Talia.

"Dammit, Cade," Bill said, "can't you get Stone on the horn?"

"I've been calling and calling," Cade replied. "The switch log at the air base has him checking out a Hummer at zero-one-thirty hours, then they drove off-post. I've tried tracking the phone. I've got nothing."

Jana drew in a breath. "You don't think he's dead, do you?"

"No need to assume the worst," Bill said. He looked over the top of his glasses at Cade. "Get me the US embassy in Tel Aviv. I want to talk to the ambassador, and I want to talk to him right now."

Cade spun around to his desk and picked up the phone as Knuckles read the last message, one that had been sent hours later:

VIPERA:
Your private liability up to date?

BILL EXHALED. "THEM, TOO."

Jana said, "What does that mean?"

Bill rubbed his eyes. "Ever since the Iran Contra affair in the 1980s, when the Reagan administration had authorized a covert action that was later deemed illegal, CIA field operatives began buying their own private liability insurance."

"Why?" Jana asked.

"Because when the political winds change, the covert action you were authorized to perform can sometimes be deemed illegal. If that happens, the agency will not back you with a lawyer."

"You've *got* to be kidding me," Jana said.

Bill added, "The handler is apparently letting the assassin know he's been disavowed."

They turned as Cade's voice escalated both in volume and sharpness. "What do you mean the ambassador is out of pocket? . . . Then who is the senior-most . . . then wake him!" Cade belted into the phone.

Bill smiled. "Looks like that young man's got some fight in him."

Cade turned with the phone to his ear. "The ambassador is on a flight to Washington. Best I can do is the Deputy Chief of Mission."

"That'll be fine, son," Bill whispered to Jana. "But it's a her, not a him."

Cade said into the phone, "Yes, thank you. Please hold for NSA Section Chief, William Tarleton." Cade handed the phone to Bill.

"Leslie?" Uncle Bill said into the phone. "What's it been, twenty years? I know we talked yesterday. I was just making small talk, you know, breaking the ice. How are you?"

Jana walked closer and smiled at the banter.

"Oh no, it hasn't. It's been thirty years since we've actually seen one another? Good Lord. . . What? oh, well, no need to bring that old story up again."

In a rare display of emotion, Bill laughed until tears formed in his eyes.

"No, no, that was all you."

But after a moment, Jana noticed the change in his tone.

"Leslie," Bill went on, "I've got a situation here. I need a favor. . ." He covered the phone and glanced at Cade. "Secure line?"

Cade nodded his ascent.

"Here's the sitrep. I've got an operative in country with a national, a friendly. Listen, we've lost comms, and they're about to walk into a whirlwind. . . Uh huh, uh huh."

Bill nodded to Jana as the Deputy Chief spoke.

"You do? Well, that would be great. It would save me an hour of red tape and those same assets would have probably been tasked anyway.

You're a lifesaver, Les. Okay . . . yes, let's do that. She'd love to see you too. Talk soon." Bill hung up then looked at the others.

"Well?" Jana said.

"The embassy has two MLEs on station. She's going to brief them now. Cade, send the embassy a package so they know who they're looking for."

Jana shook her head. "And I thought the Bureau was heavy on acronyms. MLEs?"

"Military Liaison Elements," Uncle Bill replied.

But Knuckles jumped at the opportunity. "Most US embassies traditionally include defense attaches and other military personnel. They report to the Defense Intelligence Agency. The teams are typically comprised of Army Green Berets or Rangers, but Navy SEALs are used as well, and specialized marine and air force units."

Bill said, "She's got two SEALs on-site. They're stationed there to gather intel and assist in counter-terrorism operations. They'll now be tasked to find Stone and Miss Stiel." Bill exhaled. "I'll feel better when those two are safe."

"We all will," Jana said. But then a devious little grin formed on her face. "Bill? You seemed awfully friendly with the deputy chief."

Uncle Bill cleared his throat. "Well," he said, "there wasn't *always* a Mrs. Uncle Bill," then walked off.

62

Mossad HQ, Secure Storage Facility

"Are you ready, my dear?" Moshe said to Talia as she stared at the footlocker.

She nodded.

The footlocker was closed tight by two folding clasps and a hinged lock. All three showed significant rust. Stone flipped open the folding clasps then said, "I'm going to have to pry this lock off." Talia nodded again, and Stone inserted the pry bar onto the locking mechanism and popped it open. He then slowly opened the lid. The aged metal hinges creaked in high pitched protest.

The smell of must and degraded lacquer wafted out. The footlocker was filled with various items, all tucked perfectly into place. The top was a removable drawer, subdivided into sections. On it were undershirts rolled into tubular form, all neatly snugged together. Two belt buckles were affixed to degraded woven belts. A knife, various toiletry items including a plastic comb nestled within its own case, a pair of gloves, and a small sewing kit.

Stone picked up the drawer and set it aside. In the lower compartment were military uniforms, khaki slacks, shirts, and a pair of dress shoes. A stack of envelopes containing letters, bound with twine had been stuffed in between along with several yellowed newspaper clippings. But one item stood out above the others, a leather flight jacket.

Talia picked up the folded jacket, the prized possession of every fighter pilot. The dark brown leather, once rich and supple, was cracked beyond repair. Talia unfolded it gently and looked closer at the yellowed patches that adorned the front, sleeves, and back. On one arm was a triangular patch with a likeness of the aircraft carrier. It read:

FAR EAST CRUISE, 1964-65
JAPAN, PHILIPPINES, VIETNAM
USS TICONDEROGA, CVA 14

THE ONE below it was circular and depicted a likeness of the globe split into two parts. It read:

USS TICONDEROGA
IN MARE IN CAELESTIS
GUARDIAN OF FREEDOM

TALIA SAID, "*IN MARE, IN CAELESTIS*?"

Stone's tone was reserved, reverent. "On sea, in air."

SHE FLIPPED THE JACKET OVER. On the back stitched-on letters read.

CVA-59

THERE WAS ALSO a single round patch. The patch depicted a large sailing vessel and read:

TONKIN GULF YACHT CLUB

AND BELOW IT, words that had been embroidered into the leather:

VIETNAM GULF OF TONKIN
1965

BUT WHEN TALIA folded the jacket across her arm, she glanced back to the footlocker and for the first time noticed photographs affixed to the underside of the lid.

"Oh," she said as she tilted the lid further back, exposing the underside to the dim overhead light. "Look at this." She knelt down and gazed at the images. There were four in all, each of the same woman. "She's beautiful," Talia said. The trim young woman had long brunette hair. The once-vivid Kodachrome photos depicted the woman in various poses, one in a skimpy, patterned bikini. "He must have been in love."

She picked up the stack of bound envelopes and thumbed through them. There were dozens. Each had been addressed by hand in neat feminine handwriting. Talia stared at them a moment. "Love letters," she whispered.

"Those should stay with you," Stone said. He motioned to the footlocker, "All of this is yours."

Talia looked at the personal effects, and another tear bulged from her eyelid. The love letters, photographs, newspaper clippings, and flight jacket were all she would take. Talia's throat tightened. "1965, the Vietnam war was heating up, wasn't it?"

Stone nodded while Moshe stood with his hands clasped.

"He was a soldier in the midst of a war," she said. "They were separated." She looked up at Stone. "He was serving his new country, and they murdered him for it." Her throat choked tight, and as she cried, Stone placed a gentle hand on her shoulder. "Why? So Israel could try to get its hands on its precious nuclear device?" She held one of the photos to Stone. "Look at her. Can you imagine being told your lover and his plane were dumped into the sea, in an *accident*?"

Neither of the men spoke.

Talia stood with the items in her hands. "And for Golan, can you imagine how terrifying it must have been? One second, you're in the cockpit being raised to the flight deck, the next, you're falling off the side of the ship? How horrible."

"Talia," Stone said as he approached her, "don't do this to yourself."

But she was unabated. "No! He was buried at sea, alive! Did you ever stop to think about that? What he went through? With the cockpit closed, the plane would have sunk like a rock, headed straight to the bottom. He would have been strapped in. Even if he tried, there would have been no way to get the canopy open. My God, he would have known. He would have known the plane was sinking, deeper and deeper. And then, the canopy would have crushed under the pressure. How many minutes? How many minutes do you think he had? Two, three?"

She was looking for an answer, one Stone did not have.

She looked at one of the photos of the girl again. "I bet he had a picture of her in the cockpit with him. I want the American flag placed at the head. I think he would have wanted it that way."

Stone complied then gently closed the footlocker. He lowered the lid of the casket. Both he and Moshe picked up the Israeli flag and began to snug it over the coffin.

But Talia held up her hand. "The Land does not deserve to cover my uncle. America might not be my homeland, but it was his. Israel has no right to him. And there is to be no hiding it underneath a tarp." Her sobbing came out quietly. After a moment, she stopped, her eyes locked on the casket. "They will sit *shiva*, starting today and not ending for the traditional seven days. After that, I want his casket laid to rest at Mount Herzl, with full military honors."

"Of course, my dear," Moshe replied.

They followed as she walked out the gated enclosure. She turned one last time and whispered, "Goodbye, Uncle Golan."

63

"Radiometry reports are in, sir," Knuckles said as he walked into Uncle Bill's office. "FBI's hazmat team just dropped them off."

"From the cemetery?"

"Yes, sir," Knuckles replied as he handed the sealed manila envelope to Bill.

Bill tore into it and pulled out the report, then read. After a moment he dropped it onto his desk and removed his glasses. "I hate it when I'm right."

"What is it?"

"The gravesite and storage unit at the cemetery show trace elements of enriched uranium. It's consistent with the type used in the warhead of a B43 nuclear bomb."

"The same type stolen from the *USS Ticonderoga*?"

"Exactly," Bill said. "They say the nuclear signature in the soil is nominal. Just to be safe, they're going to shut down the cemetery while they do a soil removal and decontamination. But it's not bad. The weapon is apparently intact."

"There's no doubt then," Knuckles said. "The warhead was inside that coffin."

Bill rubbed his temples. "I'm definitely getting too old for this shit."

64

Mossad Headquarters

TALIA, Stone, and Moshe rode the elevator back to the main floor. By the time the elevator opened, Moshe's phone rang. They walked into the corridor as he answered.

"Moshe Himmelreich," he said. Then Moshe stopped. "Can you repeat that?" he said as he pressed the phone harder to his ear. "It's where?"

Talia studied the concern on his face. "Aba?" she said.

"Are you sure?" Moshe continued. "All right. Has the prime minister been informed?" Moshe listened with intent then looked at his wristwatch. "Four minutes. On my way." He hung up.

"Aba, what's wrong?"

He flicked a glance at Stone then pulled Talia to the side. "It's happened," he whispered. "A nuclear device has been detected, and it's headed this way."

Talia covered her mouth. "You can't be serious." She stared at him a moment. "Where?"

"On the coast, off Sidon, Saida Port."

Talia's eyes scanned back and forth. "Sidon, Lebanon? But that's—"

"About fifty kilometers from our border, I know. I've got to go." But before speed walking away, he took her by the shoulders. "We have you to thank for this, Talia. Your technology is what detected the weapon, and it just might save us all." He was gone.

"What was that about?" Stone said.

She stood, staring after Moshe. "They've used my technology to successfully detect a terrorist weapon. It's in Lebanon, heading this way." She shook her head. "It's happening. It's actually happening."

"How far?"

"Fifty kilometers. It's on the coast. If it really is there, they won't let it get close." Talia let the thoughts play forward in her mind. "Oh, Stone, I never thought about the consequences."

"Of?"

"All I thought about was *detecting* a weapon, not what would happen if we actually found one. Oh, God. They'll carpet-bomb the area. And that means a lot of civilian casualties."

"Weren't your parents killed by a Hezbollah bomb?"

"Yes. I've hated those people my whole life. But not everyone in Lebanon is a terrorist. There are children, mothers."

"Hey, you did your job. Sometimes that's all a person can do. And think of the alternative. If you hadn't developed your technology, that nuke could have slipped through the border, and then been detonated."

"I know. I mean, I knew I would be able to make the technology work, I just never thought. . ."

"Sounds like you made it work just in time. Right now, we need to concentrate on the issue at hand."

In her distraction, Talia had almost lost sight of what that was.

"We came here looking for that casket. And now that we've found it, it's time to get you out. There's a mole somewhere inside the Mossad, and until Moshe's internal investigation routes him out, it's too dangerous for us to be here."

From behind Talia, a man dressed in a black business suit and tie approached. Stone's eyes zipped across his frame.

"Dr. Stiel?" the man said with a smile.

Talia startled at first but then smiled politely. "Yes?"

He held up a set of Mossad credentials. "Dr. Himmelreich asked me to look in on you. Would you both come with me, please?"

She looked at Stone as if to check if it was okay. "Where are we going?"

As they began to walk, he said, "Dr. Himmelreich feels until the internal investigation is completed, you'd be safer away from your office or the lab. He also mentioned he'll need to consult with you about the current developments. I assume he talked to you about that? I think he has some technical questions about the technology you developed."

"Yes, he did."

"Right this way," the man said as he led them through the crowded corridors.

Stone glanced at a bulge on the man's back right hip, underneath his business jacket. "How long have you known Dr. Himmelreich?" Stone said.

"I don't, really," the man replied. "I know *of* him, of course."

"And what do you do for the Mossad?" Stone said.

"Oh, this and that," he said with a smile.

As they reached a bank of elevators, Stone stopped the man with a hand. "I'm afraid I'm going to have to know more than that."

"Stone?" Talia said.

But Stone didn't flinch and the man glared at him a moment. "It's all right, Dr. Stiel," the man said, though his tone was not quite as pleasant. As he pressed the down button, he locked eyes with Stone. "Given the ordeal you've been through, I would expect no less of your security officer. I am Kidon, Mr. Stone."

Stone's focus narrowed, "I wasn't aware the Mossad's counterterrorism unit was involved in escort duties."

"Stone, you're embarrassing me," Talia said.

"Then let's dispense with the pleasantries," the man replied. "I am security, Mr. Stone. Dr. Stiel is under direct threat." The elevator doors wafted open. "And she needs protection. Now, if you will come with me, please?" He stepped onto the elevator, pressed a button, and held the door for them.

Talia looked at Stone. "What is wrong with you?"

"I don't ignore my gut instincts," Stone said.

"Neither do I," Talia replied as she walked into the elevator.

Stone held the door open himself and stared at the man.

"Are you coming?" the man said. When Stone didn't move, he continued. "Up here, she is exposed. Where we are going, she is protected."

Stone said, "You leave me little choice," and stepped into the elevator.

65

As the elevator descended into the below-ground levels, Stone stood between Talia and the door, a position of protection, and kept his eye on the man. But an instant before the doors wafted open, Stone saw the man crunch his eyes shut and cover his ears.

Stone let out a guttural scream. "Talia, down!"

But it was too late. The elevator doors opened, and a small metal canister hit the floor. The burst of light and cacophonous boom erupted from it so quickly there wasn't time to react.

Two men standing in front of the doors simultaneously fired Taser guns at Stone. Talia let out a blood-curdling scream as four dart-like electrodes slammed into Stone's chest at 28,000 feet per second. They impaled the flesh and delivered an instantaneous dose of 1,200 volts each.

Stone's body convulsed uncontrollably under the shock wave and he collapsed, unconscious.

Talia was pinned behind Stone, and she screamed again. The man on the elevator grabbed her by the hair and pulled her out. She kicked and flailed, but he yanked one of her arms behind her and applied upward pressure, gripping her hair to wrench her neck back. Talia screamed and winced at the pain. He force-walked her into the open side door of a white van. Adrenaline exploded into her veins, and her entire body began to shake.

The two other men dragged Stone's unconscious body to the van and threw him inside. To Talia, it looked like they were tossing a sack of potatoes. They then jumped in and slammed the door closed. The van's engine roared to life, and the tires barked against the polished cement.

Talia cowered away from the men, and her screaming continued.

"Shut her up," the driver said. The men grabbed her and used duct tape to cover her mouth and bind her hands behind her back. Her screams continued in earnest, but underneath the duct tape, they were muffled. "And make sure he's contained. I don't want him coming to and causing a problem." The men duct taped Stone as well.

Talia was forced onto the floor of the van. It was as though the men wanted to keep her out of sight. The van squealed around the tight turns of the parking deck. They reached an exit, and the van cleared past the security checkpoint. It drove into the stark daylight outside Mossad Headquarters and sped onto the street.

Talia's vision began to spin as a bout of vertigo ensued. Recognizing its intensity, she tried to inhale as deeply as possible, but since her mouth was covered, it was difficult. The dizziness increased, and a wave of nausea overtook her. *No*, she thought, *I can't throw up now. I'll suffocate.* Just the thought of it horrified her. She looked at Stone as the men rolled him onto his side and plucked four Taser darts from his chest. The van's speed suddenly increased, and the vehicle took one turn, then another, each in rapid succession.

"What are you doing?" one of the men seated over Talia said.

"We've got company," the driver said as he jammed his foot onto the accelerator.

"What?" the man in the back said. "That's impossible."

But as he looked out, he heard the roar of a military-grade Humvee engine just before it slammed into the side of the van. The van swerved, and the driver fought to maintain control. The armored Humvee slammed into the van's side again, and this time, the van spun sideways. It jumped the curb, flipped once, then crashed into a brick building before coming to a halt on its side.

In the melee, Talia could barely register what was happening. She was conscious but now lay at the bottom of a crumpled heap of bodies atop the sliding door which was jammed against the sidewalk beneath it. The weight of at least two people was atop top her, and she struggled to breathe. She heard the screeching of brakes then men outside, yelling something in English. The rear doors of the cargo van flung open, and a Kevlar-laden operator leapt in with an automatic weapon forward.

Another operator yanked open the driver's door from above and dropped into the interior atop the van's driver whose body had fallen to the passenger side. The operator cracked the butt end of an automatic weapon across the driver's jaw knocking him into a daze.

Talia could see between the seat and door jam as the operator, a brown-haired, bearded man wearing a heavy flack jacket jammed a needle into the driver's neck and depressed the plunger. The driver's eyes flickered, then closed.

Within moments, bodies were pulled off of her, and one of the operators grabbed her up and laid her face-first over his shoulder. "You're safe now," he said with an American accent. He hoisted her out of the vehicle and ran to the Humvee. As she dangled over his shoulder, she could see the other operator carrying Stone out as well.

The Humvee doors slammed closed, and the vehicle sped away. The rescue operation had taken only seconds.

66

Stone's eyes opened into sterile, fluorescent light. He found himself lying on a padded medical table in a room that looked like a physician's office. His eyes blinked once, then again as he focused on his surroundings. He was disoriented and woozy like he had been drugged. But that was nothing compared to the intense soreness permeating every muscle of his body. The relative calm of his awakening, however, didn't last.

He sat bolt upright on the exam table and clutched at his chest with his hands, looking for whatever objects had slammed into him. He was bare-chested and felt four raw, painful cut-like incisions. *Talia*! He thought. He had no idea where he was, and his next thought was *Weapon. I need a weapon.*

He stood and went first to the window, but when he looked out, he was shocked at what he saw. An expansive view of the ocean, almost as if he were in a resort hotel.

He looked down to find he was in a building just across a busy road from the beach. He estimated himself to be about four stories off the ground. The more he scanned the beach and street, the more he recognized he was in Tel Aviv.

And something else about the area triggered his memory. Just past the street, which abutted the building, and before the sand started, was a wide stone walkway about thirty feet in width. Tiles laid in circular patterns dotted the walkway which ran the distance of the beach in either direction.

"Wait a minute," he said to himself. "Am I in the—"

The door opened, and a man wearing a white lab coat with light brown hair smiled at him. "Oh, good, you're up," the man said in an accent telltale of the American northeast. "How do you feel?"

"Am I in the US embassy?"

"I take it you've been here before," the physician said. "Here, have a seat. You probably shouldn't be up yet. Let's take a look at you."

Stone wobbled toward him but said, "Where's Talia? Where's Talia Stiel?"

"Oh, Miss Stiel is here. She's fine. Take a seat." But when Stone didn't move, he said, "Believe me, she's fine. I just examined her. She's a little banged up from the accident, that's all." The physician removed a stethoscope that had been draped over his neck and motioned to the table. "Seriously, the drugs are still coursing your system."

Stone sat on the exam table, and the doctor pressed the stethoscope to his chest and listened. "What happened?" Stone said. "One second we were on an elevator, then, I don't know. I remember a flash-bang."

"Well," the doctor said, "I don't really know. You were unconscious when you arrived. The four marks on your chest, however, are consistent with Taser darts."

Stone tried to think back to the incident. "Four? I've been Tased before, as part of training, but it doesn't knock you unconscious. How long have I been out?"

The doctor moved the bell of the stethoscope to different parts of his chest. "You are right about that. It doesn't normally cause a person to lose cognitive process. When they brought you in, at first, I thought you had suffered a head injury, but that turned out to not be the case. Best I can tell is those Taser darts delivered a dose of incapacitant with them. We won't know which one until the tox results come back. Hey, where in the States are you from?"

"I need to see Talia Stiel."

"Sure," the doctor replied. "I'll send her in. In the meantime, just stay put. Whatever drug they hit you with appears to be wearing off, but just to be safe."

The doctor walked out, and the door closed behind him.

67

US Embassy, Tel Aviv

IT WAS ONLY a few moments later that the exam room door reopened.

"Stone!" Talia said as she rushed in and hugged him. Before she knew it, however, she pulled away, almost as if she felt like she had done something wrong.

"You're all right?" Stone asked.

"I'm fine," Talia replied as her eyes traced his chest and physique.

"What? Oh, the marks. It's nothing."

She continued staring, but pulled her eyes free and turned away. "I've never been so scared in my life."

"I still don't know what happened."

"Would you . . . put something on?" She turned and flicked one last glance at his chest.

"Oh, sure." He looked around the room. "Hey, where's my shirt?"

"That's right. I think they cut it off you."

Stone stood and leaned against the counter. "So what happened?"

"That was an abduction," Talia said as a shiver rode her spine. Her breathing accelerated as she thought back to the terrifying ordeal. "It all happened so quickly. I only saw them for a split second, then there was this awful explosion, and I couldn't hear, and everything went dark and," she was starting to hyperventilate, "and, and, then they . . . were, and we were in a vehicle and, and—"

Stone went to her. "Hey, hey, it's okay now." She buried her head into his bare chest. "I'm here now. It's all okay." Tears burst forth as Stone pulled her close. "Shhh. We're safe. It's all over, okay?" His voice was strong, calming.

She looked into his eyes. The terror, the fear, the adrenaline, all swirled through her body. Yet his eyes, those calming blue eyes. She stared into them, and her breathing began to slow.

Her mind was a jumble of mixed thoughts. None of the thoughts, however, would gel. Without hesitation, she pressed her lips to his and kissed him deeply.

His lips tensed at first, but then she felt him sink into it. Talia let her hands run across his chest and felt him pull her tighter. The kiss intensified. The tighter he pulled, the more she wanted this to go somewhere. She pushed him against the exam table.

"Right here?" he said.

"Yes," she said.

But then the door opened, and a tall, barrel-chested man with a full beard stepped halfway in before stopping. "Oh, pardon me, sir. We'll come back."

Talia and Stone pushed away from one another as if the reverse polarity of an electromagnet had kicked in.

"No," Stone said, a little louder than he'd intended. "No, come in."

"We didn't mean to interrupt," the man said as he and another walked in.

Talia turned to the window and snugged her shirt down.

Stone cleared his throat, and the man said, "Just wanted to check on you. You gave us a scare there. You were totally out of it."

Stone said, "You pulled us out?"

"Yes, sir," the man said. "Kind of caused a ruckus, if you know what I mean."

Stone nodded. "I do."

"Saw your file," the operator said as he grinned. "You're not the average ground pounder. Yes, sir. You've had to embrace the suck a time or two."

Stone smiled. "What outfit you two with?" He glanced between the men. "Frogs?"

The man replied with a favored motto of SEAL operators. "*The only easy day was yesterday*, sir."

"Well, you pulled our asses out of the sling, that's for sure." He glanced at Talia. "How did you find us, anyway?"

"You've got friends in high places. We got a call from Liberty Crossing. Think it must've started at the Puzzle Palace though because the intel said they'd picked up a badge scan at Gideon HQ. Then—"

Talia interrupted. "I'm sorry. I know you're speaking English, but all I hear is gibberish."

"Sorry, ma'am," the operator said. "Liberty Crossing is just a name we use. It's the U.S. Office of the Director of National Intelligence combined with the National Counterterrorism Center. We got tasked from there and then the Puzzle Palace, well, that's NSA, relayed they'd picked up the fact that your Gideon," he stopped himself, "your Mossad identity badge had been scanned."

"How would they know that?" Talia said.

"Not sure I'm qualified to answer that, ma'am," the operator said as a bit of a smirk appeared on his face.

"Or you prefer not to say?" she said.

"Any-who," the operator continued, "we knew you were at Gideon HQ, so we staked out the most logical exit point and waited. When we saw that van hop out of the underground parking deck like a bat out of hell, we knew."

"What happened to the men that abducted us? KIAs?" Stone asked.

"Can't rightly say," the operator replied. "Hit 'em with a little shake and bake, that's for sure. We didn't hang around to check their vitals, if you know what I mean."

"No one knows what you mean," Talia said.

Stone explained. "Shake and bake. Hit the enemy with multiple types of weapons at the same time. Bombs, cluster bombs, napalm, fragmentation grenades, automatic weapons fire—"

"I get it," Talia said.

"Ma'am?" the operator said, "our sole concern was your safety and the safety of Commander Stone."

"I'm not active duty anymore."

"Hey," the operator replied, "you Task Force Green pukes are all right in my book."

Stone shook both men's hands. "You saved our asses. I owe you one."

The first operator smiled as they began to walk out, "Yeah you do. And hey, one more thing. Puzzle Palace asked me to deliver a message."

"What is it?"

"They said to tell you to turn your damn phone on." The two operators laughed and walked out.

"My phone?" Stone said as he pulled the device from his back pocket and looked at it. "Son of a bitch, I turned it off at Andrews when we boarded the transport." He held the power button, and the phone blinked to life. "Oh, shit. There are a ton of missed calls from NSA." He clicked on the last one in the list to dial the number.

On the other end of the phone, Knuckles picked up. "Agent Stone? Jesus Christ, can you leave your phone on from now on?

"We're fine, by the way, but thanks for asking."

"We know you're fine."

"How do you know . . . never mind. Why all the phone calls?"

Knuckles began speed talking. "There's a nuclear device in that casket. And I don't mean *maybe*."

"Whoa," Stone replied. "Slow down there Captain McSpeedy pants. What are you talking about?"

"Talia left her wristwatch behind. Her watch has a personal radiation detector strip attached to it. She was exposed to enough radiation to light it up like a Christmas tree, or a menorah. Oh, whatever. And it's been confirmed. Bureau sent a hazmat team to the cemetery. They picked up traces of highly enriched uranium, the same type used in the warhead of a B43 nuclear bomb. The soil all around the burial plot was contaminated with the stuff. The microfilm, it's all true. They actually stole a device from us and-"

"Knuckles! Knuckles!" Stone said as he tried to interrupt the kid. Stone's eyes locked with those of Talia. He then said into the phone, "A nuclear device? There was no nuclear device in that casket. We just opened it."

"Of course, it's in there. The device would be cone-shaped. Big, heavy thing about fourteen inches long. You couldn't miss it."

"I know what one looks like. There was nothing in that casket other than a footlocker full of personals."

"Then that means . . ." Knuckles said as his voice trailed off.

Stone heard the banging sounds of the phone being dropped on the other end, then the shrill, terrified voice of Knuckles. "Uncle Bill!" the kid screamed as he apparently ran toward Bill's office.

Stone's eyes became distant, hazy, as he realized the implications. It was a Broken Arrow, a nuclear device out in the open.

68

Stone relayed everything Knuckles had said to Talia. Several minutes went by. He lay the phone on the exam table and put it on speaker so Talia could hear. He leaned toward the phone, "Knuckles? Hey, Knuckles! Dammit, pick up the phone."

"I still can't believe it," Talia said. "They're sure they detected nuclear material?"

"Confirmed."

"How do they know that? Uranium is naturally occurring. It could be uranium-238, or its decay product, 234. Are they sure the isotope is 235? A direct match?"

"Talia, I don't know my 238 from my 234 or 235. What I do know is, the FBI's hazmat team doesn't screw around. I've worked with them before. If they say its a direct match, it's a direct match. There's a nuclear device out in the open. Someone orchestrated this, and they did a damn good job of it."

"I think you're crazy," Talia said.

"Stone?" Uncle Bill's voice said across the speakerphone.

"Bill, we're here," Stone said. "There was a device in the casket?"

Bill's voice came back sounding as though he were twenty years younger. "That's an affirm. I've just spoken to the chairman of the joint chiefs. We're classifying it as an empty quiver."

Talia stepped closer. "Uncle Bill, I disagree with that assessment.

There's no way a device was in that casket for fifty years without anyone knowing. And now you're saying it was stolen?"

"Miss Stiel, I don't have time to—" Bill started.

"Not only that, but even if I did believe it, an Empty Quiver refers to the seizure, theft, or loss of a functioning nuclear weapon. That sounds to me like you don't believe it either. Under Empty Quiver status, you're not going to respond, are you? I don't know how the US categorizes it, but it would make more sense if it was something along the lines of a Broken Arrow or a Pinnacle. In Israel, if a device has been stolen, the Israeli government considers it to be an imminent threat."

Bill's volume escalated. "It *is* the Israeli government that is the imminent threat."

"What's that supposed to mean?" Talia said. "Israel couldn't be responsible for this. What would we need with another nuclear device? We've got over three hundred of them in various forms. And we sure don't need one more."

"This is not a topic open for debate, Miss Stiel. I hate to be the one to break it to you, but my sources tell me it was someone high in the Israeli chain of command that made the request to have the casket exhumed. The request went from this high-ranking official to the US Attorney General, and from there to the Chief of Naval Operations. When I pressed further about *who* in the Israeli government initiated the request, I learned it originated from the Mossad. Someone in the office of the director of political action. That department is run by a man named Moshe Himmelreich. He's the second highest ranking officer at the Mossad."

Stone looked at Talia, who, upon hearing the name, looked like she'd been hit with a bomb.

Bill continued. "Now if you'll excuse me, I've got to brief the Secretary of Defense. In the meantime, you two are ordered to stay low. Do not leave the embassy. Do I make myself clear?"

After a short delay, Stone replied. "Yes, sir," then hung up the phone. He watched Talia a moment.

She stepped backward, almost stumbling, until she fell into a chair. "You all right?" he said.

"It's not possible."

Stone didn't know what to say or even how he was supposed to act.

Talia stared at a singular point on the wall, and her eyes never flinched. "It's not possible. Moshe would never lie to me." She shook her head, gently at first, then violently. "No, no. It isn't possible." Her body began to shake. "No, no."

Stone knelt in front of the chair. "Hey, look at me. It's going to be all right. I'm sure it's all just a big misunderstanding." Though in the back of his mind, he was wondering if his gut instincts about Moshe had been accurate.

Talia suddenly stood. "You believe them, don't you?" She stepped away, and her next words came out laced in venom. "I can see it in your eyes."

Stone stood. "I don't know what I believe."

"I can see now why you worked as an operator and not an undercover agent. You make a terrible liar. How could you possibly believe that sweet man could have anything to do with this?"

Stone knew he'd been caught. "Fine. I believe them, all right? I knew something was wrong with him when I first met him."

Talia's nostrils flared. "There is nothing wrong with Moshe Himmelreich. He's a loving, kind father, and I'll not have you speak of him this way!"

But Stone didn't back down. "You're blinded by your love for him. Uncle Bill just told you the office of the director of political action made the request. And look at it from my perspective. First of all, Moshe doesn't believe its possible for there to be a mole inside the Mossad. Of course, there's a mole inside the Mossad. How could there not be? Someone on the inside is feeding information to the assassin and you know it. And next, we have the casket."

Talia squared off in front of him. "What about it?"

"How did he know there'd been a cement burial vault placed over the top of the casket when it was laid to rest?"

"Well," Talia stuttered, "the casket itself was in good condition for its age. He would have assumed—"

"Assumed, my ass," Stone belted back. "One minute he's telling us he got word the casket was in transit to Israel, and the next, he's got inside knowledge of a cement burial vault he'd never seen? And what about the flags?"

"What about them?"

"Supposedly during transit, he orders an Israeli burial flag to be wrapped around the casket, the type of flag that covers the entire surface, wrapping tightly around the corners. And then he said no one had opened the casket, right? That the casket had been sealed for fifty years?"

"So?"

"If the Israeli flag was wrapped atop the casket during transit, and he wasn't there, then how did he know there was an American flag underneath?"

Talia spat back, "Maybe someone on the flight told him."

"That casket had been opened before we got there."

"That's a lie!" Talia blurted before covering her mouth with both hands.

"There were pry marks. Pry marks that indicated it had already been opened. When I inserted that pry bar and lifted, the lid gave free so easily, I could tell the locking mechanisms were already broken."

Talia's voice began to quiet. "Well," she searched for the words, "they would have degraded after fifty years." Her lower lip began to quiver.

Stone could tell her earlier anger had given way to possibility. He put his hands on her shoulders and could feel her body trembling.

"It can't be," Talia said as a tear rolled off her cheek. She leaned into Stone, and he pulled her close. "It just can't be. I refuse to believe this."

Stone's phone vibrated. He read the incoming text message, then let out a long exhale.

"What?" she said.

"It's from NSA." He held the phone up for her.

Talia squinted at the screen.

From the digital forensics lab:
Talia's wrist watch is embedded with a GPS tracker.

BUT WHEN SHE read the last line, she gasped.

Her movements have been monitored.

TALIA READ and re-read the words.

"Now do you believe me?" Stone said.

"It can't be," she choked out. "*Moshe* gave me that watch. It was a gift." She leaned her head into his chest and cried. "I've known him my whole life. He's my Aba!"

"Talia, shhh. Look, I can't even imagine what this is like for you, but this all makes sense," Stone said. "The tracker. That's how they knew where to find you. That's how the assassin was in my apartment. And think about it, NSA is sure there was a nuke inside that casket. It was Moshe who had the casket exhumed."

"No, no."

"It's true. And didn't you say Moshe went to undergrad with the US Attorney General? That's what Uncle Bill just said, the order went from Moshe's office to the AG to the chief of the entire Navy. It was Moshe. It means he knew there was a nuke inside. It's the only explanation."

Talia's voice regained composure. "I can't. I can't!" She pushed back, balled her hands into fists, then started pounding Stone's head and chest.

Her tears erupted again as he gripped her arms to stop her. But as suddenly as she had started, she stopped and looked into his eyes.

Stone caught the change in expression on her face, and his head cocked back in surprise.

She grabbed the back of his head and pulled her face to his. They kissed deeply for a moment.

When it was over, Stone said, "What was that?"

The door opened again, and the same two Navy SEALs walked in. "Commander Stone?" the operator said as he handed Stone a shirt. "We've got a situation. Please come with us, sir."

69

The operators departed the US embassy. Uncle Bill, still on video conference from Ft. Meade, said, "Miss Stiel? Everything hinges on you finding that device. The SEAL team won't be able to wait off the coast until you have the exact location. The first phase of the Israeli invasion into Lebanon is imminent. In SEAL parlance, they're not going to be able to *standby to standby*. There's not enough time."

She nodded at him.

"We know the general area where the device is currently located, but we need you to pinpoint its exact location. To intercept, the teams will deploy immediately into an area just south of Sarafand, Lebanon. That way they'll be in close proximity to the device, and possibly be able to intercept it as it moves south toward the Israeli border."

Talia stepped closer to the monitor. "Sarafand is well south of where the device was apparently inserted at Sidon, Saida Port." She crossed her arms. "How do you know the general location of the device, much less what path it's taking?"

"The tracking device you developed was deployed by the Israeli Defense Force using an IAI Heron unmanned aerial drone. I won't bore you with the specifics, but we're tracking the drone. We can tell which direction the drone is pointed, so presumably we have a fair idea where the device is. You'll have to fill in the details."

Talia said, "I won't let you down."

She and Stone departed. Once the door closed behind them and they had walked clear of the Marine guards, Stone said, "Don't tell me we have to go back to Mossad headquarters. That's pure suicide." Stone pressed the elevator call button.

"There's only one way to access the tracking system, and it's from within Mossad HQ."

As the elevator doors opened, Stone jammed a hand in to stop them from closing. "We might as well go back and tell them we don't have access. Going back to the Mossad is not going to happen."

"Would you let me finish?" Talia said as she pushed past him and boarded the elevator. She pressed a button and stared at Stone. "Would you get on already?" Stone walked into the elevator, and the door wafted shut. "The system can be accessed remotely. We won't have to go to HQ. But there's a problem."

"Yeah, I bet. What?"

"Since the tracker has been operationalized, only a few people with operational clearance would now have access to it."

"Please tell me you're one," Stone said as they got off the elevator and made their way toward the exit doors.

"My role is pure research. I may have developed the thing, but they'd never let me near the controls if it was being used in an operation. But I can think of one person who does."

"Don't you say Moshe's name."

"It's the only way, Stone. Come on, he's got a workstation set up at his home, but it will take a bit of luck. If I can log on to his computer, I might be able to access his work computer remotely. But if he's sitting at his desk at the Mossad, he'll see."

As Stone heard the words, he stopped walking and shut his eyes. He then mumbled, "I don't know how I get myself into these situations."

70

They drove an unmarked US embassy loaner vehicle across town. Talia said, “How long will it take for your Navy SEALs to be on the ground in Lebanon?”

“Well, the team would have already gotten its tasking, and they’re pretty much balls up at this point. Sorry, I mean they’re already in motion. The MH-60 those two just boarded can do better than two hundred knots. The carrier is a hundred miles off Lebanon. It’ll take around thirty minutes from the carrier to their drop zone.”

“That doesn’t make sense. Those two SEALs have to get to the aircraft carrier to join the rest of their team, and then fly all the way to Lebanon. That means it’s probably one hundred and fifty of your miles from here.”

“Those two are not going to the carrier first. Command will hot-load a second bird off the carrier with the rest of the team and head straight toward the coast.” He looked at his watch. “In fact, they’re probably taking off now. The two birds will rendezvous at their incursion point, then punch into Lebanese airspace.”

Talia’s blurted, “You mean to tell me we’ve got half an hour before we have to give them an exact location of the device?”

“Less,” Stone replied. “We need to get them the coordinates as soon as possible. They’ll want to put the operators straight on top of the device so they can grab it and get it on board one of the helos.”

As they drove through traffic, the sun dipped below the horizon. The darkening light cast an eerie yellow glow across everything.

"Stone, my God. How do you think we're going to get the location that quickly? It's twenty minutes to the house. It'll take me several minutes to log in to his workstation, if I can log in at all. And I told you, if Moshe is on his computer at HQ when I do it, we're dead in the water."

"First thing's first. Let's just get to the house and get on his computer. It's getting dark. How late does Moshe usually work?"

"Not to worry; he won't be home for hours."

"Will there be guards in the house, even with Moshe at the office?"

"Outside, yes. But inside? Very unlikely."

"What about that one guard?" Stone said. "The older guy, friendly. What was his name?"

"Shimon," Talia replied as they crossed a massive thoroughfare. "He won't be at the house. He's by Moshe's side at all times."

"Isn't he a little old to be a bodyguard?"

"Shimon and Moshe go way back. They served in the Mossad together for years. Shimon was apparently injured in the line of duty and was about to be medically discharged. Moshe stepped in and gave him a job so he could qualify for his retirement. He's very loyal."

As Stone followed Talia's directions to the estate, rounding corners and accelerating around slower vehicles, Talia glanced at the clock on the dashboard. "By the time we get there. . . "

"I know," Stone said as the vehicle's tires screeched around another turn. "We're almost there?"

"Yes," Talia said as she braced for the turn. "Slow down, you're going to kill us."

"Those operators are in a helo right now cruising at two hundred knots, about seventy feet off the deck. They'll be getting close. If we don't get them the exact locale, they'll dust off at NSA's best guess as to the location of the device. We've still got the Lebanese military response to worry about you know. They'll be sitting ducks."

"This is it," Talia said. "Seriously, slow down as we turn into the neighborhood. The guards at the gate would open fire on us if we came in at this speed."

Darkness had settled in earnest. Within another minute they were at Moshe's gate and were waved through. They parked, and Talia went inside. But Stone stopped on the porch. He stared at the metal door knocker, the one forged in the shape of a venomous snake's head. Talia said. "What?"

"Vipera," Stone said.

"What are you talking about?"

He shut the door. "The codename on the microfilm. *Vipera.* In Hebrew, it means *viper*, right?"

"I told you, I don't want to hear your theory of how my Aba is the mole. Now come on!"

Stone followed her up the stairs and into Moshe's office. "Who has a door knocker in the shape of a snake's head? Every piece of evidence points to him," Stone said. "He's Vipera."

Talia spun around in one swift, violent motion and slapped him across the face. But the instant she had done it, she cupped both hands over her mouth. "I'm sorry," she said. "I didn't mean that."

"Never mind," Stone said as he shook his head. "Just get on that computer." But in the back of his head, the evidence was lining up. *Moshe ordered the casket exhumed. He denies there's a mole inside the Mossad. He knew things about the casket he couldn't have known. The casket had been opened before we got there. Moshe was the one who gave Talia the watch with a GPS tracker embedded inside.*

Talia sat in Moshe's desk chair as Stone closed the door. She moved the computer mouse, and the screen blinked to life.

Talia tapped at the keyboard but then looked up. "It's changed. I was going to log on as myself and connect remotely to Moshe's computer at the Mossad, but it won't let me in."

"We don't have time for guessing. I'm calling NSA." Stone pulled out his phone and dialed. He put the phone on the desk and hit the button for speakerphone.

It was Knuckles who answered. "It's about time," the kid said. "We've been tracking your location. We're out of time. The Israeli Air Force just launched a full contingent of fighter-bombers. They're headed across the Golan right now."

"Knuckles, we're having trouble-"

"Logging in? Yeah, I know."

"How did you—"

"Not my first rodeo," Knuckles replied. "Been attempting to hack that workstation for half an hour. It can't be done remotely. Believe me,

I've tried. But now that you're physically there, it shouldn't be a problem."

Talia looked at the wall clock. "Knuckles, are you tracking your strike team? How much time do we have?"

"They're sixteen nautical miles off the coast of Lebanon. The two transport helos rendezvoused and they've got two helicopter gunships in support. They're slowing down. ETA, four minutes."

Talia's breathing rate accelerated. "That's not enough time!"

Knuckles said, "Stone, I'm pushing a download onto your phone. Find a USB charging cable and physically connect your phone to the workstation."

Stone fished in one of Moshe's desk drawers and pulled out a cable. "Done," he replied as he connected the cable to the computer, then to his phone.

"Okay, the download is compiling. Wait, wait. Now, click the new icon on the phone. It will run an algorithm that will use a hash to decrypt a series of... oh, never mind. Are you in yet?"

The computer monitor blinked once, and both Talia and Stone watched as a series of characters appeared in the password box. Talia then said, "Yes! We're in. Let's see, I'm logged in as . . . as Moshe. How did you do that?" She tapped several keys. "Here we go. I'm going to remote into his workstation at Mossad." She looked at Stone. "If he's sitting there, he'll see on his screen. I can't believe I'm doing this." She maneuvered the mouse and clicked.

"Wait. Does his laptop at work have a camera?"

"Sure," Talia replied. "Great idea." She clicked the mouse to remotely enable the laptop's camera. The view from the camera on Moshe's laptop displayed and they could see inside his office.

Talia let out a long exhale as they saw the desk chair was empty. "All right," she said, "now I'm going to access the tracker control panel." Several clicks later and a user interface displayed on the monitor. She said, "Here, this is the GPS coordinates of the drone. And this," she said as she pointed to a section that read *Photonuclear Inspection and Threat Assessment*, "this is what I've been working on for the last seven years." She studied the monitor a moment. "It works, look at that. I almost can't believe it."

They heard a voice across Stone's phone that sounded like Uncle Bill. Knuckles answered him, "I know, I know!" then said into the phone, "the coordinates?"

Stone leaned into the monitor. "Latitude, thirty-three degrees, sixteen minutes, nineteen point one seven one niner seconds, north. Longitude, thirty-five degrees, twelve minutes, five five three two seconds East."

Knuckles read back the coordinates to confirm, then said, "We're tasking the strike team right now. Good work, now get off that computer and get the hell out of there."

"Way ahead of you, pal," Stone said, as he motioned for Talia to log off. He heard a small commotion on the driveway in front of the house and walked to the window to look down. But when he didn't see anything, he said, "This isn't over yet. I want to know what's happening with that weapon."

Talia closed the application and logged off of the computer. "Let's get out of this room so no one finds us in here. There's a sitting room just over there," she said as she pointed.

With the phone pressed to Stone's ear, they walked out of the office and to the other side of the banistered hallway. Talia opened a door, and they went into a well-appointed room. There were two plush couches, a large television, and a wet bar.

"Thank God that's over," Talia said as she dropped onto one of the couches. "I was so scared Aba was going to walk into his office at work while we were doing that. What's happening now?"

Stone covered the mic on his phone. "They've tasked the SEAL team to the coordinates. Sounds like the helos were already pretty close. They'll be dusting off any moment now. Hey, you did good. They'd have never identified what vehicle the device was traveling in."

"I've never felt so guilty in my life."

"Well, you can relax now." Stone pressed the phone harder to his ear. "Sounds like NSA put a drone of their own on the scene. They've ID'd the vehicle. So far, there's no air response from the Lebanese military."

"That's a relief."

"Hold on. Team is on the ground." He listened a minute then looked up again. "This is it. They've got the vehicle stopped. It's a van. Oh shit! There's a firefight." As the tense moments ticked by, Stone crunched his eyes shut and then mumbled, "Come on guys."

"What's happening?"

Stone held up an open hand as he listened with intent. A few moments later his whole posture loosened and he flashed her a thumbs up. "Firefight is over. None of the SEALs are hit. They just breached the vehicle. They got it! They have the device."

Talia stood.

"They're loading it on one of the helos. Almost there. . . they're away!" Stone spoke into the phone. "Great work, Knuckles. What's that?" Stone said as he smiled. "Oh, come on, without you guys, this would have never worked."

"It's all over?" Talia said as she watched Stone nod to her. "They've really recovered it? Thank God."

"Tell Uncle Bill I said great work," Stone's smile widened. "All right, talk to you later." He hung up the phone. "You did it, Talia. You really did it. I mean, the chances this operation was going to be successful without you were almost non-existent."

"I just can't believe it's all over. Are you sure?" She shook her head. "I don't think I've felt like I could breathe for a week."

"Then take a good long deep breath. You deserve it. It's over, and you just saved who knows how many lives."

"They're going to call off the invasion?"

"They'll have to," Stone insisted.

They both stood a moment, smiling at one another. It lasted until the silence became awkward.

"Stone?" she said. "Listen, things got kind of . . . intense. That kiss? I just think I was overwhelmed with—"

He held up a hand. "Say no more. It's partly my fault. I mean, you may have initiated it, but if you hadn't, I would have." His hands found his pockets. "I darn sure didn't move to stop it."

"You know, you're not such a bad guy, John Stone." She smiled and focused into the depth of his blue eyes. "So . . . you would have initiated it?"

"Yes."

"Then you wanted to?"

But she found her answer when his eyes ran down her body then back up.

To Talia, it seemed as though she could hear nothing but the pounding of her own heart.

She unbuttoned the top button of her shirt and watched as his eyes became magnetized there. But then Stone looked to the closed door.

"I'm over here," she said.

Stone's face hardened. He held a finger to his mouth. "Shhh." But no sooner had he said that did the door burst open.

Talia looked in horror to find a man in the doorway with a gun in his hand. It was pointed right at her. It only took an instant to identify him. The deathly pale blue eyes, the scar running down his cheek, the pock-marked skin, and that sickening grin.

It was him.

71

Adrenaline exploded into Stone's system and leapt at Talia just as gunshots rang out. His body crashed into hers, knocking her clear. As they crumpled onto the carpeted floor behind one of the couches, Stone felt as though the breath had been knocked out of his lungs.

The assassin fired round after round in repeated succession. Bullets slammed into the couch and wall. Splintered wood, tufts of stuffing, and drywall dust peppered them from both sides.

Stone shielded Talia with his body. But his gun was out in a flash. He popped three rounds through the back of the couch toward the threat. A muffled grunt was audible, one of the rounds had struck its target.

The gunman hit the ground but continued firing as he began backing out of the room.

Stone leaned over the top of the couch and fired again, this time taking clear aim.

The gunman was into the hallway and leaned an arm into the open door and fired back.

Stone continued shooting but saw his rounds hitting the wall and doorframe in a somewhat wild pattern. *What the hell?* he thought. But when he saw his hand covered in blood, he withdrew behind the couch. More gunshots rang out. Bullets zipped through the couch and one shattered a window behind them. Stone shifted the gun into his left hand and fired back.

Talia saw the blood covering his arm. "You're hit!" she said as she leaned up.

"Stay down!" Stone belted as he fired a few more rounds.

But Talia pulled off her belt and snugged it around the upper part of his arm to stem the bleeding.

Stone leaned over the couch once again, but a round from the assassin gun slammed into his Glock, mangling the gun's trigger mechanism and Stone's hand with it.

"Your hand," she said as Stone grunted against the pain. "Oh my God, your hand."

She picked up the gun but realized it was no longer operable. And that's when she felt a sharpened heat press against the back of her skull. The look of sheer rage in Stone's eyes told her without a doubt, the assassin was standing on top of her.

His voice came out cold. It matched the deadness she remembered in his eyes. "Put the weapon down," the Raven said through gritted teeth. He pressed the muzzle of his gun harder into her skull. The broken Glock dropped from her fingers. "I never fail an assignment, ever. And I will not fail this one."

Talia held as still as she could, but the terror coursing her veins caused her entire body to shake. A moment later a wave of fresh nausea roiled her system and her vision began to shift as the impending vertigo episode took hold.

Stone was covered in his own blood. He glared at the man through eyes of granite and his jaw muscles flexed hard enough to crack a tooth.

The killer held the gun to Talia's head but looked at Stone. "You. You have caused me disgrace. And now you will pay for your transgressions."

But the instant he raised the gun at Stone, Talia exploded off the floor into the man. Stone launched up as well, and the three toppled over. Talia wrenched at the man's arm, and the gun fell from his hand.

Stone slammed an elbow into the man's face, but with his injuries, the blow was ineffective. He turned to launch at the man's throat, but before he could lean all his weight onto it, the assassin yanked his stiletto dagger from his shirt sleeve. He smashed the butt end of it across the back of Talia's head. She went down, and before Stone could stop it, the assassin buried the sharpened ice pick into his side.

Stone rolled off, and the killer stood with the bloody ice pick in his hand. He picked up his gun. Before raising it, he stared at the two of them as they lay on the ground. Talia was face down, unconscious, but Stone was trying to stand. His efforts, however, were in vain. Stone clutched his side and grimaced against the pain.

"So much the warrior," he said. "But why bother? This will all be over soon."

Stone stared into the muzzle of the gun. "You burn in hell," he said as bright frothy blood spat from his mouth.

The Raven straightened his arm and looked at Stone over the top of the handgun's sights. "This is my favorite part, you know?"

Stone refused to close his eyes and stared at the man through slits of rage. When the shot rang out, he flinched.

72

The bullet tore into flesh and blood, and tiny shards of bone peppered the room. The Raven spun and fell to his knees. The gun had fallen out of his hand and Stone snatched it.

Stone saw Jana standing in the doorway. A tiny wisp of smoke eased from the barrel of the gun in her hand. She tucked the gun into its holster and tackled the Raven to the ground. She yanked a hand behind the man's back and snapped a set of handcuffs onto them as a uniformed soldier ran in to assist.

With the assassin subdued and bleeding, she turned to Stone. "Jesus, Johnny. You don't give a girl much time, do you?" She pulled his shirt up to inspect the knife wound in his side. She yelled to the group of uniformed soldiers in the hall behind her. "We need a medic up here, now!"

One of the Israeli soldiers stepped back and spoke Hebrew into his radio to call for help.

Two others came in and knelt to Talia. One said, "Stabilize her neck. Don't move her until they get a neck collar on her."

"Hey, babe," Stone said to Jana as he coughed. "Kind of glad to see you. Where'd you come from?" He coughed harder. "Christ, I can't breathe."

Jana said, "Kind of figured you'd need help, and to be honest, we weren't sure who we could trust." His breathing became more labored. "Just relax, will you? This looks like a sucking chest wound." She pressed her palm against the hole and turned to a soldier standing in the doorway. "We've got to stabilize the air pressure in his chest. Go to the kitchen. Find some Saran wrap. Hurry!"

The heavily-armed soldier cocked his head. "Saran wrap?"

"Cellophane wrap, plastic wrap, whatever you call it here."

The soldier nodded and ran off.

"Hey, don't you die on me."

Stone gasped at the air, and a wave of pain swept his face. Ever the warrior, he said, "I can hack it."

"Yeah," Jana said. "Sure you can. Just stay quiet and try to be still."

His jaw muscles clenched. "Starting to think that when you left all this and moved to Antigua, you had the right idea."

Jana smiled. "I think about it every day."

He craned his neck to take a look at Talia's motionless body. An Israeli soldier had positioned his knees on either side of her head to hold it in position while pressing a field dressing over it.

"Is she?"

"No," Jana said. "She's unconscious. Pretty bad gash on her head though. Hey, I thought I told you to shut up."

"You're mean right after you shoot people."

Jana shook her head.

A soldier ran in with a roll of plastic wrap.

Jana said, "Cut away his shirt. He's got a chest puncture."

The soldier nodded and pulled out a knife, then began cutting the top of Stone's shirt. He said, "What's the plastic wrap is for?"

They leaned Stone up, and Jana began wrapping the plastic around the width of his chest. She said, "With a sucking chest wound when he inhales, air can travel into the chest cavity through this new pathway. If we don't seal it off, the air will build up in there until it collapses his lung." After they'd encircled the plastic wrap around his chest twice, they cut it off. "Lean him down." She turned and yelled out the hallway. "Where the hell's my medic?"

"Coming up the stairs now, ma'am. And I've got an evac helicopter inbound."

"We've got to watch for signs of a pneumothorax, a collapsed lung," she said to the soldier next to her. "One side of the chest can look bigger than the other, veins on the neck might bulge, the lips, neck, or fingers can turn blue."

"What do we do then?" the soldier asked.

Stone gritted out the answer himself. "You'd have to release the seal to allow air to escape."

Jana said to him, "I thought I told you-"

"To shut up?" he said. "I know."

"Looks like you'll have some fresh new scars to add to your collection," she said.

"I'll gladly take them over medals."

Two military medics rushed in. Each carried a flat-board stretcher and bag of gear. They dropped the gear and began examining the two.

The sound of thumping helicopter rotors could be heard in the distance.

The medic said, "Sucking chest wound? Nice work." He examined Stone's injuries and began taking vital signs, then turned to the other medic. "Status?"

"She's stable," she replied.

The first medic said, "This one we expedite. Okay, let's get him on the stretcher."

They were out the door and loaded onto a Bell Twin Two-Twelve helicopter within minutes.

73

Tel Aviv Sourasky Medical Center

Talia awakened with a startle. Her head throbbed. She put her hand up and felt a large bandage wrapped around it. She was in a hospital room, but the prospect of *why* sent a wave of fluttering into her stomach. But then flashes of the assassin's attack exploded into her mind, and she sat bolt upright.

"Stone!" she said. But before she could reach for the nurse call button, Special Agent Jana Baker walked in. Uncle Bill Tarleton, his hands in his pockets, was just behind her.

"How are you feeling?" Jana asked.

"What happened to Stone? Where's John?"

Uncle Bill raised his palms to calm her. "He's going to be fine."

The sound of his grandfatherly voice eased the tightness in her shoulders, and she sat back.

"He's in recovery now," Jana said. "They said he did great."

"I don't understand how you—" she stopped. "What about the nuclear weapon?"

"Safe as well," Bill replied. "Thanks to you, that is. You saved a lot of lives today."

"How did you two come to be in Tel Aviv?"

Jana said, "There's a lot you don't know. We can talk about that later."

"No, tell me now. What is it I don't know?"

Bill exhaled. "Are you sure you're up for this?"

"Please, what's going on?"

"Some of this is going to come as a bit of a shock, so let me just start at the beginning." He pressed his glasses to his face. "It goes back to the microfilm. After we read through the decrypted data, your grandfather on board the *Ticonderoga*, another covert operative on board as well, the effort to convince your Uncle Golan to divert his plane to a remote island, well, one detail troubled me."

"And what was that?" Talia asked.

"Kitadaitō island, where your uncle was to land and offload the weapon."

Talia leaned closer.

"At the time, it was under US control."

Talia looked at Jana as if seeking an explanation, but then said, "Wait a minute. You're saying the United States was involved in the 1965 operation?"

"Back then, the US desperately wanted to help Israel but were prevented by international law. So they looked for another way, a way to get Israel the weapon they needed. Your uncle was being asked to hand over the weapon to officers of the CIA."

"Bill," Jana said, "we really shouldn't. Talia needs to rest."

"No, I want to hear this."

Uncle Bill crossed his arms then the fingers of one hand disappeared into his cavernous beard. "When your uncle refused, the plane never showed up on Kitadaitō. The CIA believed the mission was a failure. But as we now know, your grandfather *was* able to separate the warhead from the bomb, stow it in your uncle's footlocker, sabotage the braking system on the aircraft, and dump your uncle and his plane overboard. With the plane gone, no one knew the warhead had been stolen. Then the footlocker was placed in his coffin and shipped."

Jana said, "And then Israel's Six Day War broke out. After that, no one was left alive who knew about the stolen device, other than your grandfather, that is."

Bill began to pace the room. His steps were slow, methodical. To Talia it looked as though he were counting them. "The microfilm told us about the original 1965 operation, and that they had codenamed it *Red*

Scorpion. And then we learned of the second operation, one that took place years later, *Operation Absolution.*" His voice came out laced in guilt. "I should have spotted it then. I don't know how I missed it. I think I'm-"

Jana broke in, "Getting too old for this shit?"

Bill smiled.

"Spotted what?" Talia said.

"You see," Bill replied, "it's not at all uncommon for the name of an operation to mean something. A red scorpion is possibly one of the most dangerous creatures known to man. And given the fact that the objective was to steal a nuclear device, the name makes perfect sense.

"But *Operation Absolution*, now, that's another story. Absolution, to be free from blame. A release from consequences, penalties. To find out Israel wanted to take the nuclear device, insert it covertly into Lebanon, use your technology to *detect* it, and then use that as an excuse to invade," Bill shook his head. "There's just no excuse for that."

Talia stopped him. "You Americans. It's easy for you. You don't have someone sitting on your border lobbing mortars and missiles into the air with the purpose of killing innocent civilians. You have no idea what its like, to lose someone. To feel the sharp sting of death, close and personal." Her lower lip quivered.

Bill nodded, "Your parents."

"My own parents! I'm not saying I condone the invasion of Lebanon, killing of innocent civilians in the process, but those terrorists killed my parents. They took them away from me, forever! Do you know what that's like?"

Bill started to speak but Jana interrupted him. "Bill, we shouldn't."

Bill's voice quieted. "No," he said as he looked Talia in the eye, "she needs to know the truth."

74

Talia's voice shook. "What are you talking about?"

"Your parents," Bill said. "As you well recall, their names showed up on the microfilm."

Talia said, "Of course I do. A kill order. But why?

"Bill," Jana said as she stepped in front of him. But he was focused only on Talia. "Well, I won't be a part of this," Jana said. She walked out.

Bill said, "As we now know, that was no Hezbollah rocket. That's not what killed your parents."

Talia's breathing deepened.

"We've obtained some documents, documents that explain the whole thing. Your grandfather was deeply involved in undercover operations for the Mossad. And your parents were in close proximity to him. When you were a little girl, your parents apparently stumbled across details of *Operation Absolution*. It might be one of the reasons the operation failed. From what we could gather, they did not approve of an operation to purposely insert a nuclear device into Lebanon and use it as an excuse to invade." Bill looked down. "They murdered them, Talia."

"Who? Who murdered them?"

Uncle Bill paused a few moments as if picking his next words. "From the beginning of this investigation, we've known of the presence of a mole, deep inside the Mossad. It's the only way to explain the events of the past week."

She pointed at him as tears started to stream down her face. "Don't you say it! Don't you dare say Moshe's name. He's the only father I have left. I refuse to believe he killed my parents!"

"It's not Moshe," Bill said.

Talia's mouth dropped open.

"At first glance, all the evidence pointed to him. And I'll admit, I thought it *was* him. He had all the access necessary. He could have helped the assassin gain entry into the Mossad. He had access to alter the security tapes. He gave you that wristwatch, a watch with a GPS tracker hidden inside. And it was his personal relationship to the Attorney General of the United States that influenced the exhumation of your great uncle's remains."

"Then who?" Talia asked.

"A member of Moshe's personal security team. A man named Shimon Gurin."

"*Shimon*?" Talia said. "That's impossible, he's served Moshe loyally for longer than I've been alive. I don't believe it."

Bill cleared his throat. "It appears his close proximity to Moshe made it possible for him to clandestinely carry out his activities."

"What makes you think it was him?"

"I'd rather not get into the details," Bill replied. "Let's just say the NSA is very good at listening in on conversations not everyone else is privy to. But I'll tell you this, there was one thing that caught my attention. As I dug further into the request made to the US Attorney General, I learned the individual request didn't come directly from Moshe himself, it came from someone inside his office. Once I knew that, it opened up the possibility someone was pulling strings in Moshe's name. He's a bad guy, Talia. He has apparently been working on this project since the inception of *Operation Absolution*."

Talia's lip quivered. "My parents?"

"He was the one who issued the kill order. He is Vipera."

Talia cried, and Bill sat quietly with the gentle sobbing.

When she looked up, she said, "The air force? The bombers?"

"They were just crossing into Lebanese airspace when the president of the United States made a rather unpleasant call to your prime minister. He was furious about it being a US weapon. I wasn't in the room, but he pretty much told the PM if they invaded Lebanon, carpet-bombing civilians without justification, we'd pull our support."

He glanced over the tops of his glasses. "The bombers have been recalled, and the Israeli ground troops are being ordered to stand down.

Our estimation is that, if the invasion had gone through, Israel would have laid waste to a significant stretch of land. We believe the plan was to create something of a demilitarized zone, a no-mans land. That way, Hezbollah rockets couldn't get close enough to reach Israel. In the process though, tens of thousands of lives, innocent lives, would have been lost."

"I've lived my whole life believing a Hezbollah rocket killed my parents." Another tear rolled down her cheek. "I've hated them, hated them with every fiber of my being. But it's really not true? I'm not sure I know how to live with that."

Bill said nothing.

Then Talia looked down, as though ashamed to be sitting in her own skin. "My own government, using the technology I developed, for something so . . ." She looked up and stared, her eyes focusing on nothing. "I've never felt so betrayed. I can't go back there, to the Mossad. What am I supposed to do now?"

Bill touched her hand. "Come to the United States. Come work with us."

Her eyes met his and for just a moment she was catapulted back in time to when she was a little girl, on the dock at Moshe's lake house.

Bill nodded. "You think about it."

75

After surgery, Stone had been moved into a room. Jana was standing beside him when Uncle Bill walked in.

"John?" Bill said, "how are you feeling?"

"Like somebody punched me in the gut and then ran over me with a freight train. But on the bright side, the drugs are pretty good."

"Glad to hear it. I assume Jana's filled you in?"

"I was so sure it was Moshe."

Bill nodded.

Stone said, "And Jana said they caught the assassin?"

"They did," Bill replied, "but, it's complicated."

Stone almost rolled his eyes. "It's always complicated."

"His official Mossad codename is *Raven*, but he's better known in international circles as *the Needle*."

Stone held a hand to his side. "Yeah, figured that out the hard way."

"We don't even know his real name. But he's a contractor for hire. Works for the highest bidder. But this was a Mossad operation. So, when I say they caught him, that's true, but I'm not so sure it will mean anything. He apparently worked directly for the mole, Shimon Gurin, who was following orders. Since they weren't doing something illegal under Israeli law, it isn't likely anything will happen to them."

"It's a lovely world we live in."

Bill said, "We've talked with the Lebanese government. They were pretty pissed off we breached their airspace. They don't know the real reason. We told them the SEAL team was apprehending a terror suspect of high priority. They know nothing of the nuclear weapon."

Jana said, "But they'll find out, won't they?"

Bill exhaled. "They always do. The Lebanese Armed Forces were aware of the Israeli build-up on their border and had moved to the highest state of alert. Tensions are very high right now, but with a little diplomacy we're hoping things diffuse." Bill glanced between the two of them. "Well, I'll give you two your privacy." He looked at Jana and said, "I'll wait for you outside," and walked out.

Once he was in the hallway, Bill walked to a vending machine filled with snacks. Although it was not his intent, he couldn't help but overhear their conversation.

* * *

INSIDE THE ROOM, Jana placed one of Stone's hands in hers. "What now?"

"Just want to get back home," Stone replied. "I've only been in this hospital room for an hour, and I'm sick of it already."

She studied his eyes a moment and thought back to all the time they'd spent together on Antigua. "You slept with her, didn't you?"

"What?"

"I'm not surprised. She's a beautiful woman. I see how you look at her. It's the same way you looked at me when we first met."

"Are you *jealous*?" Stone said as a grin formed on his face.

"I won't get in the way. It's just, I've been thinking a lot about you lately, about us."

Stone's grin widened. "*Really*?" he said as he leaned back.

"Hey, don't get cocky. It's just that, what we had on Antigua was really *great*. Don't you ever think about us?"

"I think about us all the time. I had no idea you did the same."

"But Talia."

"It's complicated."

"Yeah," Jana said as she turned away, "sex can be that way."

"I didn't sleep with her."

Jana spun around, but she moved quickly to minimize the obviousness of her reaction. "Of course, you did. How could you not?" But when he made no reply, she said, "You really didn't?"

"No."

"Then maybe we can . . ."

"Wait a second, wait a second," Stone said almost beginning to laugh. "You're not going to make me watch those old love story movies again, are you?"

"I *never* made you watch—"

"Let's see, *Casablanca*, that one, *Roman Holiday* with Audrey Hepburn, *Some Like It Hot*, that was Marilyn Monroe, right? Shall I go on? Okay, *Love Story*, *The Way We Were*—"

"Stop!" Jana said with a smile.

* * *

OUTSIDE IN THE HALL, Uncle Bill grinned as he dropped a few coins into the vending machine then made his selection. "Ah, young love," he said as he watched the metal spirals holding a package of orange crackers spin to release the pack. He removed it from the machine and sat in a chair.

He tore into the plastic and popped the first one into his mouth. "What Mrs. Uncle Bill doesn't know won't hurt her."

~~~
~~~

HEAR THE TRUE STORY

Fighter pilots aboard the USS Ticonderoga, 1965

The facts surrounding the loss of Lt. Daniel Webster, his Skyhawk fighter aircraft, and a live B43 thermonuclear bomb are bizarre, but they really happened.

First there was the accident itself and the strikingly obvious question: How could a fighter plane just roll off an aircraft carrier? Why didn't the plane's brakes work that day?

Then there was the cover-up by the United States Navy who hid the truth for fifteen years, until witnesses finally broke their silence.

These true-to-life events are stranger than fiction.

If you'd like to learn what really happened that fateful day, visit the link below and I'll tell you the full story.

NathanAGoodman.com/BrokenArrow

ALSO BY NATHAN GOODMAN

The Special Agent Jana Baker Spy-Thriller Series

Protocol One

The Fourteenth Protocol

Protocol 15

Breach of Protocol

Rendition Protocol

Peyton Phoenix Thrillers

Phoenix Fatale

John Stone Thrillers

Flight of the Skyhawk

Visit NathanAGoodman.com

ABOUT THE AUTHOR

Please provide a rating for this novel on the retailer's website.

Nathan Goodman is a husband and father of two daughters and lives in the United States. The first novel in *The Special Agent Jana Baker Spy-Thriller* series, *Protocol One*, was an immediate bestselling international terrorist thriller. It was written with one very specific goal—the author wanted to show his daughters a strong female character. He wanted them to see a woman in difficult circumstances who had the strength to prevail. And he wanted them to know that if they have the guts, they can succeed even in places that are perceived to be "a man's world."

Pick up a copy of *Protocol One* today.

NathanAGoodman.com

CPSIA information can be obtained
at www.ICGtesting.com
Printed in the USA
LVHW050146040520
654931LV00004B/488